THE

FAST

OUT

TYLER COMPTON

THE FAST OUT

A Chance Harper Mystery

TSC Books
BAY CITY, CA

Tyler Compton
Los Angeles, CA 90046
www.tylercomptonbooks.com

Publisher's Note: This is a work of fiction. Names, characters,
places, and incidents are a product of the author's imagination.
Locales and public names are sometimes used for atmospheric
purposes. Any resemblance to actual people, living or dead, or to
businesses, companies, events, institutions, or locales is completely coincidental.

Book Layout ©2017 BookDesignTemplates.com

The Fast Out/ Tyler Compton -- 1st ed.
ISBN 978-0-9893845-6-8 (paperback)
ISBN 978-0-9893845-7-5 (e-book)

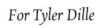

For Tyler Dille

"We live in cites you'll never see on screen
Not very pretty, but we sure know how to run things
Living in ruins of a palace within my dreams
And you know, we're on each other's team"

—Lorde
"Team"

1

FIRST LOVE

I had been sitting off in the bleachers, soaking up the warm October sun, digesting my lunch and enjoying a Coke—though it was less Coke and more Jack at that point, but who was counting?—when I felt someone's presence, off to the side, just out of my line of sight. As she approached, I had deduced whom it was by the scent of her perfume—Miss Dior Cherie—wafting in my direction, thanks to the intrusive winds blowing in from the Pacific. She was the only girl in school who wore that scent. Not because she was the only one who could carry off something so "assertive," but because no one else at Westlake High would have dared copy Jasmine Fairchild's signature smell.

Jasmine Fairchild—yes, of those Fairchilds—was of a completely different social circle than the ones I, or 95% of the rest of school, traveled in. Jasmine Fairchild wasn't just of the upper crust—she was the bar by which the elite of Westlake High had all their standards set by.

We knew each other. Had had classes together all through elementary up into our now junior year of high school. We would occasionally nod politely when passing in the hallways but had no reason to exchange words.

Not since our break-up two years prior.

Oh, did I forget to mention that we used to date? Yeah, from the seventh grade all the way until February of freshmen year, when I—um, well, until "us" ended.

I figured she'd come to see me—after all, there wasn't anyone else out on the football field during the lunch hour—but I couldn't think of any reason why she would. Juniors and seniors could do as they pleased during lunch, including leave the school grounds, which most did. Then there were the few who stayed behind, joining whatever their social circles permitted during that brief time away from raising their educational enlightenment. I, not belonging to any social circles—popular or otherwise—spent most of my days alone out in the bleachers. This wasn't a secret. After all, this was high school. People talked. Gossip was the one thing that spread throughout the student populace faster than the latest "it" craze. I'm sure if someone wanted to speak to me, they would have known where to find me. Being a loner who ate by himself every day was enough to raise awareness of my status.

But since I first began eating out on the bleachers, just exactly a year ago this month, I don't think I had ever once been approached by another student.

Not even by the few at school I did consider to be my friends.

It was probably my current isolation from any sort of social status alerts that gave Jasmine enough of an excuse to approach me. I mean, what would people say if the great

Jasmine Fairchild had been seen talking with someone of my social standing, let alone her ex?

"Either say your peace and beat it or pull the trigger and end the suspense," I said as I took another swig of my Jack and Coke. There was a time, back when I first started drinking—somewhere between freshman and sophomore years if you really want all the pieces of the puzzle—that taking a gulp that big would have burnt my throat and brought up a coughing fit violent enough to make anyone nearby concerned enough to think I was starting the spread of a violent plague.

Now?

Now, I might as well have been drinking water, all the harm it did my throat, despite the good I felt it doing to my brain.

"How did you know it was me?" Jasmine asked, most likely not surprised I knew she was there, but still feeling the need to ask just the same. She stood somewhat awkwardly, as if she didn't know what else to say or how to start the conversation she felt the need to have with me. Boy, would this be awkward.

"I can feel your eyes burning through the back of my skull just tryin' to fry my brains into Jell-O."

"But I don't like Jell-O."

"That's why I know it's what you were tryin' to do to my brains. You're bad news. You need something? There's only a few minutes left until the bell."

"That thing can tell time?" Jasmine smirked, as she eyed the Razor flip phone on the step next to my drink.

She began taking the aluminum steps up toward me, her heels echoing with each step. Seagulls usually bombarded our school, so close to the ocean we were, and while the flock that had covered the football field had all turned their heads toward us at the sounds of her steps, they had yet to feel threatened enough to fly away for safety. Perhaps they just had piss-poor eyesight. I should have warned them to fly away no matter what they thought. Or maybe to re-enact a scene from *The Birds* and attack the blond woman. Maybe I should have taken my own advice and bolted.

"Why don't you finally decide to become some cougar's boy toy and buy yourself a real phone? Like one from this decade?"

"I did the rich-girl tango once before," I replied. "But while I was dancing, she was off gathering roses from other suitors."

That would do it. Only Jasmine and I knew the truth about our past relationship and why it was no more. It would smart her that I said those words, though why I had to snap the truth in her face like that was anyone's guess. She hadn't done anything to me lately to cause me to pounce. I wasn't in any kind of a mood, so far as I could determine. It just felt like it was what we did. The back and forth.

Like the good ol' days.

"I guess I deserved that," Jasmine agreed.

She didn't have a snappy reply? A tart comeback? Now I knew something was up. She wanted me in a good mood. No matter the cost to herself.

"What do you need, Fairchild?"

12

"For starters, how about you stop calling me *Fairchild*?"

"Why? You change your name since last we spoke? Accept an indecent marriage proposal?"

"It's Jasmine, and you know it. Be civilized or I'll leave."

"I didn't drag you out here kicking and screaming."

"Chance Grayson Harper," Jasmine snapped, finally deciding to take an eye for an eye. I had always hated it when someone said my full name like that. My mother used to do it. Now she wasn't around to do that anymore. Jasmine knew this, which was why she had done it. And since she was one of the few people in the world who could call out my full name like that, she knew it would get my attention.

"All right, all right. What do you want?"

Jasmine worked her way up to just a few rows below the one I was on and leaned back against the rail. She had on a sleek green-and-yellow number—the make, I couldn't tell you—though it did compliment her figure. The dress fit her like a snakeskin. I assumed it had been tailored to fit her, as everything she wore looked tailored to her slender physique. Not that she needed her clothes to be. Jasmine just happened to have one of those bodies for which clothes had been invented. No matter the brand, the style, how expensive or cheap, she always looked exquisite in whatever she wore. Though I'm sure the dress cost her a pretty penny or two. Unlike the off-the-rack clothes I got at Buffalo Exchange or, when I really felt like spending the big bucks, one of the many logo-covered tees I found on Target's bargain shelves.

Or rather, I should correct myself, I'm sure Jasmine's dress cost her *father* a pretty penny or two. The great James

Fairchild. You've probably heard his name around town a time or two. Or seen one of his ads on TV. James Fairchild came from what one would call "old money." On his mother's side. The Fairchilds had money, owned the right property, and were seen at all the right functions and openings. He was a wheeler and a dealer, a shaker and a mover. Or something to that effect. Truth be told, I was never one hundred percent sure what he did, but I knew it had something to do with real estate and oranges. Or maybe it was lemons. Which was why he was on numerous city boards, always pushing for workers' rights and the good of the environment and small and local mom-and-pop-type businesses. Lately there had been rumors of him running for office or something higher up. Governor or senate or something along those lines. I knew he had a law degree, though I'd heard from Jasmine that he had never practiced. It was just a backup he had always said. But that didn't mean he wasn't a driven man. He had always been focused on his career more than his family. From what I remembered.

But he wasn't a bad guy overall.

So long as neither of his daughters hated you.

Luckily for me, at least back when I interacted with the man, it was when not only one, but both of his daughters thought I was somewhat dreamy. Also, luckily for me, I was considered somewhat unintimidating enough that he didn't give me a second thought. That and the fact that most of his thoughts were already preoccupied with his work.

"I've got a test in Bio next and I don't aim to miss it, Fair—Jazz," I said, stopping myself from antagonizing her any further and instead landing back on my pet name for her. Back when we had pet names for each other.

"You had Bio last year." Jasmine smiled once again. Always with the smiling. Girl knew how to throw on the charm and disarm a guy when she needed to. Pearly whites, all even and in a row, with just ever so slight a touch of lipstick, to compliment her already perfectly proportioned lips, but not enough to distract from any of the other beauty her face brought to the conversation. "You've got AP Chemistry with Mr. Clemmons this year, just like me. And you had it second period this morning. I saw you leaving as I entered for third."

"Uh-huh." I wasn't sure how to reply to that. Was she stalking me? "I was just asking the teacher a question between classes. Didn't you hear? I failed most of my freshman classes. I'm behind a year."

"You *were* behind freshman year. But you made them up that summer. You're not stupid, Chance. And you may have stumbled during freshman year but you more than caught up. Why else would you be in two AP classes this year?"

So, she was up on all current events concerning yours truly. Best to stop trying to pull the wool over her eyes if I wanted to move this along.

"Well, whatever class is next, I don't aim to miss it. You plan on spilling soon?"

"It's Madison," Jasmine answered, half biting her lip, which signaled to me that whatever she was here for, it was serious. That and the fact that she was here on behalf of her sister, who, no matter what had gone on between Jasmine and me, she would never have had an issue with approaching me about in the years since our fallout. Sure, I knew that the closeness between the two sisters had waned since I had last socialized with them. And that in public they put on airs and the show of constantly trying to one-up the other and having disdain for the other's social status. But I knew that deep down, the Fairchild sisters were madly protective of one another. Remember, I was one of the lucky few who had been fortunate enough to see behind the curtain into the private lives of the Fairchilds.

I had seen Maddie that morning in the hallways. She had had a hell of a shiner on her face and when I passed by, I had caught her line of sight. Though, now, come to think of it, it was as if she had been staring me down, wanting me to notice her face. As if she was mentally calling out for me to help her. I had almost approached her when I remembered that the Fairchilds were no longer my business, and then the class bell rang, and she disappeared into the crowd.

"Maddie? What about her?"

Jasmine stood there a moment, contemplating the situation she was in and the next step she was about to take—no doubt whether to involve me in this whole mess—when she handed over a cell phone. I knew it wasn't hers; though both Fairchild sisters had iPhones, this one had a bright-pink bejeweled protective sleeve on the back, and I knew Jasmine would never have anything she considered so tacky on one of her accessories.

Jasmine was always, if nothing else, classy.

"You know the code?" I asked before I even looked at the

phone. I knew there had to be one. Between parents, nosey friends, and jealous exes, one can never be too careful in this day and age.

"The year she was born."

I guess I shouldn't have been too surprised. It's not like I expected the first six digits to pi. This was Madison Fairchild we were talking about. And while we may not have spoken more than half a dozen words over the last two years, I still heard plenty of the rumors that went around the school. Girl was a wild one. Between her conservative father and Jasmine growing into the young woman she would one day fully become; I'm sure Madison was just doing her bit to stand out and be noticed.

Jasmine Fairchild was the junior class president, an honor student with above-perfect grades and probably the class valedictorian come the time. When this school year ended, it was known she would spend the summer traveling throughout Europe, possibly even looking at potential colleges. Despite coming from one of the richest families in school, Jasmine was a well-rounded, kind, and compassionate girl. She always made sure to include everyone in all class discussions, considered all social circles when planning school functions, and did her best to make sure no one felt unwelcomed or ignored.

Jasmine was well-liked by most everyone in school.

Madison Fairchild, on the other hand, was almost as well-liked, if just for other reasons. Like seeing who could down the most shots before blacking out. Or taking on any dare thrown at her, no matter if it got her suspended from school or even, as had occurred on two occasions, arrested. There were also the usual rumors about her and most of the football team, not to mention the other various sports teams that our school supplied growing teenage boys with so as to have a way to unleash their otherwise pent-up youthful frustrations. I may not have traveled in the same circles as either of the Fairchild girls, but I was still aware of both.

It was hard not to be. Again, this was high school, and people talked. Particularly, teen-aged people.

"What about her?" I asked as I punched in the girl's birth year and stared at the home screen.

"Go to text messages," Jasmine instructed, continuing as she saw me obeying her orders. "Open the last one. From the blocked number."

I continued to scroll through the phone when I finally paused.

Well, I had to admit it—never in a million years would I have believed I would be seeing these images when I sat down for lunch this afternoon.

2

GIRLS ON FILM

I scrolled through the various images—a nickel's worth in all—before coming to the text message connected with them demanding money in exchange for the pictures' destruction. The pictures were of Madison, each lewder than the one before, though none were taken by the girl herself, as if taking selfies for a boyfriend or suitor.

These pictures were posed for.

"So pay the piper. What's the big deal? Your dad has that kind of dough. And even if you don't want to involve him, don't tell me you don't have access to that kind of cash."

Jasmine stared at me with that stern, disapproving look on her face that used to get to me. It was interesting to know that after all this time it still could.

"Look," I said as I sat up in my seat. "You can't tell me Madison doesn't know about these. These aren't personal, intimate photos between her and a boyfriend taken late one night. She posed for them. She must know about them. And, knowing Madison, she could probably give two shits about anyone knowing about their existence. I'm assuming you and your father—if you were to ever tell him about these—are the ones who would be more bothered by them getting out into the world. Which I can understand. These aren't high art as far as my knowledge of such things goes."

"Exactly," Jasmine blurted at me. "They aren't. Those are disgusting and crude. And *vulgar*. Exactly the sort of thing I'd expect Madison to get herself wrapped up in. I don't care about her. I'm not here for her reputation. It's Father I'm here for. No, he doesn't know about the photos and I'd like to keep it that way. I'm not opposed to paying for them. I just want to make sure we get back all the other copies. In this day and age . . ."

I knew where she was going with this.

"What do you want from me?"

"I *do* have the money—that much is true. But even if I can afford it, I can't involve anyone else. Anyone else would . . . well . . . they'd talk. Word would get out. No matter whom I went to with this or threatened any action against, word would still get out. But you . . . you're one of the few people I know with actual honor to their name."

"My name's Chance Grayson Harper as you so eloquently pointed out just minutes ago. Don't remember Honor being in there anywhere."

"Don't be an ass."

"I'm touched."

"I just want this handled."

"My ass?"

"And as quickly as possible," Jasmine continued, ignoring my crude innuendo. "I trust your judgment. And I trust your senses. If you feel all is copasetic, then all is A-OK by me. I'd

20

never be able to tell if someone was pulling a fast one over on me. But you can. You always could. That's why I want you. If someone was pulling a fast one on you, I know you wouldn't let it go until you got to the bottom of it. That's just how you are. And I just want this done. In and out. Fast and over with. This is only to be a simple exchange of goods, Chance. Nothing more. I don't need you to go all Hardy Boys on me and dig into this any deeper. I just want you to do the exchange."

"What's Aiden going to say when he finds out you came to your ex with this instead of the current edition? You know you're just gonna piss him off for robbing him of the chance to pummel someone."

"Aiden never has to find out. No one has to find out. This is just between you and me. That's the whole point."

"And the photographer, makeup artist, lighting designer, craft services, techy people at the cellular company, and the person poaching you for a free college education? Speaking of which . . .?"

"Who do I think sent those photos and the message?" Jasmine asked. "I haven't the faintest idea. And I don't care, I just want it over with."

"But this isn't even your phone . . . so really, this scandal isn't even yours." I made guilty tsk-tsk noises at her. "Which goes back to my original question—why would someone bother sending this to Maddie at all? Surely, she could care less."

"Exactly. I'm just lucky I happened to have the phone at the time when that message came in."

This thought struck me dumb for a moment.

"Why *do* you have your sister's phone? You've got one of your own. And I can't see you asking to borrow hers, not when you've got Lauren or Emma's you could borrow. And I couldn't see her giving it to you to use even if you had asked. Correct?"

"My, that was a loaded question." I waited while she stalled. "Yes, I could and would just ask to use Lauren's or Emma's if for some reason I didn't have mine around. As if that would ever happen."

"I'm sure the horror of that idea makes *The Walking Dead* seem like something created by Disney." I huffed, making fun of myself for even thinking the thought.

"And you're right about the fact that Madison would never let me borrow her phone, even if I did ask. She's too convinced I'd snoop through it looking for blackmail material all of my own to use against her and Daddy."

"Hold that thought," I interrupted. "We'll come back to this real quick. But on a side note, why *aren't* you using this to blackmail or use against her?"

Jasmine stared coldly down at me, reaming me a new one for ever thinking her so low. As if I didn't know what games she played. It was a legit question. They may have been close at one time, but like I said, in the last two years I had seen the sisters grow apart. She may have tried to forget, but back when Jasmine and I dated, we spent a lot of time together. And not just with each other, but with her friends as well. The same ones I considered my friends until they weren't. I remember the way they behaved, the way they treated the other students in our classes. I can't say I don't look back every now and again and feel ashamed for some of the things I said and did. Jasmine may claim to have changed from back when we hung out all the time, but I still knew what she was capable of. And sisters were still sisters. I had seen them in action before. Jasmine had always been daddy's little girl while Madison had been their mother's favorite. And after their mother wasn't in the picture any more . . . well, Jasmine often did go against her sister with her father. So why not now? What was different about this piece of information? Unless—

"So, the rumors about your father are true? Hmmm?"

"I'm quite sure I don't know what you mean." Those were Jasmine's famous words for denying something that was true. I had those words figured out back during freshman year. They had come in real handy back then. Currently there were rumors about Jasmine's father running for governor or some senate seat. No one was sure when exactly this was going to happen, but the fires had been fanned higher as of late and word had it, he was going to announce his running sometime before the end of the year.

"So, anyway, back to the topic at hand. You can always borrow from your friends, Maddie thinks you're a hypocritical piece of doggie do-do, blah, blah, blah. So how and why did you have your sister's phone?"

"Connor Emerson gave it to me this morning between second and third period," Jasmine explained. "Said she left it at his place the night before."

"Sticky Icky? Really? Maddie and him?"

"No. At least I don't think so. Or if it is, then it's news to me. And Liam."

Liam Murphy was Maddie's boyfriend, or at least her on-again/off-again flavor of the month. Though rumor had it Liam was a flavor Maddie liked to sample repeatedly. Liam and his cousin, Aiden Murphy (Jasmine's current beau no less), were oaf jocks known for their short tempers and having arms bigger than most people's heads. Connor Emerson, on the other hand, was not known for having arms as big as people's heads. So, if he *was* having a secret liaison with Madison Fairchild, why would he go poking the bear and advertising doing so to her sister? I couldn't really see him being *that* dense, even being as high as he usually was. One would think he'd be doing as much as possible to conceal said relationship. Especially while out in public.

"Chance . . . I can see the wheels turning," Jasmine said, breaking my concentration.

I looked up at her, still considering the options and playing the various scenarios out in my head.

"Not sure quite yet. So . . . what? You want me to get the pics back? The negatives? Or memory card, or whatever. Make sure this doesn't happen again?"

"Yeah."

"This is your sister we're talking about. Even if we can clean up this mess, it doesn't mean it won't happen again."

"I'm aware of that."

"Besides, doesn't your father have professional cleanup people for something like this? I mean, if he is—"

"*If* and *when* he does what you think he might be doing,

then those people can deal with Madison's messes. Until then, it's just Father and me. And like I said, he's got enough to worry about at the moment."

"And why would I do this?"

"Because you're *that* guy. It's what you do."

"Actually, this sounds like what the cops do. Or private dicks. I'm just your average high schooler. Why not hire someone professional to handle this?"

"I think it's someone our age. The blackmailer, I mean. Possibly even at this school. You think in a million years that a professional could crack a bunch of high schoolers? Teenagers clam up around adults. You know that. I need someone who can poke their head in and around the different scenes and figure out what's what. You're good at that. People like you. Overall. When you're not being a standoffish dick. And you know how to get people to talk. If memory serves me correct?"

She was messing with me now, just as I had done with her a few moments before. If it hadn't been for my getting people to open to me and my bull doggedness for never giving up until I got the truth, then freshman year and all that came with it might never have happened. Maybe I'd still have my parents around. Jasmine, her mother. And us . . . each other. Minus the endless gossip that still paraded around me.

"But what do you need all that for if all you want is a simple exchange?"

"Again, I need to know for sure. That this is all behind and finished with. You'll do what you need to do to make sure that's true."

"You have that much faith in my abilities, do you?"

"I remember that playhouse we had out back behind your parent's yard. Your detective's club or whatever it was. No girls allowed. Yet I was there every day with you. The two of us. Out to solve the unsolvable. To correct the injustices of the world. Though I doubted we knew that's what we aimed to do. I thought it was just a way for us to spend time together. As kids. But you . . . to you it was more. You always had this drive. To know what was going on in every house in the neighborhood. When the Petersons were robbed, you wanted to know who did it. When the Fisher's house caught fire one night, you wanted to know if it was intentional or not. That was you, Chance Harper. I never really focused on it, at least not back then, but now part of me must wonder what happened to you so early in your life to drive you like that? You wanted to help people. But even more than that, you have an insatiable need to know the truth. As if everyone in the world is out to lie to you."

"Aren't they? I think I was just a scared boy who was trying his best to make sense of the world."

"Say what you will. I remember that little boy. His natural curiosity. You were born curious. And that's why."

"Again, why should I bother?"

Jasmine stared hard at me. She reached up with her left arm and caressed a scar on my face just below my hairline before dragging her finger down my brow to another nick just above my right eye.

"You're an old hat, Chance Harper. You don't belong.

26

Maybe"—she stopped and shrugged— "you could again."

"Nobody belongs," I snapped back as I removed her hand and made sure it stopped at her side. "That's why they call it high school. If everyone enjoyed all four years, then they would have called it something else."

"Well, if that doesn't work for you, then let's just say you owe me. For freshman year. Yes, I know what part I played in it all. I could have talked. Raised questions. Instead, I left it up to you. And what happened never would have happened if it hadn't been for you. So, you owe me."

I looked up at her and could see the hurt of what her sister was doing, had been doing, and would probably continue to do was having on her. Her family had been through enough, what with the loss of their mother. Their father had managed to move on when he remarried a woman almost half his age, not much older than Jasmine herself. But both the Fairchild girls were still hurting from that loss. Jasmine had learned to funnel all her hurt and anger into her schoolwork, using it to better herself. Her sister, on the other hand, had done the opposite and used the pain and loss as an excuse for acting out.

Plus, as much as I hated to admit it, the thought of my social standing at high school possibly rising, even if only a peg or two, was rather enticing. After all, I still had two years left to get through and anything to make it all that more bearable was at least somewhat desirable. Damn me for being human and weak. Besides, if anyone *could* raise my standing at school, it would have been the one and only Jasmine Fairchild. After all, she was the one who knocked me down in the first place.

"And if none of those reasons work how about I just pay you for your time?"

"Who does Sticky Icky hang out with?"

"I told you, Chance, I don't want you to figure out who's behind this. I just want you to do the trade-off."

"No, you don't. You're the great Jasmine Fairchild. Everyone thinks you're selfless and flawless. But I know you got a vicious streak deep down inside. Someone thinks they can get the best of you. You want me to find out who's doing this, stop them without making them a dime off you, and make sure they suffer for ever having thought they could do this in the first place. Tell me I'm wrong?"

Jasmine brushed a strand of hair out of her face and continued as if I hadn't said a word. "You really think Connor Emerson's blackmailing Madison?"

"In figuring out who's behind this, there are two options. First, they're blackmailing Maddie, thinking she will give in to something like this. We both know she wouldn't. So that means the person doing this, if they *are* targeting Maddie, doesn't know her. Which means it's not a student. At least not a student at this school. It also means that this all very well could be about hurting Maddie. Or your family."

"Particularly my father."

"If he truly is running, then yes. Then that means this has nothing to do with your sister. This is about him. So, then it has nothing to do with money and it doesn't matter what you pay—the pictures are going to be leaked. Just to hurt your father."

"That makes sense," Jasmine agreed. "Or . . .?"

"*Or* that the intended recipient of the blackmail message *wasn't* in fact your sister but was *you*. They know you. They knew how you'd react when you saw the texts. Which is to pay up and get this behind you. Which means this isn't about hurting you or Maddie or your father—it's simply about getting paid. That changes the facts to pointing more at a fellow student, thus someone lacking in the multiple *Ks* they're asking for. Someone who *knew* you'd have the phone on you when you did, and not your sister, making sure *you* received the message, not her."

"Connor Emerson."

"That's the start."

"That's all good in theory, but there's one problem with that."

"What's that?"

"Sticky Icky," she answered, Connor's nickname being enough to explain everything.

"Connor Emerson likes his medicinals," I agreed, nodding my head. "But it still costs, and he's not exactly known for being flush. Plus, lately I've heard he's jumped up on the food chain for a twenty-four-seven Junk addiction, which is an even more expensive habit to furnish."

"Connor Emerson isn't focused enough to tie his own shoes let alone come up with a blackmail scheme. He's more about the instant gratification and whatever fun he can get out of life. He's not a long-term-con kind of guy."

"I'm aware of all this. He's known more for being a good time. Having the right hook up. Which lately, is Junk. Which is also a higher level of seriousness and scary than the pot pool he's used to swimming in. Maybe he got in over his head and he owes someone?" I may not have been the most social kid at school, but I still heard the rumors. "That's why I asked you, who does Connor Emerson hang out with?"

Jasmine thought about this for a moment, then came up with an answer that I could tell satisfied her by the look on her face.

"Pierre Chevalier."

"That the same Pierre who has a daily vlog and is always Instagramming every moment of his life?" Connor Emerson was just about as close to white trash as a school with our high, upstanding morality would allow to enroll, while Pierre Chevalier was of the upper crust, right there alongside the Fairchilds. I was waiting for an answer when a connection came into focus. "And doesn't he take all those *pictures* for the yearbook?"

Jasmine smiled and raised an eyebrow as if to confirm my thoughts.

"The one and only."

3

AM I WRONG?

The lunch bell rang, and Jasmine went to grab the phone from me when I held it back. That was all she needed to know I'd do the job. Lord only knows why I would. Hell, even I'm not sure why I agreed to do it. But I did just the same.

She walked down from the bleachers and off the football field, the sun shining in front of her, plastering her silhouette in complete darkness as I watched her leave. Maybe I did owe her. I didn't quite see it that way, but if it helped her sleep at night what was the harm? Maybe it had to do with what those two girls had been through. I may not have agreed with all of Madison Fairchild's antics, but in some way, I could see why she did them. It wasn't like I could be considered a saint. I wasn't the same person since that time back before everything changed. I stared at the "water" bottle filled with anything but and went to pour the rest over the side of the bleachers, stopping just as the liquid hit the rim. Hell. I'd already spent the money on it. This would just be a waste. Who knew what later would bring.

I found my way into AP English, the first class I had every day after lunch, which just so happened to be the one and only class I had with Pierre Chevalier.

Pierre came from a movie family in that his family worked for one of the movie studios that were scattered throughout the city. His mother was a former model who did bit parts in daytime soaps and as a background party filler in movies. She claimed she never broke out big in the business because she never wanted to, not wanting to devote all her time to the craft of acting, instead loving her life as a mother and, more likely, as a trophy wife. Pierre's father worked as a producer of the art-house-type flicks more associated with the independent studios. Every single movie he had brought to the big screen over the last fifteen years, which was a total of six now, had been nominated for numerous Academy Awards, including the coveted Best Picture award, which Pierre's father had lost every single time.

With his parents being in the "business," and them constantly out of town on work-related trips, Pierre's house was often vacant, which he used as an excuse to throw lavish parties. The grounds had a heated pool out back, which, luckily, was deep enough, as it was often the ideal target for cannonballs off the second-story roof of his house. I always pitied the cleaning staff on the mornings after one of Pierre's infamous parties. Though I myself had never joined in on one of the happenings, I had often heard of the buffoonery carried out at such festivities and had seen the numerous pictures online afterword.

Pierre was known as the type of guy who could procure just about any item a student might have need for: be it the answers to an upcoming test, supplements to help with sporting achievements, or any other substances that might just help make the school year more bearable. Myself included, as I had found it often easier to obtain the occasional drink through him than with the fake I.D. I had obtained down on Alvarado Street. I also didn't remember Pierre to be cruel or an intolerant kid. Once, during sophomore year, during a rough time, I had found a proper and more-than-legal-looking fake I.D. inside my locker without so much as any sort of clue or hint as to who had left it or if any sort of payment had been required for such an expert job. And though he'd never admitted it and I never confronted him about it, I'd always had a sneaking suspicion that it had come from Pierre. I hoped that he wasn't involved in Madison's blackmail scheme.

After the second bell rang and class began, I noticed Pierre wasn't in class, though I could have sworn I had seen him at school earlier that day. Then again, it wasn't like I had really been paying all that much attention on him earlier. Could have just gotten my days mixed up.

I looked around, caught the glance of Rebecca Collins, and figured if anyone would know where Pierre was, it would be her. Rebecca Collins was five-feet-four of pure, natural energy, which she thought would have been wasted on the cheerleading squad (though she had still tried out for and been rejected by them freshman year) and so instead focused it on working on the student paper and yearbook, something she did closely with Pierre. This also meant she kept a watchful eye on most of the student body and often knew everyone else's business.

Rebecca pulled a strand of strawberry-blond hair out of her face as she leaned over and stared down at her desk, her pencil rapidly scrawling something out across the blue lines that striped the piece of recyclable, school-supplied paper. She was a cute girl, though not considered one of the hottest the school had to offer. She didn't know it, but I had a feeling that one day, Rebecca would more than be able to make a man's head turn 360 degrees. Forget that she had full lips and rosy cheeks that helped her Irish-green eyes *pop*—it was her confidence and low tolerance of bullshit that helped her exude the sexuality of which she was just lately becoming more aware.

"Where's Pierre? I don't see him. Is he here today?" I whispered as loudly as I dared while Mrs. Cherry began her lecture on the next class reading project. Mrs. Cherry was one of the more enjoyable teachers we had at Westlake High, trying her hardest to make the lessons relatable, as well as allowing us to have some fun while learning. She was shorter than most everyone in the student body, including the freshmen, but that didn't mean she couldn't let loose the forces of Hades when needed, often striking fear in the hearts of whomever needed to be kept in line. She was an agreeable person to anyone who cared about their education, often making herself available to her students and trying her best to help them along when they were stumped (which was more often than anyone cared to admit).

I noticed the rest of the class had their copies of *The Great Gatsby* out, searching frantically for what was probably the answer to whatever question she had asked. I hadn't heard the question, but I'd read the book before and seen both movies. I figured I could work my way through it if she thought enough to call on me. Fortunately, I was one of her better students who actually read the books and did the assignments as they were given; therefore, I was rarely called on in class.

I turned back around and Rebecca looked up at me, focused on my face through her red-rimmed glasses, and then took them off, licking her lips, which looked to have been recently reapplied with whatever brightly colored shade of red was in style that month, and smiled at me.

"Not today." Rebecca shrugged as she bounced her leg, one on top of the other as if nervous or anxiously waiting for something to happen. She tried to appear nonchalant about my request, but I could tell she was eager to talk, though whether that was simply to share some juicy gossip or to share a few words with me, I couldn't tell. Last I had heard through the grapevine, Rebecca had no romantic interest in me. My bets were on the national pastime of spreading gossip.

"You know why?"

"I'm not his girlfriend," Rebecca snipped, not with any sort of bite, but with a tone that let me know that she was saddened by the fact she wasn't.

Pierre was considered worthy of a "heart-on"—someone who turned you on but was also actually worthy of your heart—I guess, depending on who you asked. He had an even olive tan no matter what time of the year it was, with large, brown eyes, a bushy head of dark, curly hair, and a slightly uneven five o'clock shadow around the chin. Well, maybe make that a three o'clock patchy shadow. He had been on the swim team every year since third grade, so there was no shortage of shirtless pics of him floating around Facebook and in the yearbooks for all the girls to giggle over and ogle. Personally, he seemed a little lanky to me, but then again, I wasn't really one to judge, being as I looked closer to Pierre in body type than that of either of the Fairchild girls' current steroid-taking beaus.

This also struck out my theory that Rebecca may have had a slight interest in me. Which confirmed Option (a): she had something she was dying to get off her chest and I was more than willing to be that listening ear. Hell, I'd grow a third one right now just to make sure she got the hint. Sometimes girls needed a not-so-subtle push of encouragement.

"You know where he is?"

"Right now? No. Since I don't see him here and I'm in class. Trying to pay attention. Like you should be." She put her glasses back on and was about to look down at her paper when her focus returned to me. "What's your beef with Pierre anyway?"

"Nothing," I replied as I finally turned back around and faced the front of the class. "I just had some camera questions and figured he'd be the one to ask."

"Oh," Rebecca said, sounding disappointed there wasn't a more pressing reason for my wanting to know where he was. With all the "business" Pierre did dealing with the student body and the sometimes items of ill repute that were often requested, he had occasionally been seen around school looking a little scuffed up. "Well, he is. The one to talk to about that sort of stuff. He was here first period but booked it after the bell rang. Haven't seen him since. But his lackey is here, somewhere."

"Lackey?" I had no idea who she meant. While Pierre Chevalier had never particularly been someone I felt the need to keep the latest 4-1-1 on in the back of my brain, I was beginning to feel as if he and I didn't even attend the same school. I was slacking. Less than twenty minutes on the job and I was already falling behind. If Jasmine knew any better, she'd fire me and hire a professional.

"Yeah, his personal errand boy. Connor Emerson. Does any and everything Pierre asks."

"Sticky Icky?"

"What? Haven't you heard the rumors?"

I shrugged my shoulders and tilted my head to signal that I hadn't. We were still in the middle of class, and though Mrs. Cherry was going on about relating Gatsby's tragedy to our own lives, I'm sure most of the class was just wondering when they'd get to watch Leonardo DiCaprio bring what they thought was a boring book to life.

"Connor's cleaned up his act. Partially. Had to if he wanted to hang around with Pierre. And he does. Wants to carry his books. Take certain items to other students if they need it and Pierre asks because he doesn't want to be associated with it. You know. That sort of stuff. Like on *The Wire*, where one drug dealer takes the cash and another hands over the product."

"So they can claim ignorance, et cetera. I get you."

"So, you gotta be focused to do that. Can't have you off smoking the product away all day. Word has it, Pierre got Connor to volunteer himself into a rehab facility in Malibu and thirty days later, no more Sticky Icky. Anyway, Connor's kind of got a little schoolboy crush on Pierre. If you ask me, there's something gay going on between those two. Not that Pierre's gay, if you ask me. But he is French. And you know those European types. They don't have all the same 'boundaries' that we like to bog ourselves down with. Then again, Connor really could just be Pierre's bitch. Though I've yet to figure out what exactly he's getting out of the relationship."

I wasn't sure which guy she meant.

"Any idea where Connor is?"

"Nope. But I do know he has P.E. last period."

I jerked my head in confusion. Last period physical education classes were usually reserved for the jocks and other members of the ongoing sporting teams that our school had to offer, to allow the kids playing sports an extra hour early jump on their daily practice. If he had seventh period P.E., that meant he was on a sporting team, something I was not aware of. Then again, other than a few random football games, I don't think I've yet to attend a single sporting competition. Being as this was the fall and football was the only sporting event at the moment, I would deduce that Connor was on the team. And that, I knew for a fact, was a bunch of malarkey. Kid barely made it through school without being expelled for poor grades due to a lack of "focus"—though, apparently that had changed. Still, I didn't see how he could be on a sports team. And on one where everyone was at least three times his size. I couldn't help but smile to myself at the mental image when I paused a moment.

Connor Emerson was on the shorter side all right, coming up an inch shorter than Rebecca, yet still with a strong, sturdy stance that was fitting for his often-short temper. I could only see one answer for him.

"Wrestling?" I asked almost mutely.

"See . . ." Rebecca said with a smile in her voice. I could hear it as if she was beating me over the head with a frying pan. "And they say you can't teach an old dog new tricks."

Great. First, I was an old hat and now I was being called an old dog. Couldn't these girls just make up their minds already?

"I catch on real quick. Like a summer cold when you're out of Dayquil."

"Well, Chance Harper, if you ever feel like trading out of that sucking streak you've been on for the last two years for a whole new kind of sucking streak, you just let me know."

I couldn't help but flush from Rebecca's comment. Never had I expected words like those to come out of her mouth.

Um, maybe I was wrong about Option (b) after all.

4

ANIMALS

Bell rang. Class ended. Mrs. Cherry never called on me, but she did assign a fifteen-page paper discussing the various themes of *The Great Gatsby* (due the following Monday) and reminded—i.e., *warned*—that next week we would be taking our PSATs and that in two weeks we would be beginning *The Joy Luck Club*. Clearly Amy Tan wasn't writing about her high school years when she picked the title of that book. There was a severe lack of joy in school and I was sorely lucking out on moving along this project for Jasmine.

I left class and I searched the hallways.

No Pierre Chevaier.

No Connor Emerson.

I then went to sixth period Art Appreciation. S⸱ Left. Repeated my search to the same results.

Nine minutes later, the one-minute warnir I was on to my next—oh, I may have mention, I didn't have a seventh peri⸱ Work Experience. Which made ⸱ the gym and hunt down Con⸱

My current afterschool w⸱

helping my aunt and uncle take care of the motel they owned up on Cahuenga Boulevard just north of Hollywood by the Ford Theatre. This also happened to be where I lived. Where I have lived ever since freshman year, when all hell broke loose and my father and Jasmine and Madison's mother were found doing the horizontal tango by none other than yours truly, thus breaking up not one but two marriages and tearing apart both families. I was blamed for spilling the beans, Jasmine and I broke up, divorces were threatened, and before all was done, my father and Jasmine's mother decided to follow Romeo and Juliet's famous last steps and spend eternity together.

Six feet under.

Not to mention what had happened to me, leaving me with the several physical—as well as emotional and psychological—scars that Jasmine had been so kind to point out to me earlier during lunch.

I often wonder what would have happened if I had kept my mouth shut. Would Jasmine and I still be together? Would both our parents still be in loveless marriages? Or would they have maybe divorced and found new lives? Or, as I have often wondered, would some of them still be alive to live out their futures, no matter what that would have brought, be it blissful love or wretched heartache?

Again, I mostly tried not to focus on the past. Both cause I find that, no, it doesn't help oneself prepare for the e and because, why focus on something so dark and as the past? The past is for suckers who think the best d them with the future holding nothing to offer.

I am not one of those people. Or so I keep trying to tell myself. I had yet to see evidence of this in my life.

I made it to the gymnasium and poked my head in through the double doors, soaking in and almost being knocked out by the abundance of male testosterone, sweat, and various aromas of unwashed gym clothing emitting from the room as I scanned for my prey. The sounds of sneakers could be heard squeaking and squealing along the polished wooden gym floor as several games of basketball were being played.

No surprise—Jasmine's current beau, Aiden Murphy—a senior—and his cousin, and Maddie's current whatever, Liam Murphy—a junior—were both in seventh period P.E.

Will wonders never cease?

Two sisters dating cousins. I'm sure there was a Shakespearian comedy in there somewhere. Or maybe, considering past events, a tragedy.

I was praying just to find Connor Emerson and get the hell out of there without having to approach, or be approached by, either of those two. Despite her best attempts at being discreet, I'm sure by now someone would have spilled the beans to Aiden that Jasmine had been seen out talking with me during lunch. And to now be poking my head in here would probably only cause trouble.

"Excuse me," I said as politely as possible, stopping the next jock who passed by. "Connor Emerson?"

The jock was Dash Newman—yes, his parents actually named him Dash. That was not a nickname and yes, he was a highly respected and multiple-award-winning track and field star at our school. Dash made a face at me, as if he couldn't place me as an actual student there, before dashing along without an answer.

Suddenly I heard a loud "Hey" which, without even looking, I could tell by the tone and inflection was directed at me by one of the oaf cousins.

I rolled my eyes and prepared to come face to face with either Aiden or Liam, only to find both invading my personal space. They were big, sweaty, and smelly (which I guess comes with the being sweaty), the veins in their arms pulsating with anger, testosterone, and a lack of civility. They flexed their arms, something that was barely needed and yet they did with ease as their Westlake High tanks showed off more skin than they covered on those two, each one making sure the emerald-green shamrock tattoos on their right shoulders popped with each move of a muscle.

"Something I can help you two with?" I asked, hoping I was being charming, despite knowing charm wouldn't help me at all with them.

"Heard you were off talking with my boy's girl?" Liam asked as he stepped in front of Aiden. Though he was the smaller of the two, he still towered a good two shots over me and my five-feet-eight inches. "What's a faggot like you doing talking to a girl?"

At least Aiden wasn't a total Neanderthal. He had some brains going for him. He knew well enough to have Liam do the asking for him, so he could claim ignorance when word got back to Jasmine that he was roughing me up by being overprotective, something she wouldn't stand for. Even this, she wouldn't be stupid enough to fall for. She would more than know the game the two were playing.

"You have a boy? Who has a girl? Is that like when your butler has a butler? Or your pet has a pet?" Me and my big mouth. And I was going to play this politely and with respect. I might have needed to check the thesaurus once more about just what exactly those two words really meant.

Liam's patience snapped and he grabbed my shirt, pulling me up off the ground by it. I could almost hear the threads holding the cloth together threatening to abandon ship and leave me hanging there, or as would have it if they did leave, falling to the floor.

"What did you say, faggot?" Liam spat in my face through clenched teeth and bulging eyes, like a predator on the savannah just waiting to devour its prey.

"Nothing. I was just—" Liam twisted my shirt up even more in his hands as he backed me up against the wall, when a booming voice called out from behind the two cousins.

"Is there a problem here?" The voice was soft but full of edge, to the point that one might have thought it was the physical education teacher, Mr. Kingston, except everyone at school knew the teacher's voice was higher than most of the males in freshman class. Regardless, all three of us immediately knew who the voice belonged to.

While Aiden Murphy and Liam Murphy might have been a formidable force on the school grounds, it was known wide and far that senior Theo Lannapo could have crushed each student's head, one in each hand, without so much as breaking a sweat. Theo was by far the biggest kid in school, standing at six-feet-five, made up of nothing but pure muscle. He was a sweet kid, the nicest of the nice to everyone he came across, not being one to tolerate bullying of any type. This was probably due to the constant harassment he experienced all during elementary school, when he was barely four feet tall and so thin that even the scarecrow from *The Wizard of Oz* could have beaten him up. Theo was part Cherokee, part Latino and even Middle Eastern if my memory serves me correctly.

Oh, and last but certainly not least, Theo was one of the few people in school who I considered a friend.

"This doesn't concern you, Lannapo," Aiden said as he turned around, keeping Liam and I guarded behind him.

"Oh, really?" Theo smiled as he flashed his pearly whites at Aiden, appearing as if he was about to chew the kid up and eat him for lunch. "That looks like you got my friend Chance there up off the ground. And unless you plan on buying him a new wardrobe after you get done tearing apart the shirt he's got on, then I think this might be considered what one would call a 'hostile environment.'"

A *hostile environment*? Really? It was as if Theo didn't go to the same school as everyone else every day of the year. Every day of the school year was a hostile environment for three-fourths of the student-body population. But then again, it wasn't exactly like people were lined up to bully and pick on Theo Lannapo.

"What hostile environment?" Aiden smiled, trying to subtly puff out his chest while also putting on airs of friendliness. "Your buddy Chance here is groovy. Ain't that right, Chance?"

Aiden eyed me but none of us was buying what he was selling. Minimum wage didn't pay enough.

"Chance?" Theo said with the raise of an eyebrow.

"Oh, I'm all good. I mean, I obviously had a helium-rich breakfast which is helping me do the two-toe tango"—Aiden glared at me and I swallowed hard—"And I'm probably going to have to throw a funeral for my favorite shirt and go into a period of mourning, but I think I'll survive."

Aiden and Liam both glared at me.

"What?" I said defensively. "Everyone knows the GAP is seasonal. I'll never be able to find this one again."

Theo continued to stare Aiden down, his smile disappearing into a sneer that would have made a wolverine piss himself, when he took a step forward, causing Aiden's reflexes to kick in and he flinched back into his cousin. Liam quickly let me down and the two glared at each other, mentally scowling at one another for having let this happen. Liam turned to me, visually letting me know they would get me next time, when they heard a quick grunt emit from Theo, letting them know not to even bother with the threat. If anything were to happen to me, they would have him to deal with. And no one, no matter how stupid or high up on the food chain you thought you were, wanted that.

The cousins were about to leave when, at the last second, Aiden threw up his elbow, which connected with my nose and dropped me to the floor.

"I slipped." Aiden immediately grinned as he threw up his hands in surrender and bounced out of Theo's grasp.

"Accidents happen. Right, faggot?"

Aiden flipped us both the finger as the two scurried over to their side of the gym, occasionally glancing back over their shoulders at Theo, who continued to stare them down as I reassembled myself, straightening out my shirt and picking back up my book bag. The front of my shirt was covered in blood, and while my face felt like it had glass swimming around between my skin and skull, I didn't think my nose was broken. I would have dark circles under my eyes for a few days, but I couldn't think of anyone who would give me a second glance of concern.

"What? You're not going to chase after them for that little slip up?" I asked as I pinched my nose to try and stop the bleeding.

"We have two-hand-touch football today. It's amusing how often I get two-hand-touch and tackle confused for one another." Theo turned to me. "What was that all about?"

"Wha? Them? Oh, nothing. You know. We have a long-standing hate/hate relationship. Started back in fourth grade when they were both twice my size and felt the need to find someone to pick on. Hey, what can I say? I was available. And you know how much I like to be accommodating." Theo smirked and remained silent. "They're just being dickheads. That's all. You know how they are."

"Wouldn't have anything to do with you spending lunch with Jasmine, now would it?"

I let shock come over my face, though I shouldn't have been surprised. I was Theo's closest friend since seventh grade, when he was half his size, and no one gave him a

48

second glance. I shouldn't have been all that surprised to know he would have heard about Jasmine and me talking. I swear Theo had spies all throughout the school just waiting to let him know if anything was up with me. And who wouldn't want to be in the good graces of Theo Lannapo? Letting him know I had been talking to my ex would automatically ping his protective senses into overtime, for if he had heard it, then you could very well be sure that Aiden Murphy had heard the same rumors and the hunt would be on. Now, whoever had informed Theo of my doings would be owed one, as Theo would feel indebted to them for being given the heads-up on making sure I was safe.

I could pretend to be offended at having been watched over, but who wouldn't love their own personal bodyguard system in high school?

"Maybe it does. So what? Who cares if we're talking?"

"Maybe because you two haven't minced words since freshman year. You two talkin' is big news. Somethin' up?"

"Does something need to be up? What did you hear?"

"I heard Aiden and Jasmine are havin' some difficulties. Her bein' seen talkin' with you might fuel two rubbin' sticks of a rumor into a full-fledged bonfire. You should keep your eyes and body like a banana."

He meant peeled and split. Oh, that Theo. Such a wordsmith.

"There's nothing going on between Jasmine and me. We're not getting back together, and you can use that bit of information to douse the so-called bonfire of lies spreading throughout the school grounds. She and I are over. Okay? It was just business, that's all. Nothing more. It isn't like talking to her is a day at Disneyland. After a round with her, you're just begging to be taken to the dentist for a cleaning. Ya get me?"

"I dig. I'm just tellin' you what I've been hearin'. Need me for anything else?"

"Thanks, but I'm good." Theo looked down at my shirt, then started to go, when I called out to him. "You see Connor Emerson? I hear he's got seventh period gym?"

"That why you're here?" I shrugged and remained mute. "He skipped out early. Not sure why. But it was official. Office pulled him. So he's not ditching."

"Thanks."

"Not sure where he is, but Pierre Chevalier has last period off for Work Experience. He should be at his job up on Sunset near the strip."

"Who said anything about Pierre?" Sure, I was playing dumb, but where had this come from?

"I can still add two plus two, Chance," Theo said as he looked over one of his cantaloupe-shaped shoulders at me. "Much as there ain't a reason in the world you should have two words to mix with Jasmine Fairchild, there's even less a reason you should with Connor Emerson. And if I were you, I'd steer clear of that speed-freak. He may be little but he's ruthless like a baby rattler. Don't know when to stop. But I can totally see Jasmine havin' issues with Pierre, via her sister, hence her conversation with you earlier today. And since you and she were just talkin' business . . ."

There was no reason to play dumb with Theo. He'd be the

last person to go spread rumors about me or snitch to anyone about anything I was up to. Plus, it might be good to make sure someone else knew what I was up to and where I was scratching around at, just in case. You never knew.

"I don't know what you're talking about." I winked at him, letting him know, *Thanks for the heads-up.* "But just in case I felt like doing some shopping . . . you said up around the Sunset strip?"

5

FIREBALL

I left the gym and headed for the closest restroom. I tried my best at cleaning my face and shirt, then finally gave up. My school day was over, and I was headed home. What did I care? Plus, I was sure I had a spare shirt in my car. I stared at my bruised and bloody face when my backpack caught my attention. I opened it and dug in for the bottle of refreshment left over from lunch. I downed a swig, coughed, downed another, then sealed the bottle up and left the restroom. I wandered through the hallways, wondering where Madison Fairchild's locker was. Sure, I thought I knew, but in this day and age, who really knew anything? I had the area where she hung out down pat, but that was about it. And if I planned on not getting caught snooping through a student's locker, then time was of the essence. That was when I decided to go to my backup plan.

Backup for me came in the form of Skye Ford. Even if she wasn't yet aware of it.

Skye Ford worked in the main administration office, particularly the front desk alongside Mrs. Reagan, helping with attendance records and other such paperwork and filing duties. I get paper cuts just thinking about what all she does for an hour every afternoon, five days a week. But to each their own. Skye and I weren't exactly *close* friends, being as she was new to the school, with less than a year under her belt, but we're associated through the high school grapevine known as the social pecking order. That and how we met, which was through the joyous rite of passage all high schoolers must go through at some point or another in order to truly feel like a man or woman: detention.

It had been a rainy-day last March (sophomore year for both of us) and detention that afternoon consisted of only Miss Ford and myself. And even though we tried our hardest to ignore one another, when Mr. Kingston left the room for a "personal call," which we both knew to mean the restrooms, we broke down and exchanged words. The only things we knew about each other, myself being the mysterious moody boy whose family was the talk of the school and ate lunch by himself, and her the new girl with a short temper, shorter hair, and no shortage of sticking up for herself against anyone, particularly anyone she saw as the Man (or, in our case, anyone who was post-colligate in age). We spent the next thirty minutes talking and, more importantly, listening. We had found, in one another, someone who not only knew pain in a way no one else at that school could understand but was also a compatriot who somehow made the other feel a little better about themselves.

Rumor throughout school had Skye's family not as well off as most of the rest of the student body, with her single mother working long days at a health spa. Her father had run off on her mother and Skye when she was barely able to walk. Though no one knew officially, rumor had it her father was a one-night stand her mother had had with a famous movie star. Skye liked to pretend she was rebellious and tell people her mother named her after what she was staring up at while little baby Skye was being conceived in the back of a Lamborghini up on Mulholland late one night. I had it on good authority—namely, Skye herself, from that rainy afternoon in detention—that her mother had named her after an actress in her favorite movie, *Say Anything*. Skye had often defended her mother, saying she wasn't a bad person—she just made bad choices.

Skye often found herself in trouble, whether it was from a lack of parental guidance or be it just her nature in life, I couldn't tell. But I could tell you she was one of a kind and I was kinda drawn to her. I would have liked to tell you it was in a protective, big-brother sort of way, though truth was, Skye could probably kick the shit out of most everyone who came across her path, myself included.

She loved manga comics, particularly those with excessive amounts of blood and sex, but I copped that up to being a rational, everyday teenager. She also had a talent for drawing herself, often making characters of her fellow students, playing out just as graphic depictions of violence as our mascot (we were the Westlake Warriors, whatever *that* was) attacked and chewed and clawed apart those Skye deemed less than worthy of living. I'm sure her school-appointed therapist had much to say about her artwork, but I knew it was just another way for her to act out and pretend her rebellious streak had any sort of street cred. Skye would no sooner harm a fellow student than Mr. Rogers. Well . . . unless she was backed into a corner. But self-defense is a far cry from being a bully. And I feel I'd know the difference.

Skye was the type of girl that, had I been entertaining the idea of even considering attending junior prom at the end of the year, I just might have asked out, though we would probably end up skipping it altogether to spend the night drinking, joyriding, and causing trouble somewhere.

Or so I would like to think.

Truth was, after that rainy afternoon in detention, we rarely tossed words again, with most of our communication restricted to simple smirks as we passed each other in the hallways or as we rolled our eyes at our mundane classmates through various classes.

I decided a personal, one-on-one visit was way past due.

I poked my head in through the main doors to the administration office, saw Mrs. Reagan manning the desk, and so decided to wait a minute out front, trying to figure out how best to approach with my request when, just as luck would have it, she decided to take a powder. Maybe there was such a thing as good luck in high school. Oh, that smart Amy Tan.

Skye had also disappeared toward the back offices, and when she came back found me standing there, peering over the counter as I tried reading whatever graphic novel she was currently into—something with a green-faced man with a tree coming out of his head on the cover—when I felt her eyes piercing my soul. I looked up, still leaning against the counter, a wide, heart-melting smile plastered across my face, though from the look on her face, maybe my smile was only able to melt butter that had already gone a round in the microwave. Though I may not have had the Murphy cousins' Hemsworth-like bodies, my plain white T-shirt fit just nicely, and I could turn a head or two when needed, if I do say so myself. Like a young Robert Redford, as I had been told by several adults over the years. Even if I never did get the appeal there.

Maybe I had something in my teeth.

"What is it, Harper?" Skye asked as she slapped a folder down on the counter and then sat at her computer and began to type away. She paused momentarily as she took in my face and the front of my shirt, then went back to her job. "Looking for the nurse? I thought your standing appointment was for Wednesdays? I see we're starting early this week, huh?"

She had a cute little pixie haircut that worked perfect for her jet-black blue-streaked hair and bright-brown Bambi eyes that totally could have melted a heart or two. Shit, she could have melted steel with her eyes. She looked like a character from one of her manga comics. But I wasn't here to flirt, dammit. I had a job to do. And maybe the connection I felt between the two of us wasn't quite as strong as I had first suspected. This could be more work than I had anticipated.

"Skye. Ford. What's the word?"

"Fairchild was playing footsie to get you wrapped around her phalanges, which got you into hot water with the Murphys until Lannapo showed up and pulled a Superman. If not a minute or two too late from the looks of it." She hadn't looked up at me during her speech as she quickly sorted the various papers on her desk.

"I don't know what you're spewing but I think the grapevine got a little rotted by the time I reached you here at *oficina central.*"

Skye stopped moving about and squinted her eyes as she both gave me a once over and judged me before raising herself up out of her seat and reaching for my shirt, pointing out that there was a tear around the seams of my left shoulder. I may have wandered around the boys' restroom and the hallways for a bit before visiting her, but I wasn't exactly sure how she had heard all this so quickly, and I think that was the point. To prove just how good she was.

"Well, you know?" I blushed. "A man will do whatever he can to hold onto his pride. Even if it is his last shred."

Skye jerked her head back and forth, as if looking for someone we were talking about before winding back to me.

"Men? I thought we were talking about you?"

She winked at me. Maybe this wouldn't be so hard after all. She was just toying with me. I could handle that. Who doesn't like a good ribbing every once in a while? Besides, I've got extras of those to spare. We don't need all our ribs to keep functioning, right? I'm pretty sure they're expendable like a liver or a lung.

"Besides, I think your pride abandoned ship and hitched a ride over to West Hollywood."

West Hollywood? Really, now? Gay rumors? Again? What was this junior high all over again? I would have been offended if not for the fact that the rumors at least meant someone out there cared enough to take the time to spread them. I was touched. You know, they say you're not someone in Hollywood until the gay rumors start . . .

"Naw." I beamed. "Pride parade don't float 'til June. I think I've still got my last shred pretty secure until then. Even if I do have to keep it locked up in the basement."

"Oh, poor, poor Pride. That's no way to treat it."

"What?" I pretended innocence. "I visit it every other weekend. Just like every other father."

Skye's jaw clenched and I realized I might have touched upon a sore subject. Then again, if I couldn't joke about deadbeat dads, who could?

"So, what do you need, Harper?"

Back to business. Good. I had things to get done.

"Locker number."

"Chance Harper. Are you asking me to abuse my office privileges?"

"Please, Ford. Like you're not in here cyberloafing every afternoon." It was a harmless crime in that everyone did it every chance they got. Who didn't use the Internet at their jobs for personal uses nowadays?

"For?" I could practically hear her foot tapping against the floor.

"Huh?" I was temporarily confused.

"Locker number. For?"

"Oh, yes. Madison Fairchild."

She stared at me with a face like she was about to puke. "Please tell me you aren't preparing some out-of-this-world homecoming proposal involving surprise confetti and the question baked into the top of a cupcake?"

"Dammit. Has that already been done?" I rolled my eyes at her. "As if I would ever be caught going to homecoming. What's it matter why I need it? I just do." I was ready to move on, but she wasn't giving up. "It's personal, okay?"

"I thought you were smarter than to go poking a hornets' nest?"

"Last I checked, my Wikipeda page never said no nothin' 'bout me bein' smart."

"Why ask me?"

"Why ask why?"

"*Harper?*"

"Who else am I going to ask? Mrs. Reagan?"

"Oh, I'm sure you could have batted your baby blues at any member of the pep squad, and they would have rolled over twice to tell you without a moment's hesitation."

"The pep squad? Don't you mean the next generation of Bambis, Brandis, Melodys, and Tiphinii's—spelled with a *ph* and two *i*'s, no less—just buying time until they can convince the skeazy part of Sunset they're eligible to dance around a pole?"

"Chance Harper," Skye scolded me. "What are you doing knowing where the skeazy parts of Sunset are? Tsk. Tsk. But yes. Them."

"Ew. They would have wanted baked goods in exchange for said information."

"Haven't you heard? Women like a man who can cook."

"I thought we already established I'm hardly a man.

Besides, you should have kept reading Wiki. I don't cook either. And baking is hardly cooking."

"The first step to knowing how to cook for a woman is *knowing* that baking isn't cooking."

"Well, I'm no house husband." Now it was my time to move this along, sexual banter notwithstanding.

"You want a locker number; I want an answer."

"You mean why? Or why you? As if you need to ask. Who else would I ask? Remember? This is me. The person you spent an hour in detention with last spring. Who else would I ask? There isn't anyone else." And that was the sad truth we both knew. There wasn't anyone else. I had no one else to help me.

"I'm sure you could have asked one of your friends to ask someone who knows—"

"You and I both know I don't exactly have a lot of those."

"Someone who knows someone?"

"You mean, *friends*," I answered with disdain. She knew.

"And the fact that I work in main office just happens to be a coincidence?"

"Ugh. Woman, you're killing me. Fine. What do you want?"

"I want a giant cupcake, with frosting, rainbow sprinkles, and my name spelled out in Cooper Black font." She smiled up at me, every one of her bright pearly whites trying to blind me. Girl could have used some braces—no, they weren't that bad. Maybe a retainer for a month or two, but those were the least of her problems. She was too cute. No one would give her crooked little teeth a second glance.

Besides, I thought they added character.

"For reals? What do you want, Ford?"

"What you need it for? If you plan on filling the locker with horse dung, then I'm in. Hell, I might even help you shovel."

Interesting. I wasn't aware of any animosity between Skye and Madison. Maybe I had missed something. Then again, there was animosity between Madison and just about the entire student body. Girl sure knew how to make an enemy or two. Sure, the fellas liked her, but that went without saying. Any girl who forgot to wear her underwear under her cheerleading outfit as often as she did was bound to get the menfolk on her side. And as often as she bossed everyone around and posted un-insightful meanderings online about the rest of the student body, there were bound to be a few (read: *a lot*) torched bridges.

"I'm not pulling any pranks." I thought about my answer and how it might affect my getting that locker number. "At least this time."

Skye sat there, thinking about my answer and what else she could maneuver out of me. If there weren't always one person applying pressure to another at this school, then I swear I wouldn't know where I was every day.

"Mrs. Cherry has a group project due come December. You're my partner. No ifs, ands, or buts. And you'll do as I say when it comes time to doing what's what."

I stared down at her over the counter. What choice did I have? I could have gone to the pep squad. Sure. I had thought about that already. But that would have raised questions and word would have gotten back to Madison before the day was over. And I wanted to keep this as much on the down low as possible.

"Deal." I huffed, finally giving in. "So?"

"Four-oh-five," Skye answered without looking at anything. Little minx already had the number ready for me before I had even entered the office. The games people play. Sometimes, I tell you . . .

"That all you need?" she asked.

"Not sure I can afford anything else from you, Ford." I playfully knocked my fist against her chin, winked at her, and started for the doors.

"You sure?" she called out after me as I started for the doors. "Hey, Harper?" I paused. "Go get yourself cleaned up. You look like shit."

She winked and I smiled to myself as I left the office and made my way down the hallway to locker 405. I paused and glanced around the empty hallway—not a sound in the air, not even writing on chalk boards behind closed doors or the sounds of papers being rustled. It felt like the opening scenes to *The Walking Dead*. I reached for the locker and realized I wasn't exactly sure how I would break into it when my phone vibrated. I whipped it out of my pocket and looked down at the text message for me.

It was from an unknown number. In the body of the message was the combination to Madison's locker. Great. Now I owed her *again*. Oh, this December would be a long month come English class.

I saved Skye's number and opened the locker, quickly

searching through it. On the backside of the door were numerous pictures of Madison, her girlfriends, two of Liam, one on his own and one with her at the beach, and several other magazine cut outs of celebrity heartthrobs, including a shirtless actor and some members of a boy band I couldn't identify. Typical.

Not that I expected any surprises when it came to Madison.

I moved along to the inside of her locker. Just her typical books, a small purple Tupperware container that held glitter, glue, markers, and some other assortment of school supplies used for decorating poster boards in celebration of the footballers' wins, I assumed. I found a small orange pill bottle behind some books, but closer inspection had me deducing they were nothing more than multivitamins. I put the bottle back when I noticed I had knocked something out and reached to the ground to pick up a literal puzzle piece. I wasn't sure what the puzzle piece went to, as the back of it was the typical cardboard while the front was all cherry red with the white outline of what looked like it could have been the upper half of a seahorse. It was no more than an inch in length and there were no other puzzle pieces inside the locker. Maybe this hadn't fallen from her locker?

I wasn't sure but put it back inside and went to close her locker to be done with my scavenger hunt when something caught my eye and I paused. I looked back at the pictures on the door, this time staring closer at the images of Liam. I wasn't all that interested in staring this intently at Madison's boyfriend, particularly the image of them at the beach in nothing but their inappropriate-for-their-(read: *anyone's*)-age swimming suits, but it was the other image that had caught my eye. In the image, Liam stood in jeans and a white wife-beater, his bare, tattoo-covered arms crossed over his chest as he glared at the camera. I'm sure he thought he was being sexy. Brooding. I thought he was doing his best child-predator impersonation.

But *that* wasn't what I was interested in. I got out Madison's cell and opened it back to the pictures that she was being blackmailed with. And there was my first connection.

The background behind Liam Murphy's brooding sext pic was the exact same as the one in Madison Fairchild's scandalous blackmail photos.

Maybe I was wrong.

Maybe this had nothing to do with financials. Maybe this was simply a scheme concocted by a disgruntled daughter and her money-hungry boyfriend to get back at Daddy.

6

GAMES PEOPLE PLAY

Pierre Chevalier worked part-time at an art gallery that also had a studio attached that mostly did wannabe up-and-coming actors' headshots on the side. It wasn't like some world-class museum-quality art gallery, but more the brick and mortar personally funded indie-type. Its location was less Sunset Strip and more Sunset Junction, a.k.a. exiting the Hollywood area and nearing Silver Lake. But then again, while Theo had his many pluses, who could really ding him one simple flaw like geography? Even if it did take almost thirty minutes in traffic to cover the distance.

I stayed parked in my forest-green Ford Bronco across the street from the art gallery where Pierre worked. If my online research abilities were worth their weight in gold, and I'd like to think they are, then the gallery was a family-owned establishment, run by his mother's brother, though the man rarely showed up any more, the reasons why though, I was not able to find out via online sources. I'm sure this gave Pierre free range to do as he pleased when at his uncle's establishment, including running whatever little blackmail schemes he felt like carrying out on the side.

Allegedly.

The air in Los Angeles was humid and the sky looked as if it was going to rain later that day, something we needed desperately in SoCal, so I wasn't going to complain. Just meant I needed to make sure I did my business and didn't dilly-dally all afternoon.

I got out and crossed the street. Upon entering the store, I found myself greeted by a college-aged girl with a slender build and her darkened hair pulled back up out of her face. She had on more than what I usually considered appropriate amount of makeup, including a color of lipstick that I felt was one or two shades too dark for her complexion. When I entered the gallery, she didn't smile at me; instead, she looked as if I, a potential customer for all she knew, was an inconvenience.

As I got closer, I noted her high cheekbones and a mouth that had the kind of build where her two upper teeth were always visible, as if her mouth was constantly agape. As she stood in front of her desk, tapping a pen on her left hand, I had the feeling she was annoyed at having to work with the boss's nephew, who probably did very little in the way of work. She probably thought I was just another playmate there to disrupt the, well, "potential" clientele.

For the ten minutes I stared at the gallery not a single person had entered or exited the gallery.

"Can I help you?" the woman finally asked, standing her ground by her desk. Her words were blunt, crisp, and to the point.

"I'm looking for Pierre," I answered as politely as possible.

I didn't think charm would work on this one. Better to keep it simple.

She stood there, mouth still agape, eyebrows raised, as if asking why.

"Is he here?" I added before throwing on a fake smile. It had to look fake and I didn't care. I figured if she knew I was faking it too, then maybe she'd move this along.

"No. He's not," she replied before turning back to her desk and flipping through several pieces of paper. They looked to be inventory sheets of some sort, though none of the pieces of artwork up on the walls had any red dots signaling they'd been sold. And the wall space was all full.

"Really, now?" I continued conversing to her back. It was a tight, boney back, but I figured it would be just as much in the mood to deal with me as her front. Neither side was all that inviting or accommodating. "Because he's supposed to leave school every day at about this time to come here and work."

I let the words hang in the air.

"And what are you? His parole officer?"

"Pierre has a parole officer?"

She threw her pen down on the desk and turned to me. Pierre had never been arrested a day in his life, at least not so much as I had been able to discover, and if I continued to push the subject, it would only infuriate her, which might just get her to let something slip.

"I told you: he's not here. What do you want?"

"I'm sorry. Did I just travel back a minute in time? Before we started this conversation. I said I want to speak with

Pierre." She was about to speak when I cut her off. "It's between me and him, so don't even bother. But if you must know, it's about some pictures I need taken. Figured he'd be the one to talk to."

She took me in, up, and down and then up once more for good measure. It helped that I was the same age as Pierre, so she could buy the story I was selling. If an adult had come looking for him, then things might not have gone as smoothly. Then again, if Pierre and all his actions weren't exactly on the up and up, then we'd have even more troubles.

If Pierre had taken the pictures of Madison Fairchild, or if he was the one blackmailing her, I wondered how much this immovable force standing before me just might know. I figured, when it came to blackmailing underage girls, I would trust no one.

I thanked *The X-Files* and *Criminal Minds* for that one. I figured that in the wide range between aliens taking over the world and psycho, van-driving, abducting serial killers, no one would get a jump on me. Evil doers try your best.

"Well . . .?"

"He's not here. If you'd like to leave a message," she said as she held a pad of paper and a pen in one hand out at me, "I'll be sure to let him know you were looking for him."

My attention had momentarily been distracted by a noise coming from behind a door near the back of the office. Pierre, perhaps?

"Well, if he's not here right now, as he should be, and I don't know why you'd be lying to me about something like that when you don't even know who I am, then who's that making all that noise from behind that door over there?"

I smiled at her and waited for an answer.

"Rats."

"Those some big-ass rats you got in here. Might want to consider investing in an exterminator."

"Already did. He's on the way." She smiled. "Anything else?"

"No, that's all right."

"Don't you want to leave your name?" she asked as she shoved the pad of paper back into my face.

"That's all right. I'll just catch Pierre at school. Thanks."

The front door opened, and I heard the chime as someone entered the gallery. I turned to my right as the person entering came up behind me on my left and passed me, heading straight for the door leading to the back room. I reached the front right as the person reached the back door and I stopped and turned.

"Hey, Connor," I called out.

Connor Emerson stopped halfway through the door, turned, and glared at me.

"Looks like your exterminator showed up just in time." I winked at the woman at the desk to let her know I was more than aware I was being played.

I then looked up at the camera over the door, tilted my head at it as I smiled, and left the gallery.

7

BLACK SHEEP

Connor Emerson showing up at Pierre's place of work, where Pierre was not, even though he was supposed to be, only helped solidify my theory of one or both of the two schoolmates probably being involved in Madison's little blackmail scheme. One to take the pictures—Pierre—and one to do the dirty work—Connor. Kind of a one plus two plus two plus one type of a thing. Or so I would have liked to think. Then at least this whole charade would be close to finished.

I found myself driving to the Hancock Park area until I found the Fairchild's home just south of the country club near Beverly Boulevard. Their home was one of those comfortable, homely types, with two stories and a dozen or so bedrooms, a personal bathroom attached to each one. You know, how you and I and the rest of the normal world lives. It had been three years since I had last been there and I swear the place hadn't gotten any smaller with age.

In fact, if I had to guess, I'd say it had gotten larger. Perhaps they had added on to the original structure, though it was no bigger or smaller than the rest of the homes lining the street in that neighborhood. The front yard was landscaped with lavish and exotic plants, including two rows of palm trees towering over the residence that helped identify the end of the property from the neighbors'.

I drove up the front driveway, and after what felt like five minutes of driving, finally reached the front door.

Okay, okay, I kid. It wasn't that long a drive. But you get my point. The Farichilds have funds. Like Oprah dollar funds. And yes, years ago when I dated Jasmine, I too may have been slightly blinded by what they had to offer. And no, I don't think I'm at all bitter about no longer belonging to their social circle. Sure, I'd like to say I miss my friends, but when I look back on it, I knew they were all Jasmine's friends and I was simply the acceptable tagalong. There may be parts of my past I miss, but I'm not sitting around blogging or podcasting about my lost days of yesteryear. I've grown up and moved on. It happens.

It wasn't like I was a total stranger to the area. Growing up, my family lived not a few streets over. Sure we didn't have a home or the funds anywhere near the size of the Fairchilds, but we were still well enough off.

I rang the doorbell and waited patiently, taking in the surroundings that slammed back into my psyche like a sledgehammer on steroids. I remembered to the last time I had been here. To that night. When I was spilling everything about my father and Jasmine's mother—

The door opened and there stood Madison Fairchild, looking like a child several years younger than fifteen, playful and flirty in a way a girl her age should have no knowledge

74

of. But then again, kids these days grow up so much faster than the generation before. Hell, they grow up faster than the grade before, which was all the more I was to her.

"Chance Harper. What are you doing here?" Madison asked with child-like interest and a playful smile that was almost seductive. There wasn't an accusatory tone to her question at all. She said it not like it had been two years since I'd last been there, but as if I had been there all afternoon studying with Jasmine and had just remembered I'd forgotten something when I left. She eyed me up and down several times, playing with her hair as she assessed me. She seemed interested in me the way a cat is in a maimed bird. "Here to win back Jasmine's heart? You should know better by now, silly boy. She doesn't have one. You're yesterday's news and they shut down the printing press."

Aww, sisters. Gotta love them. No one knows how to love a sister like a sister and no one knows how to hurt a sister like a sister. I think I saw that once on a T-shirt. Maybe it was a bumper sticker.

"No. Not here for that." I winked at her. "But I do need to speak to her. She home?"

I knew she was. I had seen two cars parked in the open garage—probably their father's and their stepmother's—and two in the driveway—probably Jasmine's and what I assumed was Madison's "learner" car.

"Uh-huh," she said as she swung the door open. She almost appeared to be riding the door as it opened up, though she was only stepping back to allow me entrance into the large, marble lined front foyer. "You know, I always liked you."

"That's swell. I always liked me too."

"Is that why you jumped ship? Self-preservation."

"You say that like it's a bad thing. I see self-preservation as a good thing. All things considering. Your sister around?"

"Uh-huh. Unless she jumped out the bedroom window when she heard your car coming up the street."

"You and your uh-huhs. Proving the public education is at its best in this state."

"Uh-huh. You know I never blamed you. For what happened. I was always on your side. I wish you wouldn't have run off like that. After everything that happened that night. I felt bad for you. More than us. Mother was a tramp. Everyone knew that. But we still have father. You have no one. And you were always nice to me."

"What? The Murphy boys don't treat you and your sister right?"

"Oh, they do all right. But they're a different kind of right."

"You mean the kind Daddy doesn't approve of?"

"Daddy never disapproved of you, now did he?"

"Never gave him a reason. Besides, we were in seventh grade. And even though no father wants his daughter to be stolen by some young ruffian, I wasn't exactly threatening, now was I? Probably felt his daughter was safer being distracted by me than real suitors, huh?" I eyed her, standing there in her school cheerleading uniform, the colors of cherry red and white wrapping her up like a candy cane just waiting to break every last one of your teeth. But still looking just as tempting and promising to be extra sweet if you made the attempt. "Speaking of which, how exactly did you get hooked up with Liam Murphy?"

"Why? Think you can take him?"

"I don't jump from sister to sister. Not my style."

"I think you're sayin' one thing with your mouth while your brain is thinkin' another."

"It happens. It's called being a man. So?"

"Liam?" She shrugged as she thought. She wasn't trying to make something up because she didn't want me to know the truth but rather because maybe even she wasn't aware of how or why they were together. "He was around."

"Yeah? You go cruzin' through a junkyard there are plenty of pit bulls around. Don't mean you gotta go takin' one home with you."

"But pit bulls are good protection."

"Yeah? You need that? Good protection?"

"Doesn't everybody?"

"Yeah, but the kind of protection the Murphys provide means you'll be trading up for another kind of protection in order to keep him."

"So? You ain't my daddy. What do you care?"

"I don't care squat. Like I said, I'm just makin' small talk. You go do what you gotta do. I won't be stoppin' you. What about Pierre?"

"Pierre?" She said his name as if she didn't know who he was.

"Yeah. Pierre. Why? You know more than one?"

"Who says I know one?"

"I says you know one. Pierre. From school."

"Oh, *that* Pierre."

"Yeah, that Pierre. Sorry if I mixed him up with Pierre from the tennis club or Pierre from poker nights. I meant Pierre from school."

"I know him. What of it?"

"Well . . .?"

"Well? What? I ain't a mind reader, you know. What you wanna know about Pierre?"

"His shoe size."

She stared up at me, her big brown eyes staring with boredom like I was forcing her to sit through a four hour foreign film whose words were out of focus.

"You know him?" I continued.

"Didn't we establish that already?"

"But I mean like more than just as someone who goes to our school. You hang?"

"With Pierre? Yeah. Sometimes. When he's around. Or when I've nothing better to do. He throws some kickass parties up in the Hills."

"The Hills? I thought he lived in Los Feliz?"

"Who? Pierre? No. I mean, his parents have a place in Los Feliz. But his brother lives off Laurel Canyon up near Mulholland. Mountain Look Drive. Or Overpass Way or something like that. It has a view."

"What? His house or the name of the street where he lives?" She didn't reply, looking confused so I continued, "You go to his parties often?"

"When he has them. When I'm free. When I'm in the

mood."

That was B.S. and we both knew it. Madison Fairchild was at every party Pierre Chevalier threw, just like the rest of the popular kids who all came from homes with funds, as they were the only place around to score free booze or other more forbidden medicinals. They were practically a social event worthy of a secret Facebook invite if it wasn't for the fact that the kids who went to his parties wanted the kids who hadn't been invited to know they hadn't been invited in the first place.

I could tell she was bored with me. Much like the cat with its maimed bird. Only so much fun to be had. Best for me to move on before she did so she was left thinking she wanted more for the next time I came around a'knockin'.

"Well, thanks, kid. Guess I'll move along and see your sister now."

"Don't say I didn't warn you," Maddie said as she looked up the stairwell and then walked away.

8

HABITS

I found Jasmine surrounded by lavender pillows and several candles, as she rested in a nook by a window that overlooked the front yard. She stared out, at what I couldn't tell you, as she sipped away at a glass containing something I was willing to bet she was too young to legally drink. But considering when she approached me earlier that day I'd been doing the same thing, who was I to judge?

Her bedroom was somewhat the same as I remembered it from two years before, with shades of greens and lavenders now accenting the room as opposed to the pinks and whites that used to be there. There was a sophistication to the room that was somewhat unusual for a girl Jasmine's age, though not all that shocking. All the furniture looked custom made, nothing in the room having come from Target or Ikea. There were no pictures of hot men or the latest boy band crushes adorning the walls. Instead, black and white photography of Paris and New York were tastefully framed and displayed. On another wall near one of her dressers was a family photo that was at least five years old. Her mother was in it. I wondered how often she stared at that picture and thought back to the good ol' days.

I had known Jasmine since the second grade, though we had been in classes since the year before, both of us having gone to different kindergarten schools. I had known her practically my entire life, her family just as long. That was what had stung so much about what had happened between our parents. Jasmine's family had been a second family to me growing up and mine a second one to her. The betrayal that had happened had hit every one of us hard.

"Should I could come back later?"

Her shoulders moved slightly, as if she was letting out a slight laugh as she finished her drink.

"I'd like another," she said as she held the glass out, still not looking at me.

"And I'd like a first."

She motioned her head toward what looked like a makeshift bar and I couldn't help but wonder whether her father could care less that she drank that regularly or if he just never visited his daughter in her personal space.

I ignored her glass and walked over to the bar, perusing the bottles. I picked up a bottle of Jack and poured it into a glass followed by two ice cubes. I noticed a shaker off to the side, the sides of it perspiring with the remains of her drink she'd yet to consume. If she wanted another let her come and pour it. I squeezed a recently cut lime into my glass and turned to find her still sitting there, arm outstretched with her glass aimed at me. Girl could be one of the most stubborn people in the world. But I knew if I wanted this conversation to continue it would have to happen with a full drink in her hand and she wasn't going to get up. She had nowhere else to be, and although I was doing her the favor, this was still her game and I worked for her. So to speak.

"You know, I don't exactly have the free time to be zig-zagging all over town digging up leads for you," I began as I stepped toward her and grabbed the glass. "I do have nocturnal papers of my own to earn."

"Afraid those motel beds won't be waiting for you to turn them over when you get back later tonight?"

"What if I'm too tired? Tired costs more than work these days."

"Envelope's on the dresser."

I picked up the envelope on the dresser next to the makeshift bar and opened it to find it filled with five crisp one-hundred dollar bills. I glanced over at her and made the envelope disappear into my back pocket. I picked up the shaker, gave it a shake to mix things up, and poured the rest of what was inside into her glass.

Suddenly, I felt accommodating.

I knew why she faced away now. She didn't like the sight of money being talked about or passed around. She had always been like that. Despite having always had more than others.

"What's this cover?" I asked as I nudged her shoulder with her glass.

She turned and graciously accepted the drink. God, that girl had a smile that could melt steel and I could feel my entire insides immediately warm up, though that may have also been my drink working its magic on me.

"Expenses," she said as she took another sip. I saw her entire body relax as the drink attacked her senses. "Plus whatever other expenses may come up along the way. Just let me know and I'll pull some more for you. In addition to that there's five k's waiting for you once this job is completed and buried."

I whistled in disbelief. She didn't know how much I needed this right about now. Sure I worked, but it was barely for minimum wage and even at those wages I think I was still being stiffed on.

"What?" she asked. "Don't believe me?"

"It's not that. I know you're good for it."

"I know it seems like a lot, but it's nothing compared to what *they're* asking for. And I figure I'd rather give the coin to someone who would do good with it than some junkie just going to blow it all on street trash or whatever."

"You want this back?" I asked holding up Maddie's cell.

She shrugged and tossed her hair to the side. "No. Why? Don't you need it for the blackmailer's instructions when they come later? They did say they'd text where to take the ransom later tonight, didn't they?"

"You let me worry about that. Won't she miss it? Need it? Isn't it an appendage or something?"

"I'm sure she simply thinks she left it with Liam or something. She's got several. Probably hasn't even noticed it's gone yet."

"Really?" She shrugged again and continued to stare out the window. "Speaking of which, what do you know about Liam?"

"You mean as someone behind this little scheme? He's a lug head, like you'd expect. But he's not entirely dumb. A simple blackmail scheme would seem like something he'd do. But he's got it made pretty comfortable here with us. And Aiden would never allow it, so if he really is the one behind it, then he's doing it on his own. Which I'm not so sure he could come up with himself."

"What do you mean, he's got it comfortable here?"

"The Murphy's aren't exactly made of funds. Or brain cells. They're school superstars for their sporting accolades but they're not of the upper crust. They still need to work twenty-four-seven to get by, even if that work does consist of mostly illegal activities. Crime still takes time. I'd say summers lounging by a pool and drinking top shelf liquor with everything being paid for is a comfort."

"And Liam has that while he's with Maddie?"

"Even when he's not. You know how many times I've caught him over here, out in the back by the pool even after Maddie had dumped him? But she doesn't care because all that matters is the fact that Daddy doesn't like him. That's good enough for Maddie. Though, truthfully, Daddy's so consumed with work lately I'm not even sure if he's aware of the Murphy boys."

"I see. Just trying to get some attention from Daddy. And you? What's your excuse? The same?"

"Maybe I just like to live on the edge. You get?"

"I get," I replied. "You're playing Russian Roulette. Only the Murphy's aren't the edge they're over it. Average working-class people don't have rap sheets by the time they're fifteen."

I had heard the rumors through the grapevine. Nothing severe. A few public intoxications and whatnot. Property damage. Vandalism. The sort. They're underage so nothing would have stuck too permanently. But still I couldn't see Liam jeopardizing all this for a few more ks when, if he just stuck it out, he could have a lot more in the long run.

"Why are you asking about Liam?"

"I found a somewhat . . . compromising photo of him. The same as Maddie's. So . . ."

"If Liam did this then it would have been at Maddie's suggestion. He couldn't do this on his own. You think Maddie's trying to extort from Daddy? But why? She's got a trust of her own. And even if she needed more, she could always ask him for it. Even if it was an embarrassing reason, he'd still pay it. There's really no shame where Maddie is concerned."

"I thought the same thing. Plus, what you said about Liam. Even if Maddie had concocted a plan like this, what are the chances Liam would go along as opposed to talking her out of it in order to stay in the good life?"

"Blackmail's the only way if she wanted him to do it. She could have threatened to kick him out of her life completely," Jasmine said thinking the situation through. "But I just don't see it. He'd be acting strangely, and I haven't noticed anything. And Aiden's always looking out for me. If he noticed anything, he would have said something."

"Doesn't want to lose his meal ticket either?" I finished my drink and set the glass down on the sterling silver tray. "I don't think it's him. But I had to ask. I think the two lovebirds simply took some pics for each other and someone outside the two got a hold of hers and thought they could make some easy money. I was just checking. Maybe you heard something."

"I don't know of any trouble that Maddie may be in. She's always in hot water. But nothing that's gotten back to me. And it always gets back to me in the end. Besides, in order for her to be behind it, then that means she would have had to plan to have Connor Emerson have her phone, make sure it got to me and make sure I actually got the blackmail message and then was actually willing to do something about it. That's a lot of maybes."

"Actually, that's a lot of actuallys. But I agree. That seems somewhat complicated for her. Especially, like when you said, she could just ask for it. My gut's sticking with Connor Emerson and Pierre at the moment. I stopped by Pierre's afterschool job today and was given the runaround. I'm going to stop by his place later tonight and check things out. You have an online connection to him? Like Twitter feeds and whatnot. It would be good to be able to track his last few days and know whatever he's got coming up."

"You don't already follow Pierre? Doesn't everyone?"

"I'm not talking about his public feed. Everyone follows that. I know you follow his private one. The password protected one. I need that one."

"The only way to be accepted as a friend on his feed is through someone who's already been accepted who gives you the password. It's like a mafia thing, I think. That's how the mafia works, right?"

"Cuz I'm Family?"

"I know you know people out in Palm Springs. Don't deny it." She winked at me as she extended an arm. She wanted my phone and I handed it over. She grabbed my arm with one hand while she played around with my phone in the other like a mother who refuses to let her child out of her sight. "Ugh. I just can't with this phone." She handed it back and then reached for her purse and retrieved a few more hundreds and handed them over. "First stop when you leave here is to go get yourself a real phone. One that can do apps. Get one. Then I'll get you hooked up with Pierre's secret accounts."

"What's his handle?"

Her big baby-blues stared at me from over the face of the phone and I could feel my knees begin to buckle. Jazz didn't have normal blue eyes like you and me. Hers had a life and vibrancy to them like the photo-shopped eyes in a magazine layout. Or those ice-zombie things from *Game of Thrones*. I think that might have said something about what I thought about her, comparing her eye color to those of demons.

"Nightingale underscore one-one-four," she answered.

"I thought the numeric code for information was four-one-one?"

"It has some connection with *Eyes Wide Shut*," she replied as she finished off her drink. "It's his favorite movie. Don't ask me. He's French, remember?"

"And his favorite movie is *Eyes Wide Shut*?"

"Never seen it. But it's Kubrick. He thinks he's being artsy or high class for liking it."

"For liking Kubrick?"

"It's got nudity in it, Chance. He may be French but he's still a teenager. When you get a phone with Twitter access send a request and it will ask you for the password and then you're in."

"Okay. Okay. What's the password then?"

"Apparently it's the same password used in the movie to get into the secret club." She stood there, mere inches from me as she bit her lip and ever so slightly turned her head from side to side as if making sure her honeysuckle scent wafted its way to me. As if I could have missed it. Could have cut off my nose and I still would have caught it. Girl had that effect on me. Have I mentioned that before?

I raised an eyebrow at her to answer and she did.

"Fidelio."

And like that, I was granted access to a secret club all my own.

9

ORIGINAL SIN

I **left the** Fairchilds with Madison's cell still in my possession, still waiting for another text with the details of the exchange of goods, occasionally wondering if the damn thing's battery still worked.

I checked. Still a third battery life left. Go figure. Maybe our lil' blackmailer had stage fright.

I wasn't lying when I said I had work to do after school. I worked at my aunt and uncle's motel just north of Hollywood off the freeway leading into Burbank. It was one of those *Psycho*-looking hotels. I don't mean as in crazy people designed it but rather it looked like the Bates Motel, clientele 'n all. It was rather quite hidden off the freeway, as one was barely able to see the roof of the motel as one drove by it at over seventy miles an hour. We were situated just between the suburbia of Burbank and the happening scene of the Sunset Strip and Hollywood & Highland (if those places contained *your* scene). The motel was idyllic, recently painted—I should know as I helped repaint the entire thing last summer—with thirteen perfectly decorated and cleaned rooms just waiting for guests.

My aunt and uncle run the place and do the upkeep of the rooms and I help when I can after school and on the weekends. Thus the reason behind my last period drop out for what was commonly known as "Work Experience." Which, in all honestly, I don't rightly mind. Keeps me busy. And probably out of trouble.

My aunt and uncle live in a home just off the motel grounds while I live in the one bedroom-style office just behind the main check-in office. Some might consider it a little cramped. Personally, I love it. It's perfect for me, just roomy enough to house all my earthly belongings—which, let's be honest, isn't all that much to begin with—while also allowing me room to grow.

Speaking of room to grow, you'd be surprised at the things people leave behind in their rooms. The vast assortment of paperbacks that now line the check-in office are all from various renters over the years. I've read a variety of mind-numbing words from the likes of Tolstoy to Stephen King, from biographies and history to the latest and greatest in stamp collecting and other various forms of antiquities. Not to mention the vast chick-lit arena that covers everything from the *Twilight* series to *Gone Girl*. Lately I had been tugging around a paperback of some Elmore Leonard comedic crime caper that had been left behind in room three not two months prior. I've never been sure if people do this accidentally or on purpose, as I couldn't imagine how one could leave behind a book they were in the middle of. There have been a few people over time who have asked to borrow a new book off the shelves in the office, of which I politely nod and ask that in return they leave it behind or something equally (though usually less) stimulating.

Now you might be asking yourself, how I wound up here instead of living a normal teenage life all *Leave It To Beaver* style. But let's be honest here, if life were a TV show, I think mine would be a little closer to *Alfred Hitchcock Presents*. Maybe even *The Twilight Zone*.

It all started back in the summer before freshman year. Yeah, that year, the one I've teased you so much about. That was the summer Jasmine and I were going steady and everything seemed perfect. We spent many a day together, and even late into some nights. We hung out with our friends—read: *hers*—being as she had always been the more extroverted and engaging of the pair of us, as opposed to me who grew up in my own world, imaginary friends 'n all. We'd also spent time with each other's families when the occasion called for it. Maybe that was why she had brought up the idea.

My father. And her mother.

I've never been able to determine if she truly thought there was something going on between her mother and my father or if she was simply stirring the pot so as to cure her boredom. She claimed she had seen them talking out one day in her front yard after my father had dropped me off. My bike had a flat and I wasn't legal to drive just yet being as I was only fourteen. She claimed she saw them up from her bedroom window as I worked my way through her house, stopping to chat with Maddie for a second before finally reaching her. She hadn't brought it up right away, now mind you. No. Instead she sat on this information and let the thought mull through her mind like dirty laundry that just keeps spinning and spinning without and chance for reprieve.

The point wasn't whether she believed there was anything between our parents. The point was, she knew once she introduced the thought to me that there was no stopping me from pursuing the subject until I had concrete evidence one way or the other. That, I think, is the reason she also approached me about the Maddie situation going on right now. She knew me. She knew that once I got a thought in my mind there was no dropping it without knowing the whole truth. Personally, I think I had been a little too obsessed with *The X-Files* at the time, having discovered the reruns on some cable channel, and it had probably had an unhealthy effect on me concerning my trust for the adult world. A distrust that would only continue to grow as I did.

They were simply lying. *They* all did it. *They* being everyone over eighteen.

And so, I began my pursuit. And I didn't end it until six months later when, on an ice-cold day near the end of December, I finally discovered the truth about my father and Jasmine's mother. The problem wasn't my father's infidelity, not that I'm excusing his actions. Nor Jasmine's mother's for that matter. The problem was my inability to comprehend an adult situation between two sets of partners and, though it did influence their children, how it was not necessarily about us. It was about them. I, unfortunately, hadn't seen it that way. And so, I did what any fourteen year old would do in my situation.

I blabbed.

James Fairchild, Jasmine's father, had been the first to act. He had literally thrown his wife out of the house and then immediately called his lawyers and had a restraining order put on her against him, the house and their daughters.

The things the rich can pull off overnight when they're connected.

With nowhere to go and all her funds cut off, Stephanie Fairchild turned up on our doorstop. Much to my mother's tears, and over the loud yelling and breaking of many valuable things, in the end my father had chosen his lover over his wife of fifteen years and son of fourteen, and both him and Stephanie Fairchild had disappeared.

Well, not so much disappeared as they drove to his brother's motel and checked in to room number two. Though, at the time, none of us had been aware of this.

Life had been miserable during this time in my life. Jasmine had turned cold and stopped talking to me. Even Madison, whom as she had admitted always liked me, was careful not to speak to me whenever someone who knew her sister was around. Like she had spies out on the loose to make sure the big evil Chance Monster didn't continue to infect the Fairchilds.

My girlfriend had dumped me. Her father threatened legal action against my family. My mother had turned into an alcohol-induced zombie that refused to eat or speak to me as well, never leaving the house and doing nothing but watching TV all day. That was until one day when I came home, and my mother simply was gone. Kinda like in that *Gone Girl* story. The house was trashed, and though things were broken (I believe most of that had occurred the night my father left), I came to believe that nothing had happened to my mother so much as she had simply packed up and left.

Left her former life.

Left *me*.

That, ladies and gentlemen, is what I call Valentine's Day. No, really, this all happened *on* Valentine's Day. My mother had left me, to who knew where, and I was left on my own. I wasn't against the idea, but somewhere deep down inside I'm sure I still thought there was a chance for my mother and father. Maybe that's where I really got my name from. I was a second chance for my parents, never realizing just how broken they truly were.

Instead, I was given yet another reason to distrust yet another adult.

I had come to learn where my father had been staying the week or so before when he stopped by my school one day to make sure I was okay. After storming past him, wanting nothing more than to yell and hit him myself, he told me where he and Stephanie were staying until they could figure things out. A future that I, he repeatedly assured me, was going to be a part of.

I had a few suggestions, though I thought I might not be allowed to speak to an adult in such a tone while on school grounds. My, how times have changed over two years.

So on that Valentine's Day, back during freshman year, when my life fell apart and turned to shit, after my girlfriend had dumped me and my mother had abandoned me, I turned to the last person I thought I could still depend on in my life.

My father.

Now I need to admit something. I don't actually remember every detail surrounding that day as most of it is fuzzy and probably has been psychologically blocked from me having to actually face it. But as I have best been able to put together and what has been told to me is this:

I made my way up to my aunt and uncle's motel north of Hollywood. My aunt and uncle were nowhere around, but I had spent enough free time at that point in my life around that motel that I knew how things worked and I was able to figure out that my father and Stephanie Fairchild were in room two. So, I went, with a key in my hand, not even pausing to knock.

Looking back on it, I'm not even sure taking the extra few seconds to knock and wait for an answer would have helped me. I still would have seen the same scene. And my life would still never, from that moment on, be the same.

10

HOME

I forgot to do the grocery shopping today, so you'll have to go out and fend for yourself for dinner," my aunt said from over my shoulder as I finished changing the linens in room #5. She stood in the doorway, as if the room was haunted by some soul-sucking demon. Either that or it was me. It was the room, right? Had to be the room. Never the nephew who uncovered the darkest family secrets and aired them out for all to judge us by. Nah.

"Changed the linens in rooms nine, six and five," I said without looking up at, my latex glove-covered hand momentarily caught between the pillow and the case before I freed it and set the pillow back down on the navy and gray bedding. "Everything else should be satisfactory. I'll sweep the hallway before I finish too."

I didn't hear a reply and wasn't sure if my aunt had left when I looked over my shoulder to see her still standing in the doorway. I saw my aunt as an average woman, with a mousy face and piercing eyes that always looked disapproving. Her midnight-colored hair was always pulled back out of her face in a ponytail, though there were usually a few loose strands that managed to make their way into her face, giving her the look of a crazed person. She had cold, bony hands and every time she went to show me how to "properly" do something I had failed to comprehend the first time, I shuddered to myself, not wanting to get any closer to the woman. I think her cold hands were just a symbol for the rest of her demeanor. No matter what she may have said to my face, I knew I was the last person she wanted hanging around her place of business. I nodded and thanked her for the commissary funds before she disappeared.

That was how it went with me and my aunt and uncle. He never spoke to me. Not even if it was just us in the same room. I figured this was probably because my uncle, being my father's brother, probably felt some sort of reminder to what his brother did by me being around. I wasn't sure. Maybe it was something else. Maybe he just didn't like my jive. My aunt spoke to me, but usually only to relay the important things. Every now and again she'd ask about how school went or if I needed anything when she went out to do the shopping, usually with a scowl on her face, but otherwise we rarely tossed words. Never having had any children of their own, I swear they took their parenting skills from the early chapters of every Harry Potter book.

What did I care? I was just thankful I had a roof over my head and wasn't in the foster system. I wasn't here for snuggly-warm feelings and moments of familial bliss. If I wanted the perfect family I'd watch *Leave It To Beaver* on late night reruns in my room. My aunt and uncle weren't exactly warm and caring people. But it wasn't like this was something new to me, something since what happened with my parents. As far back as I can remember they had always been this way. Maybe this was why they didn't have any children of their own. Or maybe this is why they chose not to have any. From what I had witnessed they never felt comfortable around children, as if they didn't know how to relate to them. Like they were from a different planet. And though I was far from being a child myself, I knew that in their eyes I was still considered one. One of those *things* they didn't know how to communicate with. As if I spoke a foreign language. I wasn't sure if my aunt and uncle felt guilty about what had happened to me or if they blamed me in some small part for uncovering what probably happened more often than not in many families across America. While to many people they may have seemed cold and distant, as far as I knew they were just who they were. Either way, who cared?

I finished my chores and then went back to my room to finish my homework. It may have been a Monday in October, but I had the PSATs the following week, several papers due before the Thanksgiving break (not to mention the numerous others due before winter break) and figured I should get some early research done on them.

I had finished five chapters of *The Joy Luck Club* when I felt my stomach talking to me. I had been chewing on some jerky I found stashed away for just such an occasion and decided it was time to hunt down some food. I had a microwave and small refrigerator in my room, but I had found both to be empty of any fulfilling nourishment.

An hour later, I found myself sitting in the courtyard of the West Hollywood Gateway shopping center on La Brea and Santa Monica as I finished a sandwich, while I finished downloading numerous apps to my recently purchased iPhone from the neighboring Best Buy. At least Jasmine had been right about that. I did need an upgrade. And boy did it feel good.

Once I had my phone situated and connected, apps downloaded and set up with my numerous Facebook and Twitter accounts, it began to vibrate, alerts going off left and right. I had just finished setting my social media accounts to alert me to any activity that Jasmine, Madison, or either of the Murphys may have been up to as well as Pierre Chevalier and Connor Emerson.

I wonder who was up to no good now.

Pierre had sent out several cryptic tweets via his Nightingale_114 Twitter account and I had to admit that though I may have had access I still didn't have the keystone to solve his ridiculous riddles. I was able to deduce that something was taking place later that evening, but I wasn't quite sure what just yet. Nor where. Only that, as usual, Pierre was organizing the details. That was when I noticed Madison checking herself in via Facebook to the Target in the same shopping center I currently occupied. She first got a drink at the Starbucks, thank you Instagram for that frivolous update, and was now browsing the magazine selection at Target.

With no other official plans for the evening, and getting tired of waiting for the blackmailers to give instructions on how to receive their payment, I made my way over to Target, casually browsing through the isles until I found Maddie at the checkout counter wrapping up her purchase. I made sure she didn't spot me as she left the store and I followed her out and down the connecting escalator where she walked to her car. I stood there a moment and considered my options when I went back up and out on the street where I had parked and got into my car, pulling it around over to the back entrance/exit of the parking garage.

There are two entrance/exits to the parking garage, and truth be told I had no idea which one she would emerge from and figured if it wasn't the one I was guarding like a pit bull in heat then that would be the end of my stalker activities for the evening. But apparently lady luck wasn't done with me for the evening as two minutes later Maddie's pristine, recently washed, BMW pulled out of the parking garage, her without a care in the world and no realization that I was close behind.

She drove north to Sunset and turned west, me not more than a car length or two behind. I was sure she had no idea what kind of a vehicle I drove, nor would she ever pay attention to such a car even if I was at her side, being as I drove a jeep that was over a decade old. She turned north on Laurel Canyon and I immediately knew where she was headed as she took me deep into the Hollywood Hills.

I may not have been able to decipher the tweets, but I still knew something was going on at Pierre Chevalier's that night. And I planned on finding myself with a front row seat to all the happenings.

11

SHOT AT THE NIGHT

I parked across the street and up two houses from Pierre Chevalier's parents—or was it his brother's?—home that hung off the side of the canyon with a view of the city below that most would have killed for. The Chevaliers lived in prime real estate territory, where people cared more about what the views had to offer than what damage an earthquake could do if the big one ever decided to hit. The property was covered with oak trees, each one appearing to be a hundred years older than the one before as they shaded the entire property and kept most of the house hidden from the public's view as if hiding some celebrity fresh from rehab. As if.

I noted Madison's car parked on the street just below the house as she worked her way across the stepping-stones to the front door. Despite the overcast and the sun mere minutes from setting, she wore large Prada sunglasses that concealed most of her face while she glanced around as if she expected to be followed to whatever clandestine affair she was headed to. I saw her disappear behind an iron bar gate that blocked the front doorway and I settled back in my seat and waited.

Half an hour later, I was still fooling around with setting up new apps (and numerous false identities on them—hey, you never knew) on my phone when I almost missed a car drive into the Chevalier's driveway and pull all the way up to the garage door. I couldn't see who was in the car other than it was some man who exited the car and disappeared behind the numerous trees that camouflaged the property, and more importantly, the walkway to the front door. I almost caught a glimpse of him when he disappeared through the front door.

The sun was now completely hidden below the horizon when I noticed several lights inside the house go on and music began to play through the open windows in the home. Disrupting the neighbors didn't appear to be a great concern around here. At least now I knew for sure there was something going on.

I wondered what my next move should be when I got out of my car and casually made my way across the street, right up to the Chevalier's driveway and quickly took a snapshot of the license plate of the vehicle in the driveway. I wasn't sure why I had done this. It wasn't like I had some inside guy at the DMV or LAPD who could run the plate's numbers and let me know who the car belonged too. I figured there had to be an app for just such an occasion and figured if there was that at least I'd be prepared. I may never have been a boy scout but that didn't mean I didn't respect their motto. It was still sound advice.

Maybe I was just excited I finally had a phone that could do something like take a picture and so I was just overcompensating. So sue me.

I could hear Maddie's laughter coming from one of the open windows when thunder shook the ground. There had been rumors of an oncoming rainstorm all day, but the skies were still free of anything more than a slightly building marine layer.

I listened for a few more seconds when I realized there were more voices than people I had originally thought in the house. Pierre. Maddie. The mysterious third person whose license plate I was photographing (and whose voice I could not identify over the noise) and another, also mysterious, woman's voice. Guess Pierre's little soirée had been going on since before I had arrived via Maddie.

I continued to wait in my car when I dug through my school bag and found my almost empty bottle of liquid courage and several sheets of Origami paper. I glanced at the house then took a swig and began to fold the paper into animal forms. I had been taught Origami back in the third grade by a teacher who loved the Japanese culture and spent every summer in Japan. Throughout the school year, she liked to educate her students as to the ways of the Japanese, from their religious beliefs, to cuisine options and various forms of entertainment. While only a few words of dialogue may have stuck in my head, the one thing I still carried with me to this day was Origami. It sort of calmed me whenever I felt myself becoming tense or agitated.

I folded and stared at the bottle lying on my dashboard, wondering what the irony was that I was drinking it outside of Pierre's house when he had been the one who had originally supplied me with the fake ID to help me procure such substances in the first place. It had, in fact, been one of the few interactions the two of us had had over the last few years and I think the only reason he had obliged me was due to the circumstances surrounding my parents. Whatever reason he had; I was forever in his debt. This made me almost hate that I was fingering him for the blackmail scheme. Man, I hoped my gut was wrong on this one.

As I folded what I thought to be a bird of some sort, my phone chirped and buzzed with the announcement of an incoming text message. I checked my cell to see that in fact no one had text me. Or called or voice mailed or tried to contact me in any way shape or form. I put my phone back down when I heard the buzzing sound again and remembered that I had Maddie's cell on me, and I picked it up from the console and saw that in fact there was one new message. I opened it up and read:

```
Have money ready by tomorrow
night. Will give instructions
     on where to leave it.
```

I waited to see if there would be anything further, though I figured there wouldn't be. Why should there? The message said it all. Just had to wait now. At least they were considerate enough to assume Jasmine needed the time to gather said ransom. How thoughtful.

An hour later a white-faced mouse, a duck, a seagull and a (legless, deformed) parrot sat across my dashboard while I attempted a crane when another car drove up to the Chevalier's, this one pulling into a drive port on the side of the residence. I never saw who got out of the car but could tell someone had by the way the vehicle lifted from the ground after it had parked. I heard a door open and close and another man's voice began within the Chevalier residence.

I waited a solid five minutes before looking both up and down the street and, upon seeing no one about, I once again exited my car. I finished off my bottle of Jack & Coke, mentally cursing myself for not having refilled it earlier, as I looked around and noticed no neighbors' houses all alit with lights like the Chevalier residence. It was as if the whole neighborhood was on a vacation somewhere at the same time. Or else they had all been murdered. Which, being as we were up near where the Wonderland slayings had occurred was not all that farfetched a thought to have.

Well, okay. Maybe it was a little bit of a stretch.

I worked my way across the street, up to the newest set of wheels, and quickly snapped another photo of a license plate with my iPhone when I figured, what the hell? and began to snoop around the property. Though the windows were all open, music blaring out of each one, the latest and greatest that pop and rock had to offer, I hadn't been able to see anyone or anything going on inside, and the few windows I could see through had nothing to offer in the way of partiers.

This was a bust. I checked my phone when I noticed it was after eleven and figured if nothing exciting happened soon, I'd turn into a pumpkin come midnight. I made my way back to my car and searched through the various social media apps on my phone when I came across Pierre's video-blog. With the windows up, I figured I wouldn't disturb or alert anyone to my location when I began playing, skimming and skipping around before settling in and watching several of Pierre's videos. He was personable, that was for sure. I wasn't talking about an attractive face, though I'm sure he had that in spades. Rather I meant his demeanor, his voice and personality when talking about what foods he liked, places he frequented or when he interviewed various students at our school. I was hoping the videos were a true look at the Pierre Chevalier I needed to speak to about Madison's little blackmail scheme when Facebook pinged in the corner of my phone, alerting me to a friend being nearby. Oh, that Facebook. Helping stalkers and not-yet-over-it jilted lovers in getting closer to their obsessions and exacting plans of revenge. I already knew Madison was across the street and was about to dismiss the notification when I saw that it was Jasmine's boyfriend—Aiden Murphy—who was in the vicinity.

Funny. I hadn't seen him.

Or had I?

Perhaps that mysterious third (or fourth) person who had arrived and disappeared before I could catch sight of him or her was him?

Of all the Murphys to be nearby, I would have expected Madison's boyfriend Liam to be the one. Not his cousin. Oh, and in case you were wondering about the irony of being online "friends" with the Neanderthal, considering I had next to no association with them, let it be known it wasn't actually "me" who was friends with them, but rather a fictitious "student" at school whom was graciously becoming friends with everyone. For just such an occasion. And since most everyone at school didn't look at who they added so much as simply pressed the accept friend button when it popped up and then went back about their day, I figured, why not?

I glanced at my phone, noting the time at ten after midnight and saw a light sprinkling of droplets spattered about my windshield. Looks like that storm was coming after all. I put my phone away with the intention of starting my car and calling it a night when suddenly a gunshot went off and shattered the silence of the evening. Well, the silence if you ignored the blaring music coming from the Chevalier residence, which was also where the gunshot came from.

I froze, not sure what to do. Surely, I was mistaken. It was starting to rain, after all. It had to be thunder, right? I don't know who I was fooling, though. I knew the difference between thunder and a gunshot.

All the lights within the Chevalier home suddenly went out and I heard a door open and slam shut. I could hear several sets of shoes, one of them heeled, clicking along the stone pathway from the front door to the neighboring drive port. I opened my car door and stood out when the car in the driveway started and peeled out and down the road, the other car in the side drive port not a second behind, neither driver noticing me in the shadows across the street. This also hadn't helped me in identifying either of them.

I ran across the street and through the bushes, ignoring the stepping-stones, and up to the front door, only to find it locked. I wasn't sure what I was thinking, or why I was intent on entering, but I was determined to do so just the same. I looked to the side and found a window I could reach that was open just enough for me to pry open some more. I looked around and noticed that no neighbors' lights had flipped on; no one seemed to have noticed that a gun had been fired in their neighborhood.

Had the police been alerted? Or had the blasting music done such a good job at hiding the gunshot that everyone nearby, but not too close, was oblivious? Maybe the music, plus everyone asleep, really hadn't alerted anyone to any misdoings on their street. Or maybe, people didn't want to know or become involved. Though I doubted that. This was, after all, Hollywood. People loved to get all up in each other's business.

I sighed and hoisted myself up through the window.

And into the fire.

12

WASTED

Now this wasn't a literal fire, lest I make you think the Chevalier house was burning down before my very eyes. Just so you know, had it been, you would have never found me jumping in through a window. Not for anyone on the planet.

No, I meant it figuratively. Like, there's a storm coming. Gross. Is there a more overused phrase in all of film, television or literature than, there's a storm coming? I hate that phrase. Every time I hear it, I want to tear my ears off my head. Not cut them off—*tear* them off. Anywho, back to my metaphoric fire.

The inside of the Chevalier home was pitch black, save for the moonlight coming in through the floor to ceiling glass walls that overlooked the southern side of the house. The side of the house with a view of the city of Los Angeles below it. The air inside was thick and humid, as if all the windows hadn't been opened all night, but rather shut up and collecting the sweaty smells of the bodies that had been trapped inside all evening. A mixture of gunpowder and something medicinal attacked the air and I couldn't help but wonder if Sticky Icky had been one of Pierre's visitors earlier that evening.

I stumbled my way from the window I had entered through toward the center of whatever room I was in—and I'm sure the little amount of booze coursing through my bloodstream wasn't helping my steadiness—when I began to hear what I thought was crying. I stopped and concentrated and then corrected myself. Those weren't sounds of tears. It sounded more like a drunken laughter with the occasional slurred hiccup.

I stumbled on something on the floor as I made my way to the neighboring room and began to feel around for a light switch of some sort by the doorway. I finally flipped a switch that illuminated enough light to show a body on the floor of the living room—probably the thing I both tripped over and had been at the end of the gunfire I had heard go off just moments before.

I found another light switch and, wondering how smart it was to alert anyone that someone was inside the Chevalier home, flipped it on to find Madison Fairchild sitting on the sofa not ten feet from the body on the floor. She was making the cry/laughing noises as she rocked back and forth on the couch. Her eyes were red and gummy, evidence of having been drinking hard and, from the smell in the air, doing something more. I walked over to her and she was vaguely able to determine something in front of her as she looked up at me then lopped her head back down, her chin slamming against her chest, her jaw making an echoing sound that rattled her skull.

On the dining table next to her were three old-fashioned

martini glasses, each filled with various amounts of a green substance that, upon closer inspection of its licorice-inspired fragrance, I came to deduce were not appletinis.

There was a fresh shiner on her face. Not a new one so much as someone had decided to reopen the previous strike against her beauty that I had noticed earlier that morning at school. Despite the blemish, she was still a sight to behold. Damn those Fairchild girls. Even all bloody and bruised up they still just made you want to grab hold of them and kiss them. Hard.

That's when I noticed the silk Japanese kimono she was wearing and, from the look of it, not much else, save for the Christian Louboutin or Christian Dior or Christian someone's shoes on her feet. So long as the Christian's name was followed by dollar signs, I'm sure a Fairchild wore them. She fell forward, stopping herself from falling to the floor by grabbing her knees. She was a mess.

I turned away, shaking my head, and walked over to the body on the floor. He was young, my age I'd guess, with a mass of black stylish hair that covered the side of his face. He lay on his stomach, the back of his white Armani jacket soaking up the blood from his wound. I knelt down next to him, making sure not to step in any blood or disrupt any part of the crime scene, let alone leave any evidence that I had ever been there and with my pinky moved aside a lock of his hair to reveal Pierre's face.

Resisting the urge to cough, let alone throw up, I retreated from the body and tried to catch my breath. I looked over to Maddie, who was still dazed and out of it, and then began to look around the room.

I made my way over to a desk that was behind the couch Maddie sat on, finally realizing that we were in a study of some sort.

It was Pierre.

In the study.

With the revolver.

I had all three Clue cards. Now I just needed the Whodunit?

I reached for the phone on the edge of the desk with the inclination of calling the police. I mean, who was I kidding? I had a dead body here. It wasn't like I was the police. I couldn't handle this. I was surely in over my head. I picked up the handset and went to dial the number when my vision blurred for just so ever slight a second before coming back to focus. But it was enough to give me pause. I had been drinking. That was when I looked up and over to Madison. So had she. This wouldn't be good. And even worse, with Madison's father possibly announcing . . . well, whatever it was he was planning on announcing in the upcoming month, I'm sure a scandal like this wouldn't look good. And what would Jasmine say? She'd probably never speak to me again. And more importantly, what about the rest of my money? I slowly set the handset back down on the cradle and wiped the phone of any of my prints.

What the hell was I doing? The police needed to know what had happened here. That Pierre's dead body was lying across his living room floor. And they would, I told myself. Just not quite yet. First, I'd get Madison and myself out of here and then place an anonymous call. They'd still be in the loop. They'd just be a few steps behind.

So what? It's not like I was really putting them all that far behind where they already put themselves.

I snapped back to reality and quickly glanced through the various items on the desk, noticing nothing noteworthy. Someone else had already been through this desk, though if they had found what they were looking for I'd never know. Each of the desk drawers had been opened and gone through, the searcher apparently in too much of a hurry to clean up after themselves. I went to kick one of the bottom drawers closed when it stopped an inch before closing all the way. I pulled the drawer back open and tried to close it once more to find that something behind the drawer keeping it from closing. Apparently, something had been dislodged when the intruder ransacked the desk but having been in such a hurry they didn't try to tidy up after themselves and so hadn't discovered what I had. A secret compartment behind the drawer that had become dislodged when the desk was manhandled. I pulled the drawer out and reached around in the darkness for God only knew what when my hand came up with a ledger of some sort.

It was the size of a day planner; the cover made of a black leathery material, and I quickly flipped through it. In it were lines of not letters, but symbols along the likes of @ and ^ and * and #. I tried to make out what the various symbols stood for when I noticed on the edge of the desk a puzzle piece. Not just some random puzzle piece but almost the exact same one as the one I had found in Madison's locker earlier that day at school. It was cherry red but the white design on it was a swirl like the inside of a seashell. I noticed the top drawer of the desk was slightly ajar and I opened it up to find it filled with other puzzle pieces, each a different color with a different design on it. Blue, pink, purple, orange, green and yellow. The designs on the various pieces consisted of an eye, of the symbols from playing cards, swirls, a pair of dice, a fly and other little insect like designs. I had no idea what the full puzzle picture could have even started to become. I paused a moment, holding the piece up as I focused on it when I finally got the whole picture. Not about the puzzle piece. Though this was still a piece of the puzzle to be sure.

Rather, across from Maddie was a chair in front of the same background that I had noticed in both her and Liam's provocative pictures: a giant red rug with gold and navy Asian characters stitched across, hanging from high up on the wall. At least now I knew where Madison's blackmail pictures had been taken. And that somehow Pierre had to have been involved. Though he was now a dead end. Had maybe Madison's blackmail problem died out as well?

I was about to turn when I noticed for the first time a row of theatre-style masks that had been lined up on a dresser on the backside of the couch, each one facing the hanging red rug. There were five masks in all, each one from a different culture. I could identify one as Japanese (or possibly Chinese) in origins, with brilliant red, black and white designs all over it, giving it an almost menacing, intimidating look. The second one over I thought of as having some sort of African origins. The third had a white jaw to it, while two golden birds circled around the eyes, their golden wing/tails/feathers spread out and off the mask. The fourth mask was of Latin origins while the last one looked to be some sort of exotic masquerade mask, which immediately made me think of Pierre's favorite movie. I noticed that this mask, which was in the center with two on either side of it, had been moved so that it wasn't facing the wall with the rug as the other four were. Had it been moved? Intentionally? Accidentally? I also noticed it was the only mask on display that wasn't hallowed out to be worn but had a cover of some sort applied to the back of it.

I reached for the mask and picked it up, noting it was heavier than I would have imagined a mask made for wearing to be. I began to fiddle with it when a door on the back side slid up, revealing the inside of the mask to be hallowed out, though not empty. Inside was a miniature camera of some sort. The camera was intact, and I snapped the back of it open and saw a flashcard inside and quickly made it disappear into my pocket.

Oh, I just knew this might come back and bite me in the ass, but so what? Maybe it wasn't harmful that I took it. Maybe it was insurance of some kind. Though for what and against whom I wasn't quite sure just yet.

I put the mask back on its perch, lining it up to match the other four, and noticed a fifth, near empty, martini glass on the windowsill. I suddenly remembered that there had been three people visiting Pierre that night, plus Pierre himself. That was four people. Madison parked on the street just down from Pierre's home. The man who had parked in the driveway and the last person who parked in the side carport. So why was I counting five used martini glasses? Was there still someone there? In that house? With us? Me? The killer perhaps?

Whipping my head around, I listened hard, trying to remember if I had seen or heard or noticed anything to indicate that I was not alone. Even the hairs on the back of my neck and arms began to stand on end.

I made both the puzzle piece and ledger disappear into my pockets and made my way over to Madison, who still seemed in no condition to move. I hated to do what needed to be done, though if all those women in all those gangster movies had survived it why not lil' ol' Madison? I winced and held my breath as I smacked her quickly and somewhat forcefully across her face, hoping that would help. Unfortunately, I think I ended up only bruising my own hand without leaving so much as a rush of blood in her cheeks.

Damn those Fairchild girls.

I looked around and, hoping to be alone in the house, reached for Madison and hoisted her up over my shoulders, my right arm wrapped around her legs to keep her from falling. She was light as a feather. At least that's what I would have told anyone had I ever been called to testify about the events of that night. Truth be told, she was as heavy as an ox.

Maybe it was time to get back to the gym.

Or maybe, find a gym. And get a membership. Baby steps, Chance. Baby steps.

I looked around, found Madison's purse, grabbed it and

made my way to the front door. I opened it and stopped as I saw that the rain had indeed arrived. A fine steady mist had begun to fall but as for any serious downpour that was still to come. I looked around, across the street and both up and down it, listening for any proof that anyone else was around. The killer still in the house? A neighbor out walking their dog after midnight? Oh, who was I kidding? I needed to get the hell out of there.

I made my way to Madison's car, shuffled my way through her purse until I found her keys, opened the door, and rested her inside in the passenger seat.

Huffing and puffing, making myself feel like the wolf up against three little pigs, I closed the door as gently and softly as possible then hopped my way back to the house. Maybe hopping isn't the right word, as it probably never is unless you're the Easter bunny, but I still feel that's how I moved about. I reentered the house, feeling the stupidity rush through my brain as I closed and locked the front door and wiped down the handle that I had touched just moments before. I then walked to the back room and up to the desk, wiping down any knobs I may have touched. I had heard it once that less than five percent of all crimes are ever solved by fingerprint identification but figured I didn't need to be part of that tiny percentage. I had a feeling my luck would run out here soon enough.

I then glanced across the room, noticing nothing else I needed to make note of, my eyes finally settling on Pierre's body. I felt bad that I was about to leave him, but what else could I do? Even I had my limitations.

I flipped off the lights, rubbed down the switch with the cuff of my sweatshirt and made my way across the room, this time without stumbling across Pierre's body, and back out the window I had first entered in through, making sure to wipe that down as well.

Then I ran to Madison's car, started it up, and headed down the hill toward Hollywood.

13

ANGEL IN BLUE JEANS

I made it down Laurel Canyon and had just turned onto Beverly when the rain began to fall with enough force to make most every driver on the streets question their mobility and mortality. Don't ask me why, I'll never be able to figure it out, but year after year, once it begins to rain, L.A. drivers turn dumb. Like they've never driven in the rain before in their lives and it's a phenomenon to behold like finding a woman in L.A. over forty who hasn't had any sort of cosmetic surgery done to enhance their body in any way shape or form. Or a three-legged unicorn.

I was about three-fourths of the way back to the Fairchild's residence when I realized that I was driving Madison's car and had left mine back up at the scene of the crime. I'm not saying I didn't know I was driving someone else's car, only that it had just occurred to me that I still had to go back and retrieve mine. Hopefully, before the police were notified and arrived to make a note of it, despite the fact that it was across the street and up two houses from the Chevalier residence.

That also got me thinking. Where were the Chevaliers? I

meant the parents. Were they out of town? Perhaps on location for a film shoot? Not only was I lucky in not coming face to face with the shooter, but I hadn't noticed anyone else at the home either.

I stopped at a red light on Beverly and Highland and took out my phone, making sure to keep it below the steering wheel and out of sight of any passing police officers and began to flip through several screens while keeping an eye on the road. Remembering those crazy L.A. drivers and the rain. Luckily, it was already after midnight and even in this city the traffic was at a bare minimum. I looked up both Uber and Lyft to find the wait for a pickup ride was at least ten minutes away and let's not even talk about the surge pricing at that time of night. Thank you, rain!

I would just have to bite the bullet. Maybe I could expense the ride out to Jasmine, when it occurred to me, if I didn't want my car to be seen at the scene of a crime then leaving behind a trail of my whereabouts might not have been the smartest idea either. I also hadn't set up either app with my credit card information just yet. Realistically, I had only one option open to me. I needed a friend.

I just hoped it wasn't going to cost me my soul. Or worse, some vital body parts.

Twenty minutes later, I pulled up to the Fairchild's home and parked all the way up the driveway, practically on the front door itself. I walked around to the passenger door and got Maddie out to find Jasmine standing in a robe at the front door. I had texted her on the way, briefly informing her of the situation at hand.

The whole house was dark inside and out, not a single light on, save for the streetlamps outside shining in to illuminate my path. Rain pattered against the numerous windows in the home as I made my way up the flight of stairs and into Madison's bedroom where I left her in her bed. I couldn't see much in the room beyond her bed other than the faint slivers of pinks and whites which I guessed would be the colors that still adorned her walls.

"What's wrong with her?" Jasmine asked forcefully over my shoulder.

"The usual." I shrugged. "Or so I would guess." I didn't really know what the usual was, but I was sure it wasn't far off from her current condition. "Booze. Pills and maybe something more."

"Where was she?"

"Here. All night. That's the story and you need to stick with it. Once I leave, you need to fix her up, so she looks like she fell asleep here. Where are your parents?"

"Out. Still. Father had some benefit party."

"It's almost two a.m. When did they leave?"

"Earlier, before Madison."

"Perfect. Your parents left and you and Madison snuck into the liquor cabinet and she blacked out. Here. End of story. You hear me?"

"Snuck? Really?"

"Whatever. You get what I'm saying."

"It's that bad?"

"Since she was here all night it won't be."

She wanted more but I didn't think it was smart to get her

involved any more at this point. I turned from her for the door when she placed a hand on my shoulder to stop me.

"I still have to clean a few things up," I said quickly. "I'll see you tomorrow."

"Is this whole mess finished?"

She waited until I realized she meant the blackmail.

"I'm not sure. It could be. Looks like it might. But I'm still not sure. Let me put some things together and I'll let you know tomorrow. I need to call the police."

"The police? What for?"

"I . . ." I looked up at her, not sure if I should continue or not. What the hell. Word would spread throughout the school by the morning anyway. "Pierre Chevalier is dead. Shot tonight. Not sure by who."

She didn't say anything as she dropped her hand from my arm. I could see her eyes widen and her breathing become shallow. For a second I was worried she might fall to the stairs when I saw her stiffen up.

"Was he . . . was it Pierre? Blackmailing me?"

"I honestly don't know."

"Don't call the police."

I turned to look at her. "I have to. We know him. His body is just lying up there. Someone needs to know what happened to him. This is way over my head. I agreed to help you with negotiating a blackmail scheme. Not deal with murder."

"Don't . . . just . . ." I saw her search for the proper words as she glanced up the stairs at Madison's bedroom then out into darkness.

"Don't worry about her. I got her out of there and no one else was around. And whoever else was there earlier that evening, I doubt they're talking. So, make sure you stick to the alibi I told you and you two shouldn't be involved in this mess at all. But I still have to call them. I'll still try to figure out what I can. Maybe Pierre was behind this whole charade. In which case this mess is over, and we can all move on. But let me make sure just the same. Okay?"

I walked out the front door, pausing for a moment, not sure if my ride was here or not when a set of high beams flashed from a car across the street.

I pulled my jacket up over my head and ran through the rain down the driveway and across the street, not looking back to see if Jasmine was staring out after me or not.

I don't know why I cared one way or the other. She may have been finally communicating with me but we both knew once this job was finished life would go back to normal, i.e. me being on the outside.

"Harper," came the female voice from the driver's seat as I got into the '89 Toyota Corolla.

"Ford." I smiled at Skye as I ran a hand through my hair to shake off the water.

"Where to?" I could tell by the tone in her voice she was pissed. Regardless, she was still here. And that counted for something.

"You don't happen to have anything to drink on you, do you?" She glared over at me with a look at told me to move this along. Time was of the essence. "Laurel Canyon. Up near Mulholland."

When she didn't change from Park to Drive, I looked over at her and could tell she was contemplating the different ways in which she would injure me for forcing her in on this late-night drive.

"What?" I asked as innocently as I could.

"I'm not sure poor ol' Bessie here can make it all the way up that hill."

"Tell me you did not name your car Bessie?"

She glared at me with a stare that almost made me lose my bowels right there in her car. I can only imagine what look *that* action would have brought.

"And what's wrong with Bessie?" I knew she hadn't named her car Bessie, but rather used the phrase to let me know she needed incentive to move the car along. Mainly, she needed gas funds. And who could blame her? I mean, it's the least I could do after waking the poor girl up in the middle of the night.

I almost burst out laughing right there. Who was I kidding? Like Skye Ford had really been sleeping.

I dug through my wallet and retrieved two twenties and handed them over. She stared at them then looked to me.

"Plus, dinner afterwards, if you're hungry," I added.

She quickly made the two twenties disappear and started the car.

14

ONE OF THESE NIGHTS

We made it back to Casa de Chevalier to find the street was still just as dark and deserted as I had left it. Strange. Still no reports of gunshots? Really? Guess I would have to call this into the police after all. I got my car and Skye followed me down the crooked and winding hillside back toward civilization. We made it to Laurel Canyon when a police car with its lights flashing raced up the street and passed us both. If they had thought something suspicious of our cars on the street that time of night, they gave no indication.

We both made it back to Hollywood without any further incidents and had decided on a late-night bite to eat at a Denny's on Sunset near the freeway so as to be close to where both Skye and I lived.

I had been sitting there, staring off into space, when I noticed Skye staring just as intently at me, though, while my thoughts were of the events of the evening, I couldn't quite tell what hers were about.

"So," Skye began as she finished half her midnight black coffee with three swallows. "You going to tell me what's really going on? Why did you leave your car up at Pierre's place in the middle of the night and why did you need a ride from the Fairchilds?"

"What are you doing knowing where all these people live so you know where I was?" I shot back as I sipped my Dr. Pepper.

"Oh, please. Everyone knows where everyone lives. It's called Facebook or whatever. It's no secret that Pierre lives up off Laurel Canyon or that the Fairchilds live in Hancock Park. Besides, I work in the office. I have access to everything. You're avoiding. So, stop it. Spill."

I thought about telling her everything. Maybe a second opinion on the current events might be helpful. Besides, no matter what Skye Ford may have felt about the Fairchilds, she still wouldn't have approved of what was being done to them.

"Someone got a hold of some sketchy photos of Madison Fairchild from her phone and now they're blackmailing her into forking over a hefty sum of cash to sit on them as opposed to selling them to TMZ or whoever else would want them."

"Why would someone want them? Not to be harsh, but the Fairchilds aren't exactly celebrities. I mean, outside our school and the proper social circles."

"True. But their father being who he is this could hurt him."

"I knew it." Skye snapped as a smile covered her face. "I knew he was running. No matter what everyone said, I knew he was going to run for governor."

After everything I told her the only thing she cared about

what who ran for office? Oh, I will never understand girls. "Since when and why do you care who's running for senate seats or governor or whatever?"

"So, what's your deal in all this?" she asked, controlling the topic of conversation.

"Jasmine asked me to find out who's doing this and if possible, to get the photos back without them seeing the light of day."

"Why doesn't she just pay the ransom? Princess can't afford it?"

"Chicken feed. She's all for it. She just doesn't trust someone who's blackmailing her into keeping their word about the photos. She's fine with parting with her cash. But she wants to make sure she's getting her full worth penny-for-penny."

"More like dollar-for-dollar if the Fairchilds are involved. Okay. What's the what so far?"

"I'm not sure," I admitted when our food arrived. I had ordered a club with a side of seasoned fries while Skye stuck with just a cup of black coffee. "I figured Pierre had something to do with the photos."

"Makes sense," Skye concurred. "Need something shot and he's your guy. Pretty good eye too, from what I've seen of his stuff. Plus, he's got the equipment to get the job done. So, you went up there to confront him about it?"

"No. I followed Madison up there earlier tonight. There was a party going on there. Two other guys and some girl had shown up."

"Who?"

"No idea. But I got their license plates." I spun my phone resting on the table. "If I . . . just cuz."

"Oh, you go Veronica Mars. Now you just need to call up your private eye father to find out who those vehicles belonged to—Oh, wait . . ."

"I know, I know," I said agreeing with her as I sighed. "Truthfully, I don't know why I took them. I just did."

"What did Pierre have to say about the pictures?"

"Nothing. He was"—I had paused for just the briefest of seconds, but it was enough to grab Skye's attention—"I didn't exactly go up and knock on the door. He had a party going on. One I'm sure I wouldn't have been invited to. But when the party did break up, he was . . . dead."

"Wha . . . dead? What?"

And with that, the cat was out of the bag. Not only to the world but to myself. I think, despite having seen the body and even inspected it, this was the first time Pierre's death hit me and I paused for a moment, sandwich triangle still in my hand.

Pierre Chevalier had been murdered and I had been no farther than across the street from him when it had happened. I stared off into space when I circled back around to Skye's face and saw the look of concern on it. She was still on her side, across the table from me, holding my hands in hers as I shook myself back to reality. Her grip was tight like a vice and I noticed the look of shock on her face. It was the first time I had noticed that she was wearing mascara but was without any other touches of makeup. I may have woken her up, and she may have protested to not giving a shit what anyone thought about her, but she was still, first and foremost, a girl. She cared. Even if it was buried deep down inside. And even if I was her only audience.

"Hey? Hey, what is it?" I said, shaking her hands, which were still griping mine. She was visibly shaken by this news and I don't know why but this had surprised me. I mean, it wasn't like Skye and Pierre were friends, but he was still a schoolmate of ours. And while being teenagers meant we were no strangers to death; murder was still a whole new ballpark. To both of us. Why shouldn't she be shocked?

"What-what?" she asked as she finally let up on her death grip.

"You weren't breathing," I replied. "I was about to smack you across the face."

"Cuz that would have jump started my lungs again?"

"Only one way to find out." I winked as she squeezed my hands harder then let go.

"What's going on here, Chance?"

"I have no idea."

"How?"

"What?"

"How?"

"How—huh? *What? How-what?"

"What do you mean how-what? What are we talking about here, Chance Harper?"

"The birds and the bees?"

"How did he *die?"

"Shot. Gun. I heard it. From outside."

"Was it an accident? Or was it on purpose? Did it have to

do with the photos?"

"No," I answered sternly, not sure if I was trying to convince her or myself. "I mean, I don't know for sure, but I'd say not . . . I don't know. I mean I was up there because I thought Pierre might have had something to do with them. But now, I don't know. And I'm not sure I ever will. What with him being . . . you know . . ."

"So, his death? That was an accident?"

"Honestly? I've no idea. It could have been on purpose. I mean . . . trust me, I've been playing various scenarios in my head to try and figure it out. Maybe it was to keep him quiet. If he found something out and wasn't for it."

"Wait? You said Madison was there. Did she—?"

"Kill him? Not likely. Not in the state she was in. But I'm not sure. That's why I couldn't question her or let her drive home. She wouldn't have made it out of the driveway. I plan to pressure her about tonight later tomorrow when she sobers up. Or"—I checked my iPhone—"later today. Not sure if she'll remember anything though. She was pretty drugged up. Might have been the point. One of our mystery visitors at Pierre's tonight might have been doing just that on purpose. No idea."

"You need to find out who those people at Pierre's were," Skye said, as if I didn't already know this.

"Actually, just like I told Jasmine earlier, I don't," I grumbled as I picked up another slice of my sandwich and dug into it. "I wasn't hired to find out who killed Pierre. I was hired to find out who's blackmailing the Fairchilds. That's all I need to worry about as far as I'm concerned."

"You're not the least bit concerned about the fact that a fellow classmate was killed and you were close enough to possibly have witnessed the killer getting away? That the killer may in fact get away unless you do something about it?"

"That's not my job."

"But what if it is? What if Pierre's death and Jasmine's blackmail scheme are one in the same? Then it might behoove you to solve the one to find the other? No?"

"I've considered that possibility. Can't you be wrong just once?"

"Never. Have any idea how you're going to go about it?"

"I've a few thoughts," I said mulling the idea over in my mind. "My phone alerted me to Aiden Murphy's whereabouts earlier when I was at Pierre's. I didn't see him but that didn't mean he wasn't one of the two other gentleman callers. Even if he wasn't at Pierre's then I want to know what he was doing up there in that area. He doesn't know anyone in the nearby vicinity. I could start with him."

Skye was silent as she picked her mug back up and sipped away at it. She was deep in thought. This I could tell. I just wasn't sure what about or why. I took a penny out of my pocket and slid it across the table in her direction.

"My thoughts cost more than that," she retorted with a raised eyebrow. "But since it's late I think I can give you the so-so friend discount."

"So-so friend? That's all I am?"

"Looking for something more, Harper?"

Great. Back to the informal last names. I rolled my eyes

and leaned back on my side of the booth to allow her enough room to proceed. I was staring out the window at the late-night traffic when I turned back and caught her staring at me again.

"Aiden Murphy already hates your guts," she said without an ounce of embarrassment at me catching her staring. "Not sure how you're going to go about interrogating him. This might take more finesse than you can handle."

"Cuz you're the textbook definition of finesse? A greased-up bull on roller-skates in a china shop has more finesse than you, Ford."

"Eh," she shrugged and set down her cup. "But we know someone with more 'finesse' than the both of us put together." I raised my eyebrows, this time in wonder rather than sarcasm. "Theo Lannapo."

Finesse my ass. That was waiving a red flag in front of a PMS-ing bull.

"Then again . . . I could always start back at the beginning."

"Which was?"

"Connor Emerson. Connor always was my first train of thought when I started this whole thing. He's who had Madison's phone in the first place. He's what led me to jump to Pierre. Maybe I should start back with him again."

"Maybe."

15

RUMOR HAS IT

It rained the rest of the night, finally dying off around six that morning, though the overcast stuck around with the promise of more wetness to come. As I arrived at school, I could feel something was up. I had seen a local news van out by the student parking lot but hadn't put it together that they might be there, reporting on something connected with the school. In the hallways everyone seemed in a rush, the whispering and gossiping even higher than usual, everyone on their phones and gathered about in their cliques, eyeing the rest of the student population. Though I tried to ignore it, even my cell was vibrating every other second with new alerts and postings.

I was at my locker, getting my Spanish II book when I saw Rebecca Collins walking down the hallway and I motioned at her. She made a face at me, probably wondering why I even bothered to associate with her outside English class, as I slammed my locker shut and ran after her.

"Hey there Gossip Girl." I smiled as I fell into step with her. "What's the word?"

"You tell me?" she quipped, not missing a beat or step.

"How would I know?" I would play dumb as long as I could get away with it. I had no idea what was going on around here and I wasn't about to give myself away out of sheer stupidity. "Seriously. What's going on?"

Rebecca stopped walking and looked around at passing students, as if she had information no one else had and she needed to be selective about who she could tell. Finally, she stepped off the main walkway under a nearby tree; ignoring the water that still trickled from the leaves above.

"I need to get to the student paper, double time. Mr. Blair needs a new front page for tomorrow's paper. But rumor has it"—she paused as she looked around, licked her lips, and then continued—"that last night Pierre Chevalier took the fast out."

"What?" I faked shock. Pretty well if I do say so myself. I've got skills. Oscar voters eat your heart out. Though truth be told I *was* partially shocked. Pierre dead? Yes. But suicide? Where had this rumor started from? "What do you mean?"

"Head wound. Gun. Yeah, well, I mean it could have just been an accident, at least that's how the police are playing it. He was drunk or high and playing around with his father's revolver. But if it was just an accident then why are the cops here going all 1984 on us? All for an accident? I don't think so. They'd just 21 Jump Street our asses and move on."

That's when I finally noticed what should have been obvious from the moment I stepped onto the school grounds. There were police officers all over the place. Well, okay not *all* over the place but enough to catch anyone's attention. I should have noticed something was up. My head was not in the game. I had been distracted and this needed to stop.

"So, you don't think it's an accident? Or suicide? Do you know what happened? Who did it?"

"No idea. At least the police aren't saying just yet. But—" She stopped and looked around again, making sure no one had ears on us. "I know I'm in AP Math, but this still seems like first grade arithmetic to me."

"Spill."

"Connor Emerson hasn't been seen since yesterday when he bailed before last period."

"Sticky Icky? He isn't here today?"

"Well, class doesn't start for another"—she stopped to check her watch—"six minutes. But so far—nada. You tell me, Chance Harper? Coincidence?"

I pondered this riddle.

"Then again . . ." Rebecca Collins leaned up and pulled my ear down next to her lips. "Neither is Aiden Murphy. Wonder what your ex would think about that?"

She then brushed her lips to my cheek, lightly grazing my skin and then was gone before I knew what had happened.

Aiden Murphy, huh? I knew Connor Emerson usually stuck to Pierre's side like glue, so even though I hadn't actually seen him around last night, chances were he could have been one of the unidentifiable voices I overheard. And Aiden Murphy? I may not have physically seen him but that didn't mean Social Media hadn't alerted me to his nearby presence. He might have been up there too. Wonder if it could tell me where either one was right now?

The five-minute warning bell rang and I rushed off to my

locker to fetch my books for my first class when I opened it and realized I was already holding them. This morning was throwing me off. Before I could close the locker door a voice came at me from behind it.

"I made Madison stay at home. Told Daddy she came down with something, but since he had to leave before she usually wakes up anyway, I wasn't sure that was even necessary. But I figured why not play along with an alibi that even the detectives on SVU couldn't break." Jasmine leaned up against the lockers, facing the passing crowd, while I stayed standing there, staring into my locker as if searching for something. "Seems that was the smart choice, given the word on the grapevine. Is it true?"

"About Pierre? Everyone's saying accident and it should stay that way. For everyone's sake. Particularly Madison's."

What was I thinking? What if Madison had been a part of Pierre's murder? I didn't know for sure. All I had to go on was a gut feeling. And my gut didn't alibi that girl out any more than saying someone in this town couldn't have committed the crime because they were in rehab. I needed to know what happened last night. I needed to find Connor Emerson. Or Aiden. Speaking of which—

"Where's Aiden?"

"Probably with Liam. Seems those two are absent more than present. Why do you want to know?"

"Liam isn't here either?"

"Unless my eyes and ears deceive me, I'd say negative. Why do you want to know?"

"Need to ask him a question or two."

"About last night? Does he have anything to do with Pierre's death? Or Madison's blackmail photos?"

"I just need to speak to him." I had to think of a legit excuse, or she'd dig into him being a part of Pierre and Madison's deal all day. "He has connections that may help me. Word has it he's not around. Can you reach him?"

As if I had to ask.

"Let him know I need to speak to him. I don't care how you set it up. But make sure he finds me. And keep it on the D.L., okay?"

"I could tell him you're giving him a free pass at kicking your ass. No consequences."

I finally slammed my locker door shut and faced her.

"Or I could spread the word that you and I were talking this morning. I'm sure that would get back to him right quick. Your call?"

"I'll get him. Either he'll contact you or I'll let you know where to meet. Keep your phone on."

"Like it's ever not."

"Heard anything new from the blackmailers?"

"They text last night. Said to have the money ready to drop off tonight. But that was before all hell broke loose at Pierre's."

"And?"

"And? I'm still thinking. I'll get back to you. Tonight's still a full day away and I have class to think about now."

She sighed, wanting to huff, but shook her shoulders and gave in to the fact that she had no control over the situation. I turned and walked for Spanish. Halfway down the hall, and three doors away from class, I saw Skye Ford walking in the opposite direction, almost with a bounce to her step. That's when I noticed her wearing my blue leather jacket.

Dammit. I must have left it in her car last night after she picked me up before we broke bread. I wasn't sure how I would get it back, as I knew directly asking for it would only gather laughter. I'd have to woo it from her.

"Adele would be proud of the rumor mill circulating school this morning." Skye winked as she almost passed me.

"I trust my name hasn't been brought up in any way, shape, or form?"

"Not that I've heard." She shrugged.

"Make sure it stays that way."

"And if I hear a spark saying the opposite?"

"Drench it, don't fan it."

"And why should I do that?"

"Like staying warm on a cold, rainy day?" I knew I wasn't going to get the jacket back any time soon, but I needed this, and Skye was good at keeping an ear to the floor around school. She had access I didn't, particularly in the main office. Besides, that jacket looked good on her, complementing the blue streaks in her hair rather nicely. It had been getting a little tight for me lately, which was why I took it off the night before in the first place.

She mulled the proposition over, as if she really had to think about it, and then winked and clicked her tongue at me as she disappeared into a doorway down the hallway.

Then the last bell rang. And I was officially late for Spanish class.

16

I WILL SURVIVE

"So, I've got some news that will blow your dick off," Skye Ford said as she walked up behind me in Mr. Clemmon's AP Chemistry class, which we both had second period.

"What? Is the non-dick-removing news option not available?"

"Whatever. So, official word around school has Pierre's death as an accident," Skye said as she sat next to me. We weren't lab partners and I did most of the class assignments on my own as we had an odd number of students in the class. But apparently, we had something important to talk about today so Skye had traded up. I'm sure Amy Song, Skye's current—*former*—lab partner was just fine with that arrangement.

The principal had made an announcement over the speaker system during first period, letting us know about Pierre, the news reporters and police on campus, as if anyone hadn't noticed them (besides me, of course), and that counseling would be available starting second period.

Counseling? Why would we need counseling? It wasn't like Pierre was the first death any of us knew and an accident wasn't all that shocking an event. It wasn't like he was murdered. At least as far as anyone else knew. Or thought.

That was just between Pierre and me.

And Pierre's killer.

"Because officially, they're saying it wasn't an accident," Skye added as she read the look of confusion across my face.

"But you just said it was?"

"I said the student body thinks it is. The official officials on the other hand think otherwise."

"That it wasn't an accident? But they said it wasn't murder, right? So, what else could it be?" I sat there staring at her for a moment, thinking this through as it finally hit me what they thought. Rebecca had been right. "They're saying he took the fast out." I wasn't sure if Skye had heard me. "Pierre? Really? Does anyone buy that?"

"I'd like to say no, but it's more salacious to think that it's possible. That's why I said, word has it as an accident. But teenage suicide is a hot topic. Happens all the time. And between *Thirteen Reasons Why, Evan Hanson* and a dozen other examples thrown at us every day in the name of entertainment, suicide is a touchy subject right now. You remember the letters the school sent home last year after *Thirteen Reasons.* They say there's a higher percentage rate of kids committing suicide after another kid they know who's done the same thing. The school's just covering its ass. In case it was suicide. You know they're pushing the police to find this an accident. That's why I said the official word is it is one. An accident, that is. But in the meantime . . . you know the counselors will pull you in for a face-to-face. I mean, they will most kids anyways, but you especially."

"Really? Why?" I stared incredulously at her when her face said it all. "You're kidding me."

"You know they will. You and all the other survivors."

Like we were the survivors of the *Lost* crash. Here we are. We tried to kill ourselves and failed, like we did most things in life. Now was the perfect time for a second attempt after our fearless leader Pierre showed us the way. We were going to be corralled up like cattle and dropped on the island of misfit toys to be avoided by the main, sane, logical-thinking general population. I really had to prove that Pierre hadn't taken the fast out. And I could. So easily. Just admit I was there. That's all it would take. Speaking out.

"Chance? Chance would you like to share something with the rest of the group?"

I had been going to the daily sessions for a week without saying a word to anyone about anything when Doctor Lopez explained I didn't have a choice in the matter. I had to start talking or they would turn to more "extreme" measures. Probably involving my medication intake. The last thing I wanted to do was spill my guts to this adult, whom I didn't trust so much as I could command her being at my will.

"Chance? Why don't you start by telling us what you did to get here? Chance? Chance, what led you to try and take your—"

Now, let me stop right here and explain some things to you, before you think I'm another emo, death-dwelling, sexually confused, bullied-against teenage suicide story. I'm not. Not that you have to be one of those things to contemplate taking the fast out. You don't. I firmly believe that there are a multitude of reasons why one considers doing the deed and why eventually thoughts turn into actions. Though I would pray most find help before turning to such drastic measures. But my story is a little more muddled than that. Mainly, in that it never happened. At least so far as I can remember. And even if I can't remember all of said events, I'd like to think I know myself enough to know I would never take such actions. Even if the rest of the freethinking world disagreed. That was part of the reason why I refused to speak to Dr. Lopez. Or the police. I just knew the more I protested, the more I tried to refute their already concluded facts, the crazier I would sound and the less they would believe me. That's just how it went. Adults never believed teenagers. We were always lying. And when it came to something this big, lies were all they expected me to tell. That was when I wised up and decided to go along with their little charade and tell them what they wanted to hear. Meaning, nothing but lies. Which, if you were to pull my official record, would be all you would read about me.

But for you, I'll try the truth. Or at least the parts of it you may be concerned about.

And that I can remember.

This all goes back to that Valentine's Day when my mother left me, and I went up to find Stephanie Fairchild and my father at his brother's motel. I had figured out where they were and got the key and barged on in on them. Only they weren't in a disruptive mood.

The Fast Out

My father and Stephanie Fairchild were laying on one of the twin beds, arms wrapped around each other, their faces chalk white, with several empty bottles of pills scattered about their bodies and on the neighboring nightstands. I couldn't tell you why. After all they had risked losing for each other. Husbands. Wives. Families. Friendships. Now everyone knew. The hard part was over. They could move on. Be with each other. No matter the costs or consequences.

So why did they have to do it? A lover's pact. A joint suicide proposal that left two families devastated and me in a psychological state that forbid me from comprehending their actions at that time and point in life. Somehow, I hadn't seen the bottles of pills. There was no letter as none had been needed. Their actions spoke loud enough. I checked their bodies, not knowing how long they had been in that condition, then ran out the room. This is where things start to get fuzzy for me. Truthfully, I can't remember most of what happened that afternoon. I'll explain why shortly.

I figured I ran around looking for my aunt and uncle but didn't find either one. Though that didn't make sense since both were around all the time and I knew afterword that they *had* been around. Either way, I didn't see either one. Or maybe I didn't even bother to look.

I was hysterical. I was confused. I know I found myself back in my father's room, shaking so uncontrollably I fell to my knees and threw up whatever my last meal had been. With my stomach hurting, my head swirling and my body shaking I forced myself to my feet, searched for my father's car keys on the table near the TV and grabbed them. Now, I hadn't been driving at that point in life. I hadn't even had a single lesson, something my father was supposed to begin doing with me later that spring. But that hadn't stopped me. I had to reach help. Why I hadn't just used on the phone on the stand next to the bed is a fact I'll never be able to comprehend. Maybe it was one of those things where it's staring you so strong in the face that you can't see it. Either way, I hadn't. And someone—that someone being *me*—had to save my father. And maybe even Jasmine's mother. I could be the hero. I could save the day. And things would go back to the way they were. Back to normal.

I don't remember starting the car. Or driving it out of the parking lot, let alone getting onto the freeway. Or trying to take one of the many sharp exits into Hollywood. On an exit that curved too hard for me to handle at that time. Inexperienced. And without control over my shaking body. Or other faculties.

I woke up the next day in the hospital. With numerous stitches and broken bones. And a severe gash to the head which the doctors claimed attributed to my lack of remembering the previous day's events.

But due to the nature of my father's intentional death, the authorities treated my crashing into a tree as intentional. I woke up restrained to my bed, confused as hell. I barely held onto the faintest threads that my father was dead. I couldn't even recall how he had died. Accident? Mugging? Intentional murder? In the wrong place at the wrong time? All I knew was that my father was no more.

Restrained to my bed, with my father dead and my

mother in the wind, I was placed under a ninety-day doctor-appointed watchful eye, also known as a suicide watch. I may not have remembered all the details of when I discovered my father and his lover eternally wrapped in a pill-induced death-coma, or my actions following said discovery, but I do know that no matter what, I would not have attempted the same path. I know myself. I knew what I was doing. I had been going for help.

Right?

Right?

Regardless, I spent the next ninety days locked up with other socially questioning Attempts, as we in our group had come to call one another, talking and reshaping the steps in our lives that had led us to attempting to take the various actions each had chosen. Talking—

—*Chance? Would you like to share*—

—admitting, pleading, blaming and regretting as had been expected. Anger. Frustration. Feelings of abandonment and shame. You name it. Confessions were made. Blame was assigned. It was always someone else's fault we had gotten to this point. Right? Or at least that's how most of us saw it. Journals were kept—though not kept private, as we would come to learn.

—*Chance? Why don't you tell the group*—

Pills were prescribed for depressions and other inconvenient teenage feelings. Watchful eyes were kept on our every moves. And when we were about to feel just as paranoid as we should have been, we were released. Set free on the world. Just when we had become just as addicted to?

Pills? Prying eyes? Listening? Concerns? Everything the adults promised us that we would no longer receive out in the real world. Or at least that's how I saw it when I was set free.

Ninety days later. Near the end of May. After freshman year had officially ended.

That summer, with only the other social outcasts around for me to corrupt and taint, I finished my freshman year. One would have thought that after missing the second half of freshman year, as well as staying away all summer, that maybe, just perhaps, things might have been able to go back to normal come sophomore year.

I would come to discover that I had never been so wrong about anything in my life. Except maybe *everything* about my parents.

I was destined to become a leper among my peers. I wanted to fight it. I wanted everyone to know that no matter what rumors had been spread; they were in fact all lies. That I hadn't tried to end my misery. That even though my father had taken such a route and that my mother had abandoned me, that I wasn't cursed or diseased. I was just like everyone else. Misunderstood and terribly, absolutely and undeniably alone.

None of my friends had stayed around. Even though Theo Lannapo would still talk with me, without having a single class or after school social activity together all of sophomore year, we were never actually seen side by side. And I honestly think that's how Theo would have preferred it.

It wasn't until the summer between sophomore and junior

years when Theo knocked on my motel office door, asking for a place to stay for a week or two that we really bonded. I never asked him why he needed a place to stay. And I think he appreciated that. Two weeks later, he left. I assumed back to his folks, though I never really did find out. Nor did I find out why he had been there in the first place. The next year it was as if we had never spoken two words. He joined football, and with it the higher ranks of the high school caste system. However, despite Theo's upward mobility within our social statuses, ever since those two weeks that previous summer, he never went more than two days without checking in with me to make sure all was well. Word spread. I had a friend.

It wasn't until near the end of sophomore year, while serving a detention sentence, that I made the acquaintance of Skye Ford. If I had to take a stab at it, I think it was what had happened with my family that made Skye open to me. I was serving detention. She was serving detention. And with no one else in the room we bonded. It wasn't some great *The Breakfast Club*-type epiphany either one of us had had about the other. More so, it was just something had had sparked that afternoon. Though we rarely tossed words, it was still comforting to know that there was someone else at school who knew the other's pain. That there was someone to go to if needed. She knew most of my deep dark secrets. Including the truth about my suicide "attempt." Not that the rest of the student body hadn't heard of my protests as well. The difference with Skye was that she believed me.

Which was why I think she showed concern for me when the announcement came about Pierre Chevalier's untimely death and the abundance of grievance counselors that would be at our disposal. Not that I felt they would help in any way, shape or form. At most, there was a student or two who would more than know how to work a prescription out of them and that was about it.

Hell, if I had really been broke enough, I'm sure I could have had numerous prescriptions filled out in my name and sold off to my fellow students to help me more than subsidize my mediocre lifestyle. Not that I hadn't done that before.

"But Pierre didn't take the fast out—"

"And with you being the only witness to that, are you going to come forward with that tiny bit of self-incriminating information? All for the sake of getting out of a therapy session or two? What's worse? Therapy or prison?" I stared silently at her as she brushed a lock of blue hair out of her face. No, more like glared at her with contempt. "So, like I said: suicide. Or, more logically, and what they'll push for once they interview the entire student body and come to realize he never could have done such an action: an accident. Happy?" I kept quiet. "But until then, they'll move forward with their self-harming theory and throw doctors and pills at anyone they fear may be influenced by Pierre's 'actions,' you included. Don't you know? Suicide's contagious."

"Great." I slumped in my seat when I heard my name called out over the loudspeaker. Skye was proving herself quite the seer.

"If they do offer any medication, hold out for the good stuff. I'm sure you're unbalanced enough to be worth it."

I rubbed my temple with my middle finger at her as I got up and left for the office.

With friends like these . . . yadda, yadda, yadda . . . you know the rest.

17

AIN'T IT FUN

Principal Harry "the Hangman" Carver, as he was known around the school, as he had no problem sentencing any student with the most severe punishment he deemed necessary in order to keep his school under a proper lock and key so as to provide the parental units with the comfort that their precious jewels were indeed safely protected. I had had several run-ins with the man, though none had been as drastic as most others, namely the punishments he dealt toward the Murphys. I think it was his lack of tolerance toward the Murphys that kept a warm spot in my heart for the man. Though I think he felt the smallest of smidges of concern for what had happened to me freshman year, I think he also kept an eye on me, just waiting for me to flip out, influencing the student body with my drug-prescribed, addictive ways. Or else burn the entire school down in a blaze of glory if I so felt the need to attempt the fast out again.

In a former life, before he became a high school principal, Harry Carver had been a drill sergeant for the marines. After having toured and survived a grenade attack that had left him partially blind in his left eye, not to mention the numerous scars along the left side of his profile, which also might have been another connection the man had made with me. Thanks to my losing game of chicken with a tree after discovering my father and his lover's bodies, I too had come forth with several physical scars of my own.

Luckily for me, twenty minutes of talking with him and the school-provided shrink helped ease their minds. I was released back into the throws of my everyday school schedule, with the promise that if I were to ever feel the "itch" to do something "drastic," to myself or anyone else, that I would contact them or the appropriate officials. Help was available. Ears were around to listen. All one—I—had to do was reach out. There were options. I promised. They tried poking and prodding around for more information, particularly my association with Pierre, as if all Attempts belong to a club with monthly dues and secret handshakes. I tried my best to persuade them as to my limited involvement with Pierre's life. I think they wanted to believe me, but I still saw doubt on their faces. Luckily, there was only so much they could do.

On my way back to class I heard locker doors being opened and slammed shut through what should have been vacant hallways. I turned the corner and noticed several officers at Pierre's locker, going through it for evidence of depression no doubt. I caught eyes with the two detectives who were no doubt working the case, making sure to appear too busy to stop and chitchat with them. I was surprised neither one stopped me. Though neither one could probably place how or why they may have recognized me, I recognized them without any hesitation.

Detectives Talia Manning and Eric Hershey. They were the two detectives who worked my father's suicide and my supposed dive off the highway. I would also come to find out they were the reason I had woken up, handcuffed to a hospital bed and under many a watchful eye. It was their handling of said case that prompted Jasmine to use me to find out who was blackmailing her sister as opposed to going to the police. Not that Detectives Manning and Hershey were incompetent per say, but they were adults. Sure, they were both in their thirties—*late* thirties—but they were still adults nonetheless.

They saw what they wanted to see. Not necessarily what happened. No matter who said what, and though she may never had admitted it aloud, I knew Jasmine never once believed I too tried to take my life.

I made it back for the last ten minutes of AP Chemistry before bouncing off to Algebra II and finally US History. I'm sure there was important character-building, life-affirming lessons being taught but I spent the two classes with my head in my marble composition book, piecing together the various chain of events from the night before and then trying my hardest to decipher the text in the notebook I found at Pierre's the night before.

Just as I was about to go mad trying to crack the secret code the bell for lunch rang and class was excused. I couldn't find Jasmine nor Skye anywhere and considered my options. I could sit alone out at the bleachers, where I was expected to be anyway in case either girl wished to pursue me, simply relaxing and pondering over the events of the previous night, or . . . I had almost an hour to do some off campus exploring. I could just make it to Pierre's studio and back with minutes to spare.

I made it to Pierre's (or his uncle's or whoever's it was) gallery in the Sunset/Silver Lake adjacent area and found myself inside and realized something was seriously different about the place. All the artwork that had hung on the walls the day before was now off their hooks, resting on the floor, covered in brown wrapping paper. There were boxes lined up on either side of the front door while a CLOSED sign hung in the front window. Guess someone forgot to lock the door. Good thing I was here to remind them of their forgetfulness. I made my way to the vacant desk when, after two minutes of waiting, the college-aged girl who had greeted me so poorly the day before arrived from one of the back offices.

"What are you doing here?" she grumbled at me.

"I realize I never got your name." I smiled back at her from the corner of her desk where I sat patiently.

"Maybe you just forgot it. Like you should forget about being here. Now. Or ever." She said the last few words while checking back over her shoulder to make sure the office door was closed. She was tense, like a board, wringing her hands together.

"We alone? Or is this a ménage a trois?"

"This is a ménage a get-the-hell-out-of-here. You're trespassing. And I will call the police."

This time she came around the desk, arms practically

stretched out in front of her as she began to push me for the front door.

"What's wrong? Boss not show up today so you're closing early? Or permanently?"

"None of your business," she snapped back at me.

"I know Pierre's dead, but I can't help but think he wasn't actually running this joint." This got her to stop pushing me, but unfortunately, it was right at the door, which she had managed to get opened around me. "His parents are probably out of the country, but I'm not sure they'd be too thrilled with closing this place up early. Unless of course this place has other sources of income that they'd much rather the police didn't come snooping around, which they might now that Pierre's moved on to his next life. Come on and tell me . . . am I at least lukewarm?"

"What you are is about to jump off the iceberg and straight into the fire." She looked down at me, her heels giving her an inch or two on me, and she grabbed my cheeks with both hands as she stared into my eyes. "You're a cute kid. Don't look like the type of trouble that Pierre usually deals with. I know the type. You're not it. So, don't object." I could tell she was counter maneuvering my accusations. "Don't stick your nose where it doesn't belong. You don't want it to end up like Jack Nicholson's in *Chinatown*, now do you?" I stayed quiet. "Now go back to school and finish off your milk and cookies with the rest of kiddies. Dream about which University you'll attend, which celebrity you'll grow up to marry and how many kids you're going to have with her, or him, as you live your semi-boring, but *safe*, life.

Understand?"

Before I could reply she leaned in and kissed me on the lips. I closed my eyes as I took in her sweet almond scent and before I knew it, she was gone, the door to the gallery closed and locked as I stood all alone on the empty sidewalk like a fool.

She may have distracted me with her charm—the little she had; I tell you. Little. But I wasn't deterred. I worked my way around the building to an alleyway behind the row of shops that lined that side of the street. There was a small parking lot in the back where I'm sure the employees of the storefront shops parked and figured one of them had to belong to college girl. I sat down next to the furthest car from where I guessed the gallery exit to be and waited.

Twenty minutes later, when I realized I would be late for English, the lovely young woman who thought she could throw me off my game with a simple kiss . . . though it had been a while since I had—*focus dammit!*

She exited the gallery with a white fold-up cardboard box in her hands. From the look of her struggling, I would have guessed it to be filled to the brim with papers, as she popped the trunk of her car and threw the box into the last available space next to all the other boxes inside. I made note of her crimson-colored Toyota Camry and then, when I was sure she wouldn't notice me, I made myself disappear back around to the front of the shop.

I went to my car, started it and waited, keeping an eye on the alley where, if she left any time soon, she would appear. Less than thirty seconds later I was proved right as the nose of her Camry poked out into the street, the blinker turned to the left. She pulled out onto Sunset, and when I was sure she wouldn't notice me, I pulled out behind her, both of us heading west.

Ten minutes later we were headed south on Vine, until we passed Melrose, where she pulled up to a large gray-stoned apartment building on the right side, waiting patiently as the gate guarding the below ground parking garage opened and swallowed her car whole. I drove past the building until I found a suitable, and legal, parking space and then made my way back to the building.

There was neither a doorman nor security guard of any sort that I could see at the front door, but the glass doors were locked just the same. I saw a couple step off the elevator into the lobby and quickly pulled out my phone and made as if I was calling for someone up in the building.

"Where are you?" I made somewhat semi-hysterically into my phone as I "hung up" on it and turned and faked being startled at seeing the couple. "Sorry. Didn't mean to look so . . ." I made a face that hoped would convey enough of my feelings that they would fill in the blanks. "Supposed to meet my *stupid* lab partner here to go over our project but she's not answering her phone. And I know she said she'd be running behind due to work but she promised she'd be here at this time and I'm already ten minutes late so I figure she should be here by now and she better be because I can't afford to get a B on yet another project because of her. She's bringing down my entire GPA and my father is just going to *kill* me. All because of her and her *stupid* new boyfriend.

They're the worst I tell you. The worst."

And all in one breath? I'll be accepting my Emmy now, thank you.

The old couple simply stared at me as if I had been speaking to them in a foreign. They wandered off, leaving me to stand there alone. Well . . . I could keep trying this with everyone that came out of the building, but I had a feeling this might get suspicious.

As I stood there considering my options, another car exited from the underground parking garage and I saw the gate slowly closing and got an idea. I looked around then quickly disappeared inside as the gate closed. There was plenty of overhead lighting, but the garage was still dark and dank as I walked around looking for my mystery woman's car. I wasn't sure what exactly I was going to find in it or that it would be any help when finally found her car. There was nothing obvious, no addressed Amazon packages left in the back seat or anything of the sort when I tried to figure out what to do next. This was turning into a dead end when I heard someone call out from behind me. Shit. I hadn't expected anyone to be down here let alone care about lil ol' me.

"Yes?" I said cautiously as I turned around to find a man in his late fifties dressed in some sort of uniform. I suspected him of working here at the complex.

"Who are you? What are you doing down here? This is private property," the guard snapped at me. As if I wasn't aware of common society etiquette.

"I, uh, yes. I know. I'm, um, visiting a friend and I was just going to leave when I . . . I saw that I had left a dent on this tenant's car," I said turning and pointing to the Camry. "I was going to leave a note. I didn't want anyone to think I was shirking my duties or something." Time to start working on that second Emmy. "I'll pay for the repairs, I swear. I'm so sorry. I didn't mean it. It's just a little scratch. I promise I'll pay for it."

"That's Malia Doyle's car," the guard informed me.

Doyle? Hmmmm. Doyle was a pretty common name. Common as in it was usually said in association with the Murphys. I think most of them were cousins or relatives of some sort.

"If you come with me to the lobby you can call her from the lobby phone."

Great. A face to face. Not what I wanted. But too late now. Best to play this through. Once inside the main lobby I found the building to be nicely decorated in a yesteryear Golden Age of Hollywood sort of style. I stood on one side of the counter at the front lobby while I noticed the man go around to his seat and pick up his phone to dial for Miss Doyle. I saw him hit 5-0-4 on his phone and I took that to be the woman's apartment number. So now I had a name and an apartment number. Time to make like Houdini and disappear. I heard the man start to speak to Malia Doyle on the phone and with his back partially turned to me I did just that.

18

UNDER THE BOARDWALK

By the time I made it back to school I was already twenty minutes late for English class and so decided to wait the rest of the period out in my car. I flipped through the images on my phone until I found the ones of the license plates on the vehicles that had been up at Pierre's the night before. I looked around, and finding myself to be alone, began walking through the rows of student's cars, hoping to catch a break (that the cars I was searching for actually belonged to my fellow students) and discover who had been up there. I was through the second row of cars when a voice startled me.

"Mr. Harper, so nice of you to join the rest of your peers in obtaining a higher education." I held my breath that it was anyone but Principal Carver, as I felt I'd already used up my good chips with him during our meeting earlier, when I turned around to find Detectives Manning and Hershey staring me down. They didn't exactly look peeved or perturbed by whatever it was they thought I was doing, rather somewhat amused as if they had expected this kind of behavior from me. As if I was always being called to the principal's office or something. As if.

Detective Talia Manning had a good twenty years on me. The fact that she was a woman, and a stunner of a looker as well, with an exotically enticing proportion of both Asian and middle eastern heritages in her family tree, probably both helped and hurt her career. She was thin, some might consider too thin, with short-cropped ink-colored hair that was always pulled back off her face and around her ears, cut off at just about halfway down her slender neck. She had sharp lips and a pointed nose, which somehow always managed to hold her sunglasses up in place. She was forceful and blunt, not at all opposed to saying what was on her mind, something I think scared most men off, though I personally found it somewhat attractive.

Talia Manning was a true alpha male, in every sense of the word, which made her paring with Eric Hershey a match made in heaven. That and the fact that he was probably the only male on the squad who didn't spend most of his time trying to get her into bed. No, I'm not saying that he was married; as I had firsthand knowledge of many a married man sleeping with women outside their personal vows. Actually, I think he was gay. Now, I'd no official proof on the matter, as he'd never made a pass at me and I'd not seen him with another man out in public ever, but there was something about him that suggested he was. Eric Hershey looked to be in relative healthy shape, and impeccably groomed, with what I assumed to be high standards when it came to personal hygiene. I had even noticed a few side glances from the man, made toward his partner every now and again when she would do something, he deemed to be below his standards of her. Then again, the two could have been lovers for all I knew. Or cared, really.

"I, uh, just forgot a book I needed for class," I said as I patted my backpack, which, luckily, I had on me.

"Wanna try that one again?" Detective Manning snapped, not pissed but challenging me to come up with a better excuse than the one she wasn't falling for. I personally thought it was a rather ingenious excuse that was hard to prove a lie.

"I . . ." Oh, who was I kidding. I wasn't in the mood to lie just then. Sometimes you just don't have it in you. "What's up?"

Detective Manning stared intently at the cars that I had just been snooping around, probably trying to figure out just what exactly I had been up to before facing me.

"How have you been?"

"I, uh . . ." I shrugged. How did she really expect me to answer that question?

There was a look of sadness that came over both detectives' faces.

"Still living with your aunt and uncle?"

I was surprised by the question. I hadn't expected either detective to show that much interest in who I was, let alone remember my name or my living circumstances.

"I am. They're just—business as usual, I guess."

"Good to hear," Detective Manning smiled. She seemed genuinely pleased to hear what I told her. As if I was some long-lost pet project that she had invested her time and effort into. Which, in all fairness, considering the pair were the ones to investigate my father's suicide and thus my adjoining connection with his car and a tree; maybe they did have some genuine interest in my well-being.

That and pigs could fly.

They were still adults. There was still an agenda. There was always an agenda with adults. Probably they were trying their best to figure out how to use me to help advance their current investigation. Obviously, being as they were here at the school, they were working the "suicide" of Pierre Chevalier. It probably helped to know a fellow high schooler one-on-one.

"And school?"

"School's school. I guess. How's work?" I could play at this game too. Just watch.

"Work's work."

"Yeah, I hear you. So, what's new?"

"You tell us," she replied without missing a beat.

"How would I know?"

"So, where were you last night?"

That stopped me, even if only for a second. Here I thought we had a nice rapport going, maybe even a little flirtatious, even if only on my side, and there she had to go and shatter my hopes and dreams by bringing up one of the worse nights of my life.

Well, third or fourth.

"At the motel. Studying. I've got the P-SATs coming up soon, you know?"

She was silent for a moment as she processed my words. I was lying, sure, but did she know that? And worse still, had she not only just caught me in said lie but was able to prove it?

"How well did you know Pierre Chevalier?"

Dammit. Something was up. What the hell was going on here?

"You mean like you want his IMDB credits or his Wikipedia stats?" I was buying time as I tried to piece together what was going on.

"You know what I mean."

"You're talking about the kid who died from an accidental gunshot to the head last night?"

"How do you know it was an accident? And how do you know it was from a gunshot wound? And how do you know it was last night? Why not this morning?"

"I hear things. Rumors and whatnot. Like how you all think he got loaded up and then ended things. Trust me when I say this, but I totally understand the need to medicate when going to start the long task of sitting through school all day. Regardless, Pierre wasn't a pothead. He seemed like getting high was more something he'd want to enjoy throughout the night, not waste on a day at school."

"Did Pierre often get loaded?"

"Look. We weren't exactly traveling within the same circles, if you catch my drift. There's a monarchy in the grand scheme of High School social statuses, and Pierre and I aren't exactly on the same level."

"I hear you. So, you two never hung out?"

"You mean socially?"

"Sure. Why not?"

"No. We never had any reason to mix words. Socially."

"What about at school? Or for school? Work on any class projects together?"

"Never had one with him before. Couldn't say as I ever said more than a hello to him in my entire life if you want the truth."

So that wasn't entirely true. We might have exchanged a few words . . . but I highly doubt Pierre kept record of our rendezvous and it wasn't like they were going to interrogate the entire student body. Right?

"And is that what I'm getting here, Chance? Right now? From you? The truth?"

"What's going on? You don't think I was off getting loaded with Pierre weeknights, do you? You think I could really sneak off from the motel for that long without my aunt and uncle noticing? Seriously. Check with them if you don't believe me."

"Did Pierre ever visit you at the motel?"

"I already told you: we weren't friends. We weren't chummy. We didn't sit around reading the latest Teen Beat and braiding each other's hair while we gossiped about who was taking who to the prom and who was cheating on whom. We weren't Facebook friends who poked each other for shits 'n giggles. We didn't Instagram each other pointless pics all day long. We never had any association outside the random hello while passing through the hallways of our greater educational careers. Okay?"

Detective Manning processed my protests, tilting her head ever so slightly to the side as she contemplated her next words.

"So, you say you and Pierre Chevalier weren't social friends. You had no reason to talk to one another, let alone meet up. Personally, or for school reasons. Then riddle me this, Chance. Why are your fingerprints up at Pierre's bungalow where we found his body this morning?"

And that's when we stopped. They were full of shit and just fishing. And I knew it. Sure, I may have left a fingerprint or two up at the crime scene. After all, I was there and it's not like I'm a professional criminal who knows how to erase his tracks one hundred percent. But even if I had they wouldn't have been able to compare them as they didn't have mine on file. At least as far as I knew. Actually, *if* anyone's fingerprints had been found up at Pierre's, the only ones they'd possibly have an ID on would have been either of the Murphys. Both of whom *had* criminal records.

"Nice try," I said dryly as I secured my backpack. "But I'll give you a B+ for effort."

"Can't blame me for trying."

"Right. Well I have class to get to."

"Ever heard of PDV?" Detective Manning asked as she focused on me, I assume to get an actual facial expression from me in case I decided to lie. But I had no idea what she was talking about. I flinched from her and made a face as if I didn't want to catch whatever it was she just asked about.

"No clue. What is that? A form of PTSD? STD? A new test they're giving the kids in order to graduate? A side street to the PCH? What?"

"I'm sorry. I meant Flush?"

"Excuse me? I'm not on a toilet at the moment."

"Have you heard of it?"

"Flush?"

"Yes."

"Flush?"

"The word won't change no matter how many times you say it."

"PDV? Flush? What the hell are you talking about?"

"You know, for a high school student currently on the scene you're not all that aware."

"So I'm being informed."

"PDV is a new drug that's been making its way through the local schools. Apparently, the higher ups on the food chain call it PDV, though what that stands for we don't yet know. It's gotten the street name of Flush."

Funny. The drug scene wasn't my scene, but I'd still like to think I would have heard about the latest and greatest craze. I'd have to ask my sources about that one. Though as I thought of it, who the hell exactly did I consider to be my source when dealing with the underworld of high school drugs? Man, I was slacking. I was practically giving away my street cred.

"No clue. Never heard of it. What's that have to do with Pierre Chevalier?"

"Chance?"

"Sorry. I got nothing." Suddenly it hit me. It was the fingerprints. "Those aren't my fingerprints you found up at Pierre's. Mostly, because I was never there." I winked at the detectives. "But you did find one or both of the Murphy's fingerprints up there." I didn't need to use first names as I knew the two detectives knew who I meant. "And they do have a connection to the drug trade at our school. Right?"

"You aware of a connection between Pierre Chevalier and the Murphys?"

Truth was I was trying to figure that one out. There may not have been connections between the teenagers, at last not in public, but there had to be something. That's when it hit me.

Madeline Fairchild. She was Liam's girlfriend and she liked to party with Pierre. I wondered if Liam liked to party with that crowd as well? At the very least, he was a supply of party goods. I mean, I knew they weren't on the same social steps as one another. Hell, I don't think they were on the same ladder. But a party was still a party, right? Like I'd know. Never even been to a high school party in my life. But I hear they're a real swell time.

"Chance?"

I knew I had to give them something. "It's kinda common knowledge throughout the school that Pierre likes to throw a good party. It's also common knowledge that the Murphys are good suppliers of party favors, if you catch my drift." I could tell by the nodding detectives that they did. "So maybe if one plus one still equals two . . ."

"Chance? We're talking about drugs here." I made a face that was supposed to read something along the lines of 'as if I'd ever have to worry about the harms that came with the big, old, bad, scary world of drug dealers.' I'm sure I just looked constipated or something close to that. "We could just haul your ass off to downtown in the interest of keeping you safe." I was about to say something when Manning continued, cutting me off. "I mean, after all, you could be a person of interest."

I knew it. See. Adults. Always finding a way to use a kid. I knew there was a reason they threw that B.S. about the fingerprints at me. They figured it was a way to scare me and use me as they saw fit. Mainly, as their inside line. But what choice did I have?

"That's all I know. I swear. But maybe . . . I'll look into it. See what I can find out."

"I'd rather you didn't, Chance. That's a dangerous world and you and I both know you've had enough of that in your lifetime. Okay?"

I nodded my head at her, turned, and left without another word.

I slipped into English class with less than ten minutes left of class and without anything more than a look from Mrs. Cherry that let me know she would deal with me later. After a few minutes of silence for studying, there started a murmur from the back of the classroom as something was gaining the student's attention.

"Mrs. Cherry?" Rebecca Collins raised her hand as she stood, a look of sorrow on her face as she held her phone in her other hand. As I turned my head, I could see that a live news report was being played on her phone.

"What is it, Miss Collins?" Mrs. Cherry asked.

"I think . . . I think something's happened."

"What are you talking about?"

"I think you should turn on the TV," Rebecca suggested as she remained standing. Each of the classrooms had a television for the occasional class video or from time to time for important news reports. I had a feeling this was one of those times.

Mrs. Cherry looked doubtful but finally found the remote and turned on the TV to a local station. There was a breaking story on channel 5. Reporters were out at Santa Monica beach where a car was being pulled in from the ocean.

Suddenly the classroom was filled with whisperings. But why? What was I missing?

It looked as if the driver had driven straight down the pier and off into the deep, blue Pacific. Evidence of the car's destruction was plastered all over the pier and two ambulances were being filled with victims while several other people sat off to the side also being tended to. All this in the middle of broad daylight? Really?

We could all hear gulls crying in the distance as waves crashed up against the beach. Music was playing from the boardwalk, with the sounds of roller coasters going full force and hundreds of people conversing and going about their daily lives as if nothing of great importance had gone on mere feet from them.

As the reporter stated what was going on, he admitted that they didn't have the identity of the driver to be released yet but that he had in fact been found dead in his car. The cause of death not yet apparent. As the camera tried to focus in on the car being retrieved, I caught a part of the license plate and it hit me like a slap from a betrayed woman. It was one of the two mystery cars I had seen up at Pierre's last night. But whose was it?

I could hear my fellow classmates talking amongst themselves. Why had this alerted Rebecca to tell Mrs. Cherry to turn on the TV? Sure, it was tragic, but they hadn't released the identity of the driver yet. Did Rebecca know whose car that was just by looking at it?

No sooner had I mentally asked the question than the officers inspecting the car opened the driver's door and sitting there in the seat, staring off into space with his mouth forever agape while his bluish white skin begin to collect the sand that blew in the wind, was none other than Madison Fairchild's boyfriend—Liam Murphy.

The camera quickly cut back to the reporter who was apologizing for the intense images and was warning the audience of viewer discretion.

Liam Murphy? Jasmine had assured me that neither of the Murphy's had been aware of the blackmail scheme involving Maddison. But supposing Maddie had spilled the beans to her boyfriend? I wonder if he might not have made a visit to Pierre's last night after making the somewhat reasonable deduction one could make concerning salacious photographs. After all, I had done the same thing.

Of course, if Liam had thought Pierre had blackmailed his girlfriend, I could see why he would have killed him.

But if that was the case, then who had killed Liam Murphy?

19

THINKING OUT LOUD

So, the car was Liam's and he was in it. Didn't mean I bought that he drove it off the pier into the Pacific. Cuz, let's face it, why would he? I wasn't buying a sudden rash of suicidal teenagers at our school. And since I knew Pierre's to be false, I wondered how real Liam's was?

Even though I hadn't seen him, what if Liam *had* been at Pierre's last night? Did he shoot him? If so, what did that have to do with him ending up in the Pacific without a lifejacket?

And if he didn't have anything to do with Pierre's death, but had simply been there, and if Maddie hadn't killed him— and with Maddie that was still a big *if* but one that I was more than willing to bet on—then our mysterious third or fourth persons there last night must have done the shooting.

And maybe, if Liam hadn't been our shooter, he was instead a witness. Which is how he ended up with the fishes. Which means—

Maddie!

She was at home still—as I checked the time on my iPhone—but who knew how long that would last before the girl got dancing feet and decided to explore. One had to assume the worst. I had to bolt.

The end of class bell rang just as I made it to Jasmine's last class, and I waited impatiently for her to exit. When I saw her friend April leaving the class without Jasmine at her side I got in her face and almost startled her into dropping her bags.

"Where's Jasmine?"

She made a face and rolled her eyes when I caught sight of Jasmine exiting behind her friend. I grabbed Jasmine firmly by her arm and pulled her across the hallway into the nearest men's restroom.

"What the hell is wrong with you?" Jasmine all but hissed at me as she jerked her arm free, almost losing her step in the process.

I quickly checked to make sure we were alone inside and then locked the door to make sure we stayed that way. I caught a whiff of what I assumed was a broken and clogged, yet still being used, toiled and swore to myself to make this as quick as possible when someone started to pound on the door.

"Chance? What the f—"

"Where's Maddie?"

"Right this second?"

"Or as close to it as possible."

"Well, I'd have to check her ankle monitor to be sure but—oh, how the hell should I know? At home, I'm assuming. What the hell is going on?"

"She could be in danger," I said matter-of-factly. I wasn't

quite sure what else to say or how to explain my actions.

"When is that girl ever not in danger?" Jasmine said as she turned from me and faced herself in the mirror. She retrieved her lipstick and began to apply a fresh coat. "Really, Chance. If I lost it every time that girl got into danger I'd never be found again."

"This is different. Could be serious." She stared at me through the mirror, putting on a show that was to have me believe she wasn't buying what I was selling let alone that she should care. "Have you heard about Liam?"

"What about him?" she all but yawned as she put her makeup away and turned toward me.

"He's dead too."

"What?" I don't think she believed me. Either that or she hadn't really heard me.

"Apparently he drove off a pier in Santa Monica and drowned in the Pacific."

"Bullshit."

"Check Twitter. Check Rebecca Collins' feed. I'm sure it's all the rage right about now."

I could tell by the look on her face that she thought I was playing some sort of prank on her and she wasn't all that appreciative of it. Despite what she may have thought, she still took out her phone and began to search through it. As she did so, I walked over to the door and shouted through it that the bathroom was out of service. I walked back over to Jasmine and she almost fell into my arms. I could feel her trembling as she rested in my arms.

"What's this have to do with Maddie?"

"I'm not sure. But I think he was up at Pierre's last night too. I promise I'll figure it out. Right now, I just need to make sure she's safe and that she stays that way."

Jasmine hit a few buttons on her phone, and I could hear it begin to ring. It went straight to voicemail and Jasmine hung up. Probably the sisters never called each other and answered when one did even less.

"She should be home," Jasmine said looking up at me, the corners of her eyes wanting to tear up. I knew they wanted to. I could feel it. Sisterly love and all that BS. Or maybe I was just making this crap up in my head to feel good about what was going on.

"Let's move," I replied.

Twenty minutes later we both pulled up to the Fairchild driveway and Jasmine marched her way through the front door, not appearing frantic in the least bit. Always the lady that one.

"Madison? Madison are you home?" she called out.

"Maddie?!" I all but barked behind her.

We both made our way up the stairs, taking them two at a time, until we reached Madison's bedroom.

Vacant. The room was decidedly more in tune with that of a teenage girl, unlike her sister's. I glanced over the various posters and pictures that hung on the walls as I made my way over to her dresser with a mirror that was almost the size of a door. On the mirror, taking up the entire center where Madison would have looked at herself to get herself ready for the day were several dozen different pictures of Maddison Fairchild, each one taped up next to the other as if making a collage of her face with pieces of her face. An eye ripped from one picture, the other from another. Her lips were made up of two different pictures, one where she smiled and the other not. From across the room it simply looked like a shrine to the teenager. Up close, it had a decidedly more haunting effect. I turned to Jasmine and could tell by the look of horror on her face that she obviously never entered her sister's room. Or hadn't in a long time.

"Where is she?" Jasmine asked me as if I could solve all the problems in the world.

"Any way to find out where she is?" I broke my stance in front of the collage and made my way out of the room.

"I can try and check with some of her friends. But I'll probably be shut out all around."

"How about you check things out on your end and let me know what you find," I suggested as I started back down the stairs.

"Wait! Where are you going? You're not just leaving me here are you?" She practically hugged herself as she said these words to me, as if I had told her that she was the one in danger and not her sister.

"I can't do anything here but wait around for her to show up again. I think I can be more productive out there."

"But where are you going to go?"

"I'll figure that out when I get going. You keep checking with her friends and let me know what you find. Okay?"

She didn't like that option but then again, I didn't like the entire situation.

"What's with all the shouting and running around?" came a sharp yet feminine voice from down the hallway that lead to the back kitchen.

I stayed where I was on the bottom of the stairs when what I at first took to be a heavenly angel, or rather a Victoria's Secret catalog model, came walking toward us. The woman was in her early thirties, with long slender, tanned legs and athletically shaped calves that were shown off exquisitely thanks to the no doubt expensive heels she clacked along the marble floor. She wore a sleek, mini skirt that barely covered her backside and a rather flowy, near transparent blouse of some sort that showed off the Victoria's Secret underwear that she wore. She had perfect lips, which were glossed over just ever so slightly with a darkened blood-red, which was even more shocking by her perfectly straight and blindingly white teeth. She had a button-cute nose and large, enticing honey-colored eyes. She ran a hand through her caramel-colored hair that was cut up short around her head, as if to show off her plummeting neckline.

I stood waiting for an introduction while the rest of me stood; I'm ashamed to admit it, for other obvious hormonal reasons.

I could see out of the corner of my eye as Jasmine rested on one hip and all but rolled her eyes at the woman whom I took to be her new stepmother.

"Chance this is my . . . father's *wife*. Selena. Selena this is my . . . this is Chance."

The woman's face immediately lit up as if she had just been handed a Christmas present. "*The* Chance?"

I was hesitant but who was I to refuse an offered hand.

"The one and only. Although I must admit, I have not yet heard of you. Selena was it?"

"It is. Pleasure to meet you," Selena extended her soft, lotioned hand and squeezed mine ever so slightly as she slowly pulled it away, making sure each of her fingers caressed the inside of my hand as she did so.

"So, you've heard of me?" I asked.

She shrugged her shoulders and then glared up at her stepdaughter.

"I have. Though I doubt ever with any words one could call favorable. Or that a woman of my upstanding pediment would dare repeat in public." Upstanding pediment? I would have questioned the woman's choice of words but didn't feel it was right to question a woman of such beauty. I'm sure most men felt that way around her. "So, what's all the ruckus for?"

"You haven't by any chance seen Maddie today, have you?"

"Who?"

You have got to be kidding me. Really?

"Madison," Jasmine offered as she took the steps down to me and placed a hand on my forearm. Selena was no fool as she had noticed this just as much as I had.

"Oh, your sister," Selena all but laughed. "Can't say that I have. Been too busy. But I'm sure she'll show up sooner or later. I've got to be off for happy hour with the girls. You kids don't get into any trouble, now you hear?"

She was leaving? Dressed like that? The only reason a woman should leave the house like that was if she planned on—well, truthfully, she probably shouldn't. But maybe that was just me.

"Oh, and if you dears do happen to sample some of the booze, try to keep it low key tonight, okay? Your father will be home late, and he's had a long day."

She winked at us and with those words Selena Fairchild was out the front door.

I must admit that since my head had turned around to follow the woman out the door that there was a good chance my jaw was wide open as well. I turned completely around to face Jasmine and figured that yes, my jaw had indeed been agape.

"Men," Jasmine sighed, though why should she have any reason to be disappointed in me was beyond my comprehension. What did she care who I looked at? She was dating a Murphy with arms like a Hemsworth. Speaking of which . . .

"Did you ever get a hold of Aiden?"

"No. Why?"

"Remember? I asked you to put us in touch. I need to ask him some questions. And now with Liam . . ."

"I, uh . . . I haven't been able to reach him. I mean he's not answering his phone or any texts or anything."

"You don't know where he is? You don't think something could have happened to him as well, do you?"

"No idea."

"Will he have heard about Liam yet?"

She simply shrugged as the thought came over her and I swore she turned a shade paler.

"Well, if you do hear from him tell him, I still have questions for him."

"What about Maddie's blackmail situation?" Jasmine asked as she got back to the subject at hand.

"Not sure if you'll need the money. But you might, if only for different reasons."

"What's that supposed to mean?" she asked as I started for the front door.

"I think our blackmailer is going to be a little too preoccupied this evening to worry about picking up a ransom. Unless they need it to help skip town."

"What's that supposed to mean? You know who's blackmailing me?"

"You mean your sister, right?" I turned and studied her reaction. Her body tensed up as if hiding something. "Don't worry about it. If you've got the money, then good. I'll let you know what's what if and when I get further instructions. Until then keep looking for your sister."

And with that I disappeared out the door.

20

TOO MANY FRIENDS

I had no idea where Maddie could or would have gone. She could be shopping at the mall or tanning poolside on the roof of some Sunset Strip hotel for all I knew. Since she was currently MIA, I needed to figure out who had killed Pierre, in hopes of staying ahead of whoever *might* be going after Maddie, and so I decided to head to the only place where I figured there might be any sort of evidence.

I drove toward Laurel Canyon and forty-five minutes later found myself at Pierre's front door. There was crime scene tape strewn across the front door though it looked as if the place had been abandoned by all form of police officials. I was wondering how to get in when I heard footsteps behind me on the rock covered pathway.

I froze, not sure if I should be ready for an attack of some sort when I heard a soft giggle. I turned to find Maddie standing there, staring up at me, her eyes glossed over and reddened, though if it was from booze or crying, I couldn't tell.

"What are you doing here?" I asked.

She smiled coyly and nodded at the front door.

"Got a key?"

"No. But you do."

"No. But I know the code."

I looked back at the front door again and for the first time realized there wasn't anywhere to put a key. Rather an expensive and intimidating-looking keypad rested on the wall next to the door.

"Why do you need in there?" she asked as she stepped past me.

"Why do you care?"

"Just inquisitive."

"What are you doing here?"

"I think I . . . I was . . . just trying to . . . I forgot something . . ."

"Here? Last night?" I finished and she jerked her head up at me.

"*You* weren't here last night?" she asked, though it sounded more like a statement than a question.

"No, I wasn't. Neither were you. Remember that."

"Oh, a wise *old* owl, huh?"

"Something like that. Just remember what I said."

"That's what father used to say he liked best about you. Well, two things. One, that you were smart. He didn't have to worry about you making bad decisions in life, or something like that. And that he could trust you. That was why he didn't care about you and Jasmine always hanging out. You were different. He liked you." She looked up at me. "I liked you too. Having you around, I mean. You always had my back. But once you left . . . and mother . . . well, there was no one left for me."

"What do you mean? You have your sister. And your father?"

"No. Jasmine was always daddy's girl. She always knew how to wrap him around her fingers. I belonged to my mother. Whenever everyone took sides. At least it all evened out. Two against two. But once mother wasn't around everything became unbalanced. Something in father broke. Have you seen him? Recently, I mean?" I shook my head in the negative. "He's not the same. At least from how I remember him. I bet you wouldn't think he was the same either. He's more closed off. Distanced himself from everyone. Even me 'n' Jasmine."

"What about your stepmother?"

"She's just arm candy. She knows how to control father just like Jasmine. I think that's why they don't get along. They're both trying to manipulate him for the most attention. I don't care. I figure, let them fight it out and when they're both gone it will just be me left to comfort him."

"Smart."

We stared at each other, me taking in her dark chocolate-colored eyes, which seemed out of place on the rest of her pale palate. I could hear birds chirping in the distance as the sounds of trees rustled in the wind. There was a moment there where I remembered the fragile little girl that I used look out for, to protect, like that one time when her father and mother were having a serious fight—

I snapped out of the past and focused in again on the present.

"You remember that code yet or are we waiting out here all day?"

She typed in the six-digit code and the door unlocked. The house had been gone over earlier that morning by the police. There was evidence they had gone through every inch of the place, with fingerprint dust over most every surface in the room where the body had been. Blood was still seeped into the otherwise pristine ivory-colored carpet near where Pierre's head had lain.

Madison almost fell back onto the sofa where she had been sitting the night before and stared down, lost in her own thoughts. I wasn't sure if she was trying to remember what had occurred the night before or forget it. She reached down with one darkly painted nail and ran it along the outline of the dried-up blood when she spoke up to me.

"I don't know what you and my sister have going on, but I can tell you it isn't good. She isn't a good person. You should leave her alone. You may miss us, and I miss you, but she's still the manipulative girl she always has been. More so now, I think. That she's gotten older."

"She's not that bad. She's not a monster."

She thought about this.

"You remember when you used to tutor me?" I did. Math. Back when I could somewhat decently decode the subject. She had been in seventh or sixth grade at the time. I had forgotten about that. "You remember why you were tutoring me?"

"If memory serves me it was because you were flunking and needed help."

"It was because I couldn't understand it, like it was a foreign language. Father had gotten tutors in the past but none of them were patent enough. Then he just stopped caring. Then you saw how I was doing, and you offered to help. You told me you'd talk to my father about it. Jasmine had overheard us. She was jealous. But she knew you'd still help just the same. She suggested to my father that you could help me and suddenly it was this brilliant idea that only Jasmine could have ever suggested."

"What's it matter who suggested what to whom? I tutored you and it helped. You passed your classes, if I remember correctly? What's it matter? Who cares if your father thought it was me being genuine or your sister kissing his ass?"

"Just making sure you know who my sister really is."

"I know who she is. Really. She may not be the same girl you know but I still know her. I just know a different side of her. Maybe, just like how I helped you, when I'm around her, I help make her better too."

I could see by the look on her face that this wasn't the reply she had been hoping to get out of me. She wanted me square on her side. Sister against sister. As always. This also meant if I was on Jasmine's side that I wasn't on hers. That I couldn't be trusted. I knew how this game worked.

I walked around the outer edges of the room, taking in everything that had gone on while the police had been there. The home looked as if they had searched through most every crook and crevice that it had to offer, including the desk where I had found Pierre's thus-far undecipherable ledger.

"Confused?" I asked, when I saw her staring down at the

bloodstain once again.

"I don't know what you're talking about," she whispered as she sniffled and looked up and over to the row of masks displayed behind the couch she had been partying on. She took a step toward them and then seemed to remember that she wasn't alone and turned as if inspecting the rest of the room.

"Don't bother," I smiled slyly at her. "It's not there."

"What isn't?"

I nodded toward the row of masks as an answer.

She suddenly didn't care that I was there and rushed for them, grabbing the masquerade mask in the middle and opening it up to find it the camera. She opened the camera to find the memory card gone.

"Where is it?" she hissed at me through clenched teeth.

"How should I know?"

"But you knew about it?"

"Did I?"

"Chancy." She changed tactics like a manic on speed. She purred like a cat as she made her way over to me and all but fell into my arms as she looked up at me with her big Bambi eyes, trying her hardest to get under my skin.

"You remember anything about last night?" I asked as I touched the tip of her nose and then set her straight on her feet. "Seriously. Who else was here with you last night? Besides Pierre, of course. The others? Who were they?"

She looked around the room, stopping on the couch where she had been sitting, appearing to be trying her hardest to remember.

"I remember . . . Pierre . . . the drinks. A knock at the door . . . Connor Emerson . . ."

"Connor doesn't have the code?"

She didn't hear me or chose to ignore me as she continued. "Then another car pulled into the driveway. Pierre could see the headlights in the mirror in the front hallway. But who . . .?"

"Liam?" I asked and she jolted forward and faced me with a look of confusion.

"No. Never. Liam would never. Why would you think that?"

"But he has been here before."

"No. Never. Why?"

She was lying, but I couldn't admit that I had seen him in the same type of pictures as her, with the same background here at Pierre's, without letting her know that I had seen the pictures of her as well. After all, why or how should I have seen them? It wasn't like they were circulating around the school and there was no reason for me to admit that I had been through her locker. In addition, she wasn't aware of the blackmail scheme. So far as I knew. Then again, maybe whenever Liam had been up here before it hadn't been with her?

"What *do* you remember about last night?" I prodded again.

"No*thing*," she all but shouted at me when suddenly we recognized someone standing in the front door.

I didn't recognize the face but there was something familiar about him. He was in his mid-thirties, maybe younger, maybe older. It was hard to tell at that moment with him standing in the shadows. He stared intently at both of us, with large soulful eyes. He ran a hand through his mane of thick hair that looked like he was petting a raven. He then rubbed his fingers across the edges of his mouth as he took a step into the house.

That was when I felt Maddie tense up in my arms.

"I might be inclined to ask who you are and what you're doing here?" the man asked us, with ever so slight a foreign lisp to his words. They were slower and more deliberate like a foreign actor who spoke with an American accent for a movie.

"And I might be inclined to ask the same of you," I responded, standing my ground.

"This is my place," the man answered as he continued closer to us, when he finally got a better look at us. "And you must be . . . acquaintances of Pierre's?"

"Something like that. And you must be . . ."

"The landlord," the man replied with a smile that immediately reminded me of Pierre. The older brother perhaps? Someone related to him. The resemblance was uncanny.

"You're Paul," Maddie said as she left my arms and walked up to the man.

"And you are?" he asked as a way of neither confirming nor denying her statement.

"A friend," Maddie said with a smile as she eyed "Paul" up and down. "You're the half-brother. Who lives out of the country. What are you doing here?"

"I am Paul-Henri," the man said by way of introduction as he looked to me. I wasn't sure if he had given me a hyphenated first name or if he was one of those people with two first names as his first and surname.

"Chance Harper." I extended my hand though the offer was not reciprocated, making me stand there like a fool before I retrieved my hand.

"And again, I ask, what are you doing here?"

"Paying our respects," I answered as I looked to the puddle of blood in the carpet. I wasn't entirely sure who this man was or why he was there. Had he been informed of Pierre's condition? Or was he simply crashing a party already in progress?

"Awww, je vois," Paul-Henri said as she shook his head. "You've paid your respects and now you can go."

"I've seen you around before," Maddie said as she stared up at Paul-Henri. She wasn't in the mood to be bullied and she fully intended on letting our guest know it. "At one of Pierre's parties. You were in the back room the whole time. But I saw you once when Pierre went to get something from the back. I saw you."

Paul-Henri didn't respond to Madison's accusation as he stared intently at me. I wasn't sure why. Perhaps he was sizing me up for some reason.

"You I am familiar with," Paul-Henri said looking down at Maddie. "You are the one Pierre called Madison. No?" Maddison smiled and blushed as she lowered her gaze to the floor. "But you"—Paul-Henri looked to me with an edge to his gaze—"I am not familiar with."

"Oh, he's okay. Bit of a square, but he's nothing to worry about," Maddison said as a way of vouching for me.

"And what's to worry about?" I asked, keeping my eyes on Paul-Henri even though Maddison was practically in his lap even though he was standing.

"Good question," Paul-Henri nodded as he looked back down to Maddison. "Why don't you be an obedient little girl and run along now. Scat."

Madison immediately looked to me as if I had the final word in all her doings and I nodded politely at her.

"Go on. It's okay. The men need to talk apparently."

She scowled at me, then marched over and grabbed my shirt and pulled me down for a kiss on my cheek.

"I know you barely knew it because they tried to never do it when you were around but mother and father fought all the time."

"I knew. From Jasmine. They just didn't like to do it with strangers around. *That's* why I tutored you every day after school that year."

There was a sparkle in her eyes, as if she knew I was telling the truth and felt comforted by it.

"I'll always remember you fondly, not as the boy in love with my sister, but as the boy who looked out for me. I'll never forget you for that."

As she passed Paul-Henri, she smiled at him before disappearing out the front door.

"Who are you really?" I immediately asked.

"I already told you," Paul-Henri answered. "I'm the landlord."

"I thought your—that Pierre's parents own this humble abode?"

Paul-Henri made his way around the room, looking at the damage that had been done by the police going over everything as he worked his way to the bar, perusing through the various bottles. He then walked across the room to the kitchen, retrieved a bottle of Veuve Clicquot from a temperature-controlled box up on one of the marble countertops, and poured himself a drink. As he went to seal the bottle back up, he held it up as if to offer me one as well.

"As you can see, this is my place. Pierre's . . . *parents* own a place over near the beach. Says it reminds them of France. Though I don't see how. This was my place they bought for me to keep me away from their doings. It works for me. Pierre likes to crash here during the week instead of making the trek all the way home from school. I let him. I'm hardly ever here. See? The landlord."

"Speaking of which, where are Pierre's parents? Shouldn't they be here?"

"They're vacationing. Out of the country. Rather, father is working, and *she* is . . . shopping. They'll be back. By the end of the week. To deal with the funeral arrangements. Touching how quickly they move to come to their son's aid, no?"

"So, it was what? Just you and Pierre here? That seems like a bit of a drive for Pierre. Wouldn't he have gone to a different school living that far away?"

Paul-Henry shrugged to let me know this was beyond his worries. He wasn't his brother's keeper and didn't worry himself with such mundane things.

"And what exactly is it you do?" I pushed.

He paused and ever so slightly looked beyond me to the middle mask on the table behind me before focusing his gaze back to me. But it was too late. I knew he knew what was going on around here. At first, I thought it was Pierre's thing. But perhaps his brother was the entrepreneur.

"I dabble here and there."

"Like your father?"

"I'm nothing like my father."

"And Pierre?"

"He's more like his mother. The belle of every ball. The face to sell what needs to be sold. The enticement to entrap the unassuming spender."

"And what needed to be sold? Or entrapped?"

"I don't remember you from any of Pierre's parties."

"Was that a question? Or a statement?"

"Who did you say you were again?"

"Leaving," I nodded with a smile.

"That's not an answer," Paul-Henri said as he moved around the counter and stood in my way, towering over me, trying his best to intimidate. He was taller than I, but not much wider. He may have had age on me, but I wasn't sure there was much else. "I'm not alone," he added, reading my thoughts.

"The voices in your head keep you company at night, do they?" I wasn't sure where this was going, and I wanted to be out of this place and away from Paul-Henri. I didn't trust being all alone with him. I pushed past him and headed for the door.

I heard Paul-Henri whistle from behind me, when the front door opened and a man I presumed to be Paul-Henri's bodyguard popped in. Now *this* was a man who took up the entire doorframe. He not only had height on me, but weight, which I assumed was pure muscle. Right about now I wished I had taken Theo Lannapo with me on my afternoon excursion. Especially when the man suddenly jackknifed me like a cheetah on speed. He had one arm wrapped around my neck while he twisted my left arm behind my back to the point that it felt as if it was going to break.

The bodyguard managed to drag/carry me over to Paul-Henri as if he was carrying nothing more than a bag of cotton. Paul-Henri stared down at me, shaking his head as he tried to figure out what to do with me.

"Do you even care that your brother was murdered?" I stammered out at Paul-Henri in-between choked off breaths. I wasn't quite sure what else to do or say at that moment and was hoping to distract him. Luckily for me, it worked.

"The police said it was suicide?"

"You really believe that?" His eyes dilated as he took in my words as the truth. Got 'em. I knew that if the two brothers were remotely close that there was no way Paul-Henri was buying the suicide story.

"Pierre is—was—is—the only person on this God forsaken planet I ever considered family. If what you say is true—*when* I find out who took his life, they will pay. Une promesse." He breathed in deeply. "Now again, who are you?"

"I'm the person who's going to help you fulfill your

promise." I wasn't sure if that was true or not, but I didn't exactly want to be kept prisoner in this glass house any longer either.

He began to nod at me, believing my words as he finished off his drink and set the glass down on the counter before reaching in his breast pocket. With the flick of his wrist he commanded his bodyguard to release me and I dropped to my knees. Paul-Henri retrieved a business card, looked over at the nearby desk for a pen and scribbled something on it.

"This is my information," Paul-Henri said as he handed over the card. "The front has my business info. On the back is my private number. You should use that. When you have results for me. You are someone efficient at procuring results, are you not?" Before I could answer he answered himself. "Yes. Yes, you are. I can tell that about you. Call me. It will be well worth your time and effort; of that I promise you."

And with those words he went back and poured himself another glass of champagne.

21

LITTLE MISS OBSESSIVE

Even though I now had not one but two employers—though I don't know how or why I obtained such opportunities other than being in the wrong place at the right time—I found myself with even fewer threads to follow. Though I was still on the original thread that Connor Emerson was somehow involved with all this, I had nothing more than my gut to go on. I also still wasn't one-hundred percent sure who had been blackmailing Maddie, or if she had even been the intended target of said blackmail, and so was stuck waiting for another text before I had that one figured out. Which left me with problem number two: Pierre's killer. Which I figured could—and hopefully did—have something to do with the blackmail scheme. Then again, the two might have been mutually exclusive and this was all just a coincidence. Though, I personally would have liked to believe that our high school wasn't really this corrupt and filled with so many vile and reprehensible occupants. This wasn't Neptune High or Riverdale.

Unfortunately, I knew better.

I went back home—the motel, I mean—and went about

doing my duties, which, being as it was a school night, were light. My aunt and uncle did most of the work, leaving the heavy and more time-consuming chores for the weekend to not disrupt my homeworking. The last thing they wanted was for me flunk a grade and be stuck around another year.

I called Jasmine when I needed a break from *The Joy Luck Club* and informed her that I had seen Maddie when she interrupted me to tell me that her sister had just gotten home and she promised to keep an eye on her for the rest of the evening. I told her it was a smart idea as I wasn't sure who had killed Liam or Pierre or why and that she may well be in danger still. I assured her I'd call her as soon as I heard anything from the blackmailers.

Then I called Skye Ford to see if she had heard anything new around the school when I was sent straight to voicemail. I might have taken it personally when I remembered that she had an after-school job at a coffee shop near the school grounds.

Maybe I just needed some coffee.

It was nine o'clock by the time I arrived at Curious Coffee, the afterschool hangout where Skye worked. She figured her options were to stay after school every day and study extra hard in hopes of one day obtaining that nonexistent scholarship she didn't believe in or else work every night and save up enough coin to one day bounce. I wasn't exactly sure how much she planned on saving before doing so but secretly hoped it would be a while. Skye Ford was one of the few people I felt the ability to properly have an adult conversation with. Loved me some Theo Lannapo, and when life was tough, he was the perfect person to help with the getbys, but he wasn't exactly waxing poetic if you catch my drift.

Curious Coffee was not far from school, with a large patio area in the back that kids liked to hang out in as it was fenced in and kept away from the prying eyes of adults. There were various Buddhas and even a pond with some sort of running waterfall leading into it in one of the corners that helped add to the ambiance, which was already quite Zen for my tastes. While it *was* a social hangout of sorts, it felt more like a school away from school where kids could also finish homework, or, more likely, not worry about what tutor they would be seen with.

I got an iced mocha and contemplated how much caffeine my body was about to intake, when I recognized that due to both my youthful age and the fact that I currently had two employers eagerly awaiting updates, that I might just be up until the wee hours of the night anyway, and continued on my merry way. I surveyed the back patio, looking for and not finding Skye when there was a voice at my side, startling me as I tried my hardest to hide it.

"She's not here," Skye said as she passed by and on to a vacant table near the back, cleaning up a mess left behind.

It might have been after nine, but Curious Coffee stayed open to the public until eleven and I knew Skye would be here until nearly midnight. I settled in, taking the vacant table that she had just finished cleaning when she tousled my hair and continued onto the next table.

"And who is it you think I'm here looking for exactly?" I asked as I took a sip through my straw.

"Your girlfriend."

"Wasn't aware I had one. I am so slick. What's her name? Is she pretty?"

"Pretty skank if you ask me. But what do I know?"

Suddenly I didn't think we were simply bantering. There was a tone to her voice that made me sit up and pay attention.

"You're talking about Jasmine?"

"Who else?"

"You know she's not my girlfriend."

"Sure about that?"

I looked to my crotch then back up at her.

"He may be confused, but"—I tapped the side of my head—"I'm pretty sure I know what's what."

"Sure that's the part of your body that's in charge?"

Arg. Women. Can't they ever just let me win one?

"What's up?"

Though she was welcome to socialize during her work hours, employees of Curious Coffee weren't exactly allowed to sit and mingle. Skye looked around as she worked her way behind my table and sat down on the rock wall that made up the planter that outlined the property alongside the wooden fence. She dragged her feet along the ground, making circle shapes with the souls of her shoes as she avoided my question.

"Ford?" I nudged.

"I just hear things. That's all."

"What kind of things? Surely not that Jasmine and I are back together again."

"No. But things. I've been listening. People talk."

"And what are they saying?"

"That the police questioned you today. That maybe you were up at Pierre's last night. What does she have you mixed up in?"

"Who says she's got me mixed up in anything."

"Because last week you were eating PB&J out by your lonesome on the football field like you always do. Then she comes and talks to you and now you're the talk of the school."

"And what are they saying, exactly?"

"Not sure. Some think you are involved. That you are behind everything. Both Pierre's and Liam's deaths. Others don't know what to think. Some think you are a God taking revenge on those who have wronged you. Like a reverse *Thirteen Reasons Why* where the victim doesn't commit suicide the tormentors do. Some of us . . ."

"Yes?"

But she wouldn't finish the sentence. Something about what she wanted to say to me. I wasn't sure what it was, but she held back for a second as if the words might hurt.

"I know you Chance Harper. I hate to say it, and I'm sorry to do so, but *do* you have any friends? People you hang out with? Play video games with. Make memories to look back on in the later years of life and laugh about. To run off to . . . oh, I don't know where . . . a museum or Disneyland or wherever.

The beaches, the mountains, you name it."

I lost focus on her as my mind began to drift. Where had this come from?

"No . . . no, I don't. Haven't for a while now. But I'm not so . . . that's not all there is to life, you know?"

"Sure."

"What about you? Do you hang out with the girls every weekend, doing sleepovers and drooling over which member of One Direction is the dreamiest? I know everyone loves Harry and his crazy-ass hair but personally I'm partial to the Liam myself."

"You're an ass," she deadpanned to me. "Besides, what the hell are you doing knowing the names of One Direction?"

"Me? Please. I'm up on all the happenin' happenings. I know them all. There's a . . . a Nick . . . and a J.C. and a . . . that's all, right? One more?" She was eyeing me with distain. "One more? A Joey? Danny? Joey. It's a Joey for sure. See? I know 'em all."

"I repeat: you're an ass. Regardless, I'm leaving this city the second I can. I have plans for a future. You . . . you I have no idea. I don't know what you're planning. But I don't see it involving you leaving. Or even considering your future. Or a future. Which makes me worried when dealing with the danger this . . . whatever it is brings. It makes me wonder . . . worry about your safety. Or your lack of concern for your own future. I'm worried about you is all."

"A real fast out? Well, I can't say I'm heartbroken over the concern. But trust me, I'm not looking for a way to end things. No plans. I'm still here and I plan on fighting for every breath this body can produce until I'm the age of a hundred. Really. I thank you for your concern. But I'm not as involved as people may think. Yes, the police *suspect* I was up at Pierre's the night before. But I'm not seriously a suspect. It's only because the two detectives handing this case are the same ones who handled my father's suicide. They were mostly checking up on me to make sure I was surviving all right. Kinda like you. 'kay?"

She wasn't sure what to say as she stood up and started away. She stopped before she hit the next table and turned to me.

"You know, you may be a major ass sometimes, Harper, but some people would still be hurt if you weren't around to level out the playing field from the real assholes."

It was a little after ten o'clock before Skye made her way back around to me. Most of the crowd on the patio had cleared off already since Curious Coffee closed their patio to the public at ten, trying their hardest to both keep an eye on the late stayers and spread the vibe that they closed soon. I guess Skye had okayed it that I be left alone to my own devices, which was good, as I wasn't aware that I had been.

I had had my head buried deep in Pierre's ledger that I had all but forgotten that I had snuck out of his place the night before when I rescued Maddie as I was trying my hardest to decipher it. Of course, the fact that I may have slipped a little something extra into that coffee I was drinking may have been muddling my brain. Maybe it was a list of names of Pierre's clients? Then again, maybe it was just Pierre's way of keeping track of who picked their noses in public on what day and at what time. How would I know? Even if I did have a gut feeling it was something more than that. I just couldn't figure out what.

"Wow, those PSAT flash cards are being worked double time, now aren't they?" Skye asked sarcastically as she sat down in the chair next to me and threw her legs up in a nearby vacant chair. She referred to the flashcards and open books on my table, each spread out for the world to see. Unfortunately, I, being who they were there for, was not looking.

"I attempted. Doesn't that count?"

"What's got you distracted?" She asked as she glanced at the ledger.

"Depends how much lying you might care to do in the future?"

"Plausible deniability, huh? Well, let's say I'm a risk-taker. Give it a shot."

"Pierre's ledger of some sort. Found it at his place last . . . sometime in the past that wasn't last night when he was murdered." I smiled at her and she rolled her eyes at me to let me know she wasn't falling for it but that she understood the plausible deniability I was giving her. "Think whoever killed him was looking for it but they missed it somehow."

"And yet super sleuth Chance Harper had no trouble finding the lost clues in the old mill up on the cliff? Think maybe it was left for you intentionally?"

"What? Why? That's just stupid talk. Why would someone

have left this for me? I can't even decipher it. And no one knew I was around last—during a time that shall remain nameless. Can a specific time be nameless? Or is it timeless?"

"Well, why don't you call Encyclopedia Brown and Veronica Mars and the rest of the Scooby gang to meet up later in the old clock tower and you can all put your heads together and solve the mystery of the undecipherable ledger!"

She was being a snot, but I got what she meant. Why was this *my* job? Oh, right. Because it could be related to the two jobs I was hired to do. One of which I saw as being potentially life threatening if I didn't complete.

"But it isn't."

"What? What isn't what?"

"I know what you were thinking. And this isn't your job. You're a high schooler, Harper. Give this over to the police. Let them handle it. Two kids from our school are dead. You wanna end up lucky number three?"

She stared at me with her deep amber eyes and I could feel the concern in her voice. But she didn't know. She couldn't. I needed to figure this out and fix this. I needed to—

"But you can't," she interrupted as if she could read my thoughts.

"Can't what?"

She stopped and considered her words. I don't know why. Maybe she thought they might hurt me. Maybe they would. But even though we'd only been friends for a short while honesty was a standing rule between the two of us. In a world filled with adults who seemed to do nothing but lie to one another we had made a pact. No matter what the costs. No matter what the reasons why, we'd argue against it. We always told the truth. She knew this. She was just building up to it.

"Get back the past."

"I don't know what you mean. But I know you're wrong."

"You lost all of them. Your mother. Your father. And Jasmine. I know it all. Remember. We've talked. And I hear things. About this all. And for some twisted reason you think if you fix whatever it is that's Jasmine's problem right now then maybe you can save her and be her knight in shining armor and maybe things can go back to the way they used to be. But life doesn't work like that, Harper, and you know it." She took a breath and then turned from me, leaning her head back over the back of her chair so she could stare up at the stars above. "She isn't going to just change because you've proved yourself, Harper. I know you think she blames you. For everything that happened. Even though deep down inside you really do think that, I think you also know it's bullshit. It wasn't your fault. All that shit that happened two years ago. Hell, if I was going to blame anyone, I'd blame her. From what you've told me, it was her fault in the first place."

I tensed up and I could see her read my body language. Something in my posture told her to shut up and mind her own business but she was on a roll and had no intention of doing so.

"She's the one who knew about your parents cheating. From what you've said. She just didn't want to be the one to spill the beans to the rest of the world. She didn't want to look like the bad guy. So, she got you, her puppet, to do the dirty work for her. And it worked. World hates you. Blames you for what happened. Plus, you look crazy in the process, and she comes out smelling like a rose. And don't you dare say anything against that. You know I'm right. Bitch has been playing you since you were kids. Sure, she may have been a little princess whom you fell in love with, but people change, Harper. They grow up and become the people they were always destined to be. No matter who's around in their lives to change their path. We always become who we were born to be. It's just the way life works. And to those who know you, like I'd like to think I do, you don't *need* to change. Unfortunately"—she turned to me, her head still arched back and facing the night sky above—"I also know that boys are stupid. Especially boys around girls. So, you're going to have to do this the hard way. The long and stupid way. I just hope it doesn't end up getting you killed in the process."

"You don't actually think there's a chance I'll get killed over all this."

"What makes you say that?"

"Because if there was actually a chance I could get killed you'd find a way to stop me. No matter what I said or thought."

"You have no idea how close I am to doing just that. But I also know that you, like all other teenagers, are a work in progress. You're not perfect. And if you don't learn now you might never do so. So, all I can do is hope that this time is the lesser of two dangers and you live to breathe another day." She paused and shrugged. "Or maybe I just don't give a shit one way or the other if you live or die."

"Bullshit."

She raised her eyebrows in doubt then turned back to the nighttime sky. A few minutes passed between us as I processed what she had said to me when she broke the silence.

"You can't make up for their mistakes. Either of them. Your father or your mother. You can't make things perfect, so *she'll* come back. And you can't do enough in this world, so people won't look at you like you're *his* son. Their sins aren't yours to atone for. Even though we go through life feeling that way. They made the mistakes. Just like everyone in this life does. They were wrong. Not you." She paused momentarily and then continued. "I know you feel abandoned. I get it. And so maybe this is your way of holding on to the past, some small part of it, that's still around for fear that it too will disappear from your life. But you know what, Harper? Even if it does, even if she leaves too, that doesn't mean you don't exist. That doesn't mean you're invisible or cursed or anything else. It's just life. It's what happens. Hard as it is."

"Finished?" It was all the more I could say. I could feel my face flushing with anger and embarrassment, and I knew if I said anything else it might just damage one of the few friendships I actually had in this life.

"What are we gonna do, Chance?"

"I can't stop. I've already committed."

"I'm not talking about your stupid project for Jasmine,

dork. I mean later. In the future. After high school. What comes next?"

"I've decided to become a weatherman." I have no idea where that thought came from, but it immediately brought almost uncontrollable laugher to Skye and I knew I had said the right thing.

"A weatherman?"

"What? What's wrong with being a weatherman?"

"Oh, nothing," she held up her hands in defense. "Weathermen bring home a steady paycheck, which is a hell of a lot more than I can say for most of the men in my mother's life. I'd worship a God damn weatherman." She stopped and shook her head at me. "A weatherman . . ."

I couldn't help it and I finally let out a laugh as I began to gather up the flashcards spread out across the table.

"Weatherman on one of the local channels is kinda cute. Only does the weekend weather, I think."

"Shut up," I said without much effort. "Like you ever sit around and watch the news. Or the weather."

"I might. If the right man was on TV doing the forecasting." Skye stood up and gathered the few cups that I had acquired throughout the night. She glanced over the table at the ledger. "Calling it a night?"

"Not sleepy yet. But I know you're closing. Probably head back to the motel and keep working away at this riddle I got my hands on."

"You're welcome to stay."

I shrugged. "It's okay."

"Are we okay?"

"Us?" I looked up and smiled. "Yeah. We're all good. I hate you sometimes but we're solid. Probably one of the few people I know that I am solid with."

"Good," she replied as she rustled my hair and started back for the café. "Oh, by the way. You think those symbols look familiar?"

"Of course they look familiar. Everyone knows the percent sign, the and sign, the at sign and all the rest of them."

"Well . . ." she waited for me to get something, but I was grabbing at fog. "Maybe your puzzle is more mathematical."

"How so?" I asked as I stood up and shuffled everything into my bag.

"All those signs in that book of yours? They're each and only the signs that pertain to the numbers one through zero on the top of a keyboard. G'night, Chance."

And with that she was gone. Leaving me to stand there alone in the back patio, staring down at the ledger which began to make sense to me. Skye had removed the pebble from the dam. And suddenly the floodgates were wide open.

22

PUMPING BLOOD

I **should have** just gone back home after I left Curious Coffee, but somewhere between Silver Lake and hitting the 101 freeway I decided to take a side trip. I wasn't entirely sure where I was heading until I found myself parked on Vine Street, opposite the building where Pierre's former coworker, Malia Doyle, lived. I sat parked in my car and took back out the ledger and fiddled with it. Skye had been right. Each of the symbols could have stood for a number, being as there were only ten different symbols to choose from. One was a !. Two was a @. Three a # and so on. So, if that was the case then I could decipher each of the symbols into a number. But what did the numbers mean?

The sound of thunder shook the city and I could almost feel my car rattle when I flipped on the radio and found a jazz station located out of Long Beach. I figured the music would be calm and soothing as I tried to focus on the numbers. About thirty minutes later, at what by my clock looked to be around eleven-seventeen, I noticed a car pull up in front of the stone-gray apartment complex and then drive past and park in the first available spot next to the sidewalk.

I knew that car. Even without identifying who was behind the driver's wheel or seeing the license plate I knew that car. It was Jasmine's.

I turned off my car so the glow from the dashboard wouldn't light up my face as I slinked back into my chair and watched Jasmine hop out of her car to make her way to the front door of the building. She pressed the buzzer for an apartment, and though I didn't know for sure whose, I thought it only a coincidence that she would be at the same building I was staking out a girl who used to work with Pierre Chevalier. I waited until she disappeared through the doors and then quickly got out of my car and made my way across the street.

The front door was still slightly ajar, the heavy glass and gold door refusing to close all the way and I pried it open. I looked around for any suspicious types and then made my way in. I saw the single elevator in the building going up and stop on the fifth floor. Malia Doyle lives on the fifth floor. I was beginning to think these coincidences were less and less coincidental.

I skipped the elevator and made my way up the neighboring staircase until I found myself on the fifth floor. I looked around and worked my way to apartment 504 where I knocked twice.

I could hear scrambling and hushed whispers from the other side of the door when it flew open. There was a look of momentary shock on Malia's face as if she had expected someone else, when that look quickly turned to anger.

"What the hell do you want?" she asked crossly as she

folded her arms across her chest.

"I heard there was a party up here," I announced as I forced my way in past her.

"Hey, you can't just barge in here like that," she spat as she closed the door and followed me into the main living room.

The apartment was elegantly, if not somewhat oddly, decorated in the colors and tones of someone stuck in the sixties. Perhaps the decorator was a fan of *Mad Men* and felt the need to bring the age back. Hell, they say eventually everything comes around again. Maybe I was just behind in the times.

I turned around and faced Malia as I sat on the arm of a brown stripped sofa.

"What do you want?" she asked curiously, keeping her sultry eyes deadlocked on me.

"I told you. I heard there was a party up here. Or at least this is the place to get a party started, is it not?"

I was full of crap. I had nothing to connect Malia to the Murphys' drug dealing trade or even Pierre's shenanigans. I was just throwing out ideas and hoping one would stick. Or else that I'd piss her off enough to get her to let something slip on accident. Her eyes widened just for ever so slight a second but that was all I needed. Confirmation.

"The question is whether or not I ask you or the other person you got hidden in the back room for the party favors?"

She began to sway in her stance as if determining whether to accommodate my request when she kept her feet planted firmly in their place.

"I think you should leave now," she said as she held an arm up and pointed at the front door as if I had forgotten where it was. As if I couldn't see it from where I was. Place wasn't that big.

"What's wrong? Don't trust me?"

"I don't know you or what you're asking about."

"Just ask your friends about me. They'll tell you."

"I don't have any friends."

"Sure you do. Just ask your friend in the other room. You know? The second door down the hallway on the left. With the door open just a smidge. She'll tell you. I'm a swell guy."

I had to hand it to the girl. She wasn't breaking a sweat over what I said any more than she broke eye contact. But she didn't need to. I knew who was in the back room and I knew she couldn't stay put.

"Hello, Chance," Jasmine said from behind me as she made her way down the hallway.

"Hiya, doll. Say, Jazz, why don't you tell your friend here I'm a swell guy."

"He's a swell guy," she said to Malia with bite. "Doesn't mean you should listen to him. Or do what he says."

"Gee, now what did I ever do to deserve that?" I asked as I turned and faced Jasmine. "So, when's the party get started around here? It's already nearly midnight. And on a school night no less."

"Who the hell—" started Malia before Jasmine cut her off.

"Chill. I'll handle him. There is no party, Chance. What the hell are you doing here?"

"Just following Hansel's breadcrumbs to the witch's house," I said smiling at Malia.

"And what breadcrumbs would those be? I'm not here about Maddie's situation at all," Jasmine said as she eyed Maia.

"Oh, I'm aware you're not," I smiled as I studied her. "You're here for PDV."

She tried to play innocent, but the look of shock was too apparent across her face.

"Excuse me?"

"PDV. Oh, I'm sorry. I believe the kids these days are calling it Flush. Though not sure why. Neither were the detectives who asked me about it earlier today."

That did it. Both women were suddenly sweating underneath their blouses and Malia immediately began to pace the room.

"What do you want, Chance?" Jasmine asked as she circled around me and worked her wayside by side with Malia.

"Flush." Jasmine raised an eyebrow with doubt at my request and I realized she'd misread my intentions. "Not the actual thing. What is it? How does it work? And how are you involved? Or why?"

"What? Do you think you know me or something?" Jasmine asked.

"I mean, I get her involvement. Now that I know my threads are legit," I said nodding toward Malia. "But you? What, are you the go between? The connection?"

"What are you talking about?"

"I mean, everyone already knows that the Murphys are

connected to the drugs in this town. At least at the high schools. Why do you think Liam and Aiden keep flunking out? No one's that stupid. They're a connection to the high school from their uncle's bars in Hollywood and on the beach. I get that. No one's shocked about that. But it was shocking that you had gotten involved with them considering the rumors about them and how much you seem to care about your image concerning your father's potential political future. Which begs the question, why?"

"You don't know what you're—" Malia had decided to throw her two cents at me when I cut her off.

"You're a Doyle. That makes you related to the Murphys in one way or another. Cousins. Brothers of sisters or something like that. I can add two plus two. I'm sure a little digging would get me all the answers I could hope for. You're older than us by a few years so I'm sure you used to be the way into the high schools but since you've graduated I guess they needed someone new. Liam and Aiden. But they both graduate this year. So . . . what? You're going to pass the baton off to Jasmine? I don't see that. The other question is how this all connects to Liam and Pierre's murders. Because, despite what Jasmine would like me to think, I *can* see this all being connected to Maddie's little blackmail scheme."

Malia looked to Jasmine with confusion though the girl didn't notice as she was too focused on me. Fine for me. I could read the signs all around us and that included body language. I'd stumbled onto something bigger with the PDV and I wouldn't even have that if it wasn't for the detectives. I should remind myself to send them a donut basket or something.

"What did you get me involved in and why?" I asked sternly.

"This has nothing to do with what I hired you for. You can leave now, Chance. This doesn't concern you."

"Oh, but I think it does. For reasons I'll just keep to myself. But this here, tonight, right now, does concern me. See, girly here works—or, I'm sorry—*used* to work for Pierre who was murdered last night. Pierre was my only link to the pictures that you're so worried about. At first, I thought he was taken out because of those pictures. But I know you didn't kill him and supposedly no one else knows about those pictures. Oh, wait—that is except for Liam. And lookie here, he's dead too. Now granted, those pictures aren't exactly refrigerator hanging material, but they're nothing so scandalous as to kill two teenage boys over. And the only other connection I've got between the two so far, besides those illicit pictures, is the drugs. So . . . why would they have been killed? Perhaps for a certain ledger containing clients' names? A certain ledger that could pose a real threat for numerous people involved with this whole Flush drug thing. Users? Buyers? Sellers?"

I shrugged. I was bullshitting, as I had no idea what that ledger really contained. But I figured those girls didn't know I was full of it.

"You lie," Malia hissed at me.

"About what?"

"There is no ledger. That's just a fairy tale. He just used that as an empty threat to keep people in line."

"He?"

"Malia," Jasmine snapped at the girl.

"It's okay, Jazz. I've figured this all out for myself already. And if this ledger is a fairy tale then how come I know about it? We all know I don't exactly travel within these circles. Hmmm?"

"You have it." Both Malia and I turned to Jasmine as she calmly made this accusation at me. The edges of her lips curled up as she shook her head. "You have it. Somehow. You were up at Pierre's last night. When you got Maddie out of there. Before the police come. And somehow you found it and now you have it. Don't you?"

Malia jerked her head at me and was about to say something when there was a knock at her front door and all three of us froze as if the person on the other side wouldn't know we were there if we didn't so much as breath.

"And you said you didn't have any friends," I said snarkily at her. "Seems like this really is the happenin' after-hours place to be." Neither girl moved and I could hear the ticking sounds of a clock counting off the seconds somewhere in the background. "Well? You gonna check it out or nah?"

Malia looked to Jasmine then back at me. There was the slightest look of fear on her face and I stood up and motioned at her that I would go with her. Though I had no idea why the hell I would. It wasn't my place and I sure as hell wasn't expecting anyone.

"Who is it?" Malia called through the closed door as I stood off to her side so when she did open the door, I would be hidden behind it.

We all waited patiently for a reply. When none was given Malia peered through the peephole then looked to me, the look on her face saying no one was there. She grabbed the handle and began to open the door right as something clicked inside me, telling me something was wrong.

Suddenly three gunshots rang out from the other side of the door, two of them hitting Malia and sending a spray of blood across the wall as she fell to the floor. Jasmine screamed as I slammed myself up against the door, catching the gun between the door and frame, causing whoever was holding it to let go. I backed away from the door and the gun fell to the floor. I knew immediately that our shooter had fled the scene.

"Stay down," I ordered Jasmine as I knelt to check Malia's pulse, my fingers sliding around her blood-covered neck. It was slight but there was a pulse. "Call 9-1-1. Now! She's still alive."

I breathed as deeply as I could to calm myself and flung the door open, trying to peer out into the hallway but also keeping myself protected from behind the door. I jumped through the doorway into the hallway and heard footsteps echoing through the stairwell on the far side of the floor. I heard commotion coming from behind the neighbor's closed doors as I immediately bolted across the hallway and down the stairs.

I was at the second floor when I heard someone below me bolting through the lobby door and I forced myself to run even faster to catch up with Malia's shooter. I made it through the lobby door just as I saw someone disappearing through the glass front doors of the building.

He had paused for a moment to look back over his shoulder to see if in fact someone was after him and that was all I needed. It was enough to identify him.

Connor Emerson.

Sticky Icky was Malia's shooter. But why?

"Connor!" I shouted as I burst through the front doors and he turned around from his spot in the middle of the street. He turned and continued across the street when less than two steps later he was hit by an oncoming car.

The sound of glass shattering and breaks squealing on the wet pavement from the rain earlier that evening all but deafened me as I heard the life being taken from Connor Emerson's body. He was flung up over the roof of the car and landed with a dull thud on the pavement behind the car as it swerved off the street, stopping up on the sidewalk, narrowly missing me as I had run in their direction.

But I was too late. As I stood there, breathing deeply, trying to catch my breath, I could tell that Connor Emerson was already dead.

23

IN THE MIDNIGHT HOUR

"We've got three dead teenagers in the last two days and you seem to be the only connection between them." Detective Talia Manning glared a hole at me with her non-existent Superman stare, but I got the point. This wasn't looking positive for me. The bodies were piling up by the day and even though I had no social connections with any of them, I did appear to be the common dominator. "Just what the hell are you doing here, Chance? You don't belong here."

Damn math and its simple addition.

"Me? Oh, you see this?" I said as I circled my face with my right index finger. "This is my I-give-a-shit-what-you-have-to-say face. I've been practicing it all month just for you and then started praying to God, Santa Clause *and* the Tooth Fairy just to get the chance to be able to use it before I forgot it. Seems as I if I'm gonna have to yank out every damn tooth I got cuz I owe that Tooth bitch some serious coinage after this."

"Don't you have any empathy for what's going on here?" Manning spat at me.

"Empathy? I'm a teenager. I'm full of nothing but empathy.

Unless I'm thinking of a different word. I could be confused. Could be the shock from seeing a fellow classmate just get run over. Or else it's that empathy sounds like a twelfth-grade level word and as we both know I'm currently a junior. Way to throw my shortcomings in my face."

Detective Manning's face grew furious as the veins in her forehead began to throb and her jaw clenched.

"What about Malia Doyle?" I quickly asked as I realized maybe I didn't want two homicides to have occurred in this exact spot in the same night.

I sat there on the sidewalk, the blue and red lights from the police cars that blocked off the street flashing off everything they touched. There had been an ambulance there earlier, but it had disappeared with Malia only a few minutes after arriving. There was a gaggle of detectives and CSIs all huddled around Connor Emerson's body still lying in the street.

After the oncoming car had struck Connor and I determined he was dead, I ran back upstairs to Malia's apartment. She was still unconscious but breathing. I looked around for Jasmine and couldn't find her anywhere. When I went to the window and looked down below, I saw that her car was also gone.

Fled the scene of the crime without so much as a second blink of the eye. At least I couldn't say I hadn't been warned about the girl.

"Unconscious. But the paramedics are hopeful. Pending they got her to the hospital in time. Which means right now it's your word against no one and time to get your story on the record. Yo comprehendo?"

"Just so we understand each other, I am *not* your inside line. But I'll give you what I got, the way I got it, and that's the way it is. The way it happened, at least as best to my recollection or my figuring out. This ain't professional and might not hold up in court but could and should be enough to keep you on the right path. I can't be doing all your jobs for you. The names, places, times and other such pertinent information may have been altered so protect the innocent, insomuch as I may know anyone who actually fits that bill, and you'll take it like that as I give it to you or you can call my lawyer now and we'll call it a night. Yo comprehendo?"

"Let's dance."

I followed the two detectives to their vehicle and slid into the back seat, leaning down deep, not to hide my identity from anyone so much as to get myself comfortable. After jumping out of the way of speeding bullets and practically throwing myself down the stairs to get after Connor I basically threw my body out of whack. I needed a chiropractor but good.

"I'd never heard of Flush before you two asked me about it. Sure, I go to school where it's dealt and taken daily, I'm sure, but it's not my scene and whenever it, or anything like it would be mentioned, I probably tuned out. Dig?"

Both detectives stayed silent and that was wise. This was my story to tell and they gave me the stage.

"So, Monday morning a friend comes to me. Someone's blackmailing her with some racy pics that were hacked from her phone. No, it's not her boyfriend or an ex, I've checked those lines of thought. But said blackmailer wanted a heavy pile of paper in exchange for keeping said photos under wraps. I was approached as a mediator to make sure all went according to plan. That the money was delivered as promised and that all proof of scandalous pics were destroyed."

"You're a regular teenage Olivia Pope," Detective Eric Hershey chuckled to himself. I let the comment slide and continued. "You do this sort of thing often?"

"Never before."

"Then why now?"

"Like I said. I was a friend of the girl whom pressure was being applied to. She didn't want anyone else she knew to find out about the pictures, and she knew I could keep my mouth shut."

The two detectives thought about this, remembered it was my story, and nodded at me to continue.

"Now I don't know who actually took the pictures. At first, I thought it was possibly Pierre Chevalier. But I've no actual proof of this and the more I think of it the less I buy it. More likely it was Pierre's older brother who was seducing the younger up-and-comings with illegal enticements. Flush, etcetera. You get the picture I'm painting."

"We're aware of Paul-Henri. So, these weren't just selfies taken for the boyfriend?"

I thought about this for a second. I had to connect Pierre but how far to take it?

"Yes. No. I mean they were not selfies. These were . . . artistic you could say."

"Of a minor?"

"You do know I didn't take these pictures, right? I'm simply the middleman. I can't control what every high school-aged girl and boy does on their free time. I was simply brought in after the fact. Which is also why I don't buy Pierre taking them. That's just not his scene. Sure, he likes a good party, but his parents keep him supplied with a steady flow of cash and that was just never the vibe I got from him. His black-sheeped brother on the other hand is s a different story. Him I can buy setting up a blackmail scheme for money."

"So, these pictures were taken by Paul-Henri?" Detective Manning continued to keep me going. I was spilling like a dam that had been blown sky high in a James Bond film. If I didn't watch it the village would flood fast.

"That's my assumption," I continued. "So, Monday night I was . . . hypothetically staking Pierre's place out as he was my original line of thinking. Well, him and Connor Emerson. But everyone who knows Connor knows he doesn't have enough brains to carry a con like this out he's more hired muscle. Short-tempered and low on brain cells kinda muscle. And he usually hung around Pierre. Which meant that by proxy he would have known Paul-Henri. Anywho, Pierre had visitors Monday night. There was a sort of party going on. Now I'm not sure about who all was there ~~ this has been more complicated than solving a game of C make a guess—or bet—on this I would s; have included Malia Doyle, Connor Emers an as of thus far unidentified third person true. I was leaving out the fact that Ma been up there, and I didn't know who that mysterious last person was just yet. "Connor Emerson had been coming and going throughout the night, so I don't know if he was there at the time of Pierre's death. Aiden and or Liam Murphy may or may not have been that mysterious third and possibly even a fourth person up at the house that night. Not sure. I think Liam was up there but not Aiden. But their connection to the drug you call Flush and Malia Doyle would easily connect the three. Anyway, I was outside. I heard gunshots and when I raced into the house, I found it empty save for Pierre's body. No, I don't know who shot him. Though I could make suspicious deductions, those don't exactly hold up in court. Then I left."

I gave them a moment to comprehend everything that I had just said before I continued.

"I think Aiden was not at the party the night before, but Liam was. The next day neither Aiden nor Liam showed up to school. I think Aiden had been looking for Liam who had been in hiding since the night before. At least he had been before he was killed."

Detective Manning turned to me. "And who do you think kill—"

"Connor Emerson. I think Connor killed Liam because Connor believed Liam killed Pierre. Again, I don't exactly have evidence of all this, mostly this is a lot of deducing based on who was where, when and how everyone knows everyone else. Everyone knew that Connor was Pierre's little lackey. Most thought he had a crush on Pierre. People also ght Connor followed Pierre around because of his connections. Particularly his connections to Flush. But I think this was wrong. Pierre didn't have connections to Flush, his brother did. I think Connor hung around Pierre so he could be closer to his drug connection: Paul-Henri. Connor Emerson was an addict. As I'm sure you're aware of."

"He has a rap sheet," Detective Hershey confirmed. I already figured as much.

"But why had Liam killed Pierre?" Detective Manning asked as she turned around to face me. "At least in your theory?"

"Not one-hundred percent sure. Probably something having to do with the drugs. Or something. They were all dealing and using. Maybe someone got in a fight over product or money or something. Who knows?" I couldn't tell them it was because I thought Liam had figured out Maddie was being blackmailed and thought he knew who had taken the pictures, so he jumped to the same conclusion I had. Only difference was I had thought out the situation with my brain and, realizing it was wrong, held back. While Liam Murphy thought them out with his fists. And a gun. But I was keeping Madison and Jasmine out of this story if I could help it and so far, the drugs seemed cover every angle.

The two detectives thought about what I was saying, had a momentary look as if they knew I was holding something back, but then remembered my words about how this story would unfold and they took it as I dished it.

"And tonight?"

"At first I thought Connor killed Liam in retaliation for cutting off his drug supply by killing Pierre. But if Pierre wasn't his supplier and Paul-Henri *was* maybe he was doing it to show his loyalty to Paul-Henri? But Connor didn't want to go to jail. Which is where I deduced that the only other person up at Pierre's the other night was Malia Doyle. So tonight, he hunted her down to take her out so there were would be no witnesses to what he had done. And again, drugs connect them all. So really, how much time and effort were you going to put into them? Just some more using teenagers caught in the middle of a drug war."

"And how had you ended up here tonight?"

"Malia worked with or for Pierre at one of his father's art galleries. I think that's how they knew each other. She was the only other person I knew connected to Pierre at the time and when I had met her the day before at Pierre's art gallery, she seemed spooked by me. So, I followed her around. I was going to confront her about it when I saw Connor going upstairs. By the time I got to her apartment he had already shot her and fled. I chased him downstairs and . . . well you know what happened from there."

I stopped and stared over at where Connor's body was being loaded onto a gurney.

"Would you say they're handling Connor's body gingerly?"

Both detectives did a double take at me as they tried to focus on what I was saying.

"Excuse me?" Detective Manning asked.

"I was just wondering if the way they're handling his body was what one would call gingerly. See, I've been reading a lot more lately and I've noticed in most every detective or mystery novel I've read the author at some point in every book uses the word gingerly. Though I can't for the life of me recall anyone in real life ever having used that word. Then again, I can't for the life of me recall having ever learned that word. Do you know what it means?" Both detectives simply stared at me." "It means to handle something with great care."

"I'm aware of what the word means," Detective Manning deadpanned at me.

"Oh? See, I had to look it up. But again, I'm only in the eleventh grade. Maybe that's another one of those twelfth-grade words I've yet to learn. Anyway, I figured since this is my own sortta mystery that I should at least use the word once so I can be like all the pros."

"You're not a detective, Chance Harper, so drop it. Now. Oh, and in case you weren't aware we are aware that there are some holes in your story."

"I know," I answered still staring out the window. "But so what? You know me. You know I'm telling the truth. And you know I'm not fleeing anywhere. You need to ask me any more you know where to find me."

I opened the door and stood out. A fine mist of water fell from the nighttime sky barely blanketing everything in a layer of dew. The stars that Skye and I had been staring up at earlier that evening were nowhere to be seen.

"Chance?" Detective Manning called out after me as I started back to my car. I turned and stared at the two. "So? Was Malia blackmailing your friend?"

I thought about that for a moment and shrugged. I had

ideas. But I thought they were all BS. "Who knows? Could have been Malia. But my guess would be on Connor. He seemed like the type of person who would stoop to something like that for a little side cash. But who knows? I haven't heard back from the blackmailer tonight and that's when they were supposed to let me now when and where to do the exchange."

"You know, Chance, you could have come to us with all this? We would have helped."

I shrugged again as I started on for my car.

"Yeah, but you know teenagers. We never trust adults with anything."

24

NIGHT MOVES

By the time I had made it back up to the motel it was well after one in the morning and the fact that I barely needed a few hours of sleep a night to still function as a semi-responsible teenager the following day was coming in handy. I noticed lights on in rooms three, five and seven. I noted this with no real interest or reason other than the tenants were still awake in the only three rooms we had rented out. Although, when you considered our location, the proximity to Hollywood and the types of people we catered too one couldn't be too surprised.

I walked around the main office and peeked back up at my aunt and uncle's place to find all the lights off. It figured that they would already be asleep. They weren't exactly what you'd call night owls, but the motel was still their responsibility overall and I could usually count on one or the other to keep a night light on.

It was times like these when I came to realize just how alone in the word I really was. My father was dead, and my mother was who knew where. She didn't care. She hadn't stayed around long enough to give two shits about what happened to me. I had been dumped on my relatives, and though they claimed I helped them around the place, realistically, I could tell I was just an unfortunate burden they'd rather not have around to remind them of the past. And I knew that a year and a half from now when I either turned eighteen or graduated from high school it wouldn't be long until they gave hints that it was time for me to move on. Hell, they were already giving hints that were about as subtle as a blow to the head with a sledgehammer.

I leaned against the motel and stared at their dark house. Would they even notice if I did just disappear overnight? How long before they noticed? And would they even do anything about it? Or did they not consider me a responsibility at all?

Mostly what scared me was I had no one to fall back on. I truly was alone in the world. If after graduation I did decide to go out into the big bad world and try it on for size and *failed* no less (as often happens in life), I had no home to fall back onto. I couldn't move back in with mom and dad and reassess my situation and give it another try later. If the college I attempted to attend (which, without the aid of a scholarship didn't seem all that likely) suddenly didn't work out due to grades (okay, so that really wouldn't happen to me) or more likely, lack of financial aid, what then? I didn't have mom and dad to bail me out. No one around to co-sign on loans for a new car. I had . . . what?

I shivered.

Both sets of grandparents, my mother's parents and my father's, had all passed away when I was younger. My father's

I didn't even remember and my mother's both lost battles to cancer in their sixties. I had been twelve when the last one passed on.

My father's parents hadn't exactly been wealthy, more living paycheck to paycheck as they lived a simple life. When they passed on, they didn't leave behind any sizable surprises in their will, but they also hadn't left behind any debt for their children to inherit. I'd call that a considerable gift. My father had worked his way through law school and his brother had gone into the motel management business. My father was dead, and though my uncle's motel wasn't exactly prosperous he was still alive, thus proving their parent's point of view that money wasn't everything in life.

My mother's parents on the other hand hadn't lived life by that rule as they had had money and had no problem spending it. They left a little debt behind, but all had been more than covered by their life insurances. My mother had only herself and a younger sister left to inherit and after all was split evenly my mother helped support my father's budding law career while my aunt picked up and pursued her dreams of living the lavish life of a celebrated clothing designer in Paris. I wasn't sure exactly how she was these days as I hadn't spoken or seen or heard of the woman since my grandfather's funeral. She hadn't even come around when my father passed on and my mother disappeared. Wonder if she might have known where my mother was though?

Standing there, I noticed the rain coming down steady, which was a good thing for the city as we were going through yet another water shortage. Someone should get

Jake Gittes on that one and figure out where it's all gone. But the real reason I noticed this was because I was standing in it and it wasn't like it had just started falling; it had been coming down my entire drive home. Boy was my brain on auto pilot. I couldn't even remember driving home. I knew I did it. Stopped at all the right stop signs and red lights. Got both on and off the freeway. But man, for the life of me, I couldn't even remember starting that car. Last thing I remembered—

Sure, I remembered my talk with the detectives. But the last image in my mind was of Connor Emmerson lying in the street. Dammit, life sure sucked sometimes. Everyone knew Connor was a foster kid, bouncing from house to house. When he graduated in a year and a half he too would be out on his own. Kinda like my own situation.

Kinda.

That was when I shuddered and snapped out of my little daydream. I rolled myself from the corner and found my way back to my front door. I walked in, saw everything to be as it should be in the front office, and made my way back to my back room. I entered and flipped on the light and got the surprise of my life.

Someone had been in my room. And I don't mean like a girl waiting in my bed for me type of someone. I mean someone had gone through and trashed my place looking for something.

Maybe my aunt and unc—hell, no. They had no reason and they had all the access they wanted (even though I did always lock the door when I left each day for school).

No. This was someone looking for something that they thought I had. That only I might have. But had they found it? How should I know? I wasn't even sure—

I stopped. I hadn't even thought about it but when I turned around to stare at the mess that had been made of my walls, I felt the corner of the ledger poke into one of my ribs from the inside of my jacket pocket. I immediately took the little black book out and stared at it, sealed tight with the five rubber bands that had been holding it together since I first found it.

What the hell exactly was this little black book? What information did it hold? And who wanted it so bad they were willing to do this and not cover their trail? Someone wanted to find this.

But most of all, they knew I had it.

And they wanted me to know they were looking for it.

I suddenly heard a creek behind me, and I froze, though I was able bodied enough to slide the ledger back into my coat pocket. I slowly turned my head around to find Jasmine standing there, drenched from the rain, sorrow and shock displayed across her face which was no less a sight for sore eyes despite the Pollock-inspired makeup job the rain had done to her.

"Where the hell were you?" I all but shouted at her as I stormed the room, yes, all ten feet of it, and grabbed ahold of her as if she was a bird daring to fly away. "Where the hell did you go?"

"I just . . . I couldn't . . ." she stammered as I saw the tears coming from her eyes. She immediately buried her head into my chest and continued to cry. "I just couldn't face it. All that blood. The guns. I feared something might have happened to you."

"Apparently not enough to stick around and make sure I was all right."

"Oh, I did. I knew you were all right. You always are. God, Chance . . . I don't know what I would do if anything ever happened to you."

Boy she was laying it on thick. But truth of the matter was I kinda liked it. It felt good to hear someone say words like that to you. Even if they were shady.

"I just . . . I'm sorry, Chance." She looked up at me with her baby blues and I could feel myself melting right there. I just felt so damn sorry for the girl. I knew she was playing me. At least chances were good she was. But I couldn't help it. She was my first love. My first heartbreak. And I'm honestly not sure if I ever truly got over that. God help me, I loved the girl. I knew it was stupid. I knew she would never bring me anything but trouble. But I couldn't help it. Sometimes I feel God messed up making all of us by not mixing the brain and heart as one single organ. People sure were stupid. And like another girl I knew once told me, boys were the stupidest people of them all.

Especially when it came to women.

"Can I stay?" Jasmine said, breaking the silence. "I'm just so . . . I don't want to be alone. And I don't think you do either. For the night? Please?"

I continued to stare down at her as she reached up and kissed me. That was it. I was done for. Stupid Chance. Never had one with her around that was for sure.

I flipped the light switch next to the door then guided her over to my little makeshift twin bed in the far corner. We laid there on the bed, listening to the rain as it slammed against the window. Despite all the mess we had been through that night—hell, our whole lives up to that point—this still felt comfortable. Good. Inviting.

I could feel her heart beating as she lay against me. She looked up at me and once more we kissed away the night.

25

LUCKY

The next morning, I jerked awake from the nightmare I was having, reliving the night I discovered my father and his lover's bodies and drove my car into a tree. Right as the car was about to hit, I awoke and fell out of my bed. My head was swirling, though not from booze but rather from the lack of sleep I'd had. I looked over to my alarm clock, which I'd forgotten to set. Luckily, I'd been reliving past horrors and I awoke only fifteen minutes later than usual. That's when I noticed I was alone in my bed. I walked around my small room and poked my head out through the door to the main office.

Nope. All alone.

I showered and then dashed off to school; stopping by one of the many Starbucks on the way.

Despite being late to school, nothing was all too out of the ordinary for me. I wasn't sure what I was expecting, police perhaps? Being taken in for more questioning because they hadn't fallen for my BS story? No idea. But something felt off to me.

When I got to my locker, I saw that Theo Lannapo was

standing next to it. I wasn't exactly sure what his face was telling me, but I thought it was somewhere between concern and being pissed off at me. I said hello to him, and he simply stared forward like he was his own totem pole. I rolled my eyes and dug through my locker without another word.

A minute later Skye had managed to sneak up beside me and grab my coffee and take a swallow of it before I even noticed let alone could have stopped her.

"Ewww, God. You and your sugary-flavored coffee drinks," Skye said with a face of disgust as she placed the cup back inside my locker.

"Hey. That's mine. I kinda need it, in case you hadn't noticed."

"Oh, I had," Skye teased while I dug through my locker, trying to find my Spanish and AP Chem books.

"And you know, if *someone* I knew who worked at a coffee shop felt kind enough to bring me coffee every morning . . ."

Skye's face told me to drop dead as she ignored my comment. "So, you haven't seen the latest and greatest?"

I couldn't tell if Skye was stating a fact or asking a question. I was off my game. Perhaps I did need more than four hours of sleep a night. Maybe I was getting old? I noticed her glance over my shoulder at Theo and nod her chin up at him as a form of greeting. Theo remained the same though I could have sworn I saw the edge of his mouth go slightly up in a wannabe smile. Just slightly. I know it was there. I could feel it.

"What's that?"

"Connor Emerson?" She knew I had to know something

and wanted to know what.

"Why don't you spill before I do."

"Fine." She rolled her eyes in protest but obeyed. "Connor's dead. Hit by a car or something. Now, no one knows why or what exactly. Some say he was high or drunk and wandered in the road. Some say that he's simply another student who opted to take the fast out. Others say it has to do with Liam's death. No one knows. But there are even more counselors on campus today to help the grieving population. So . . .?"

"So what?"

"Chance Harper. Are you going to tell me you honestly left my place last night and went straight home? Without stopping by anywhere? Cuz you and I both know that's bull. I don't know why or where Connor was run over, but I refuse to believe you weren't anywhere near him when it happened. Three dead students in the last few days? That's not a coincidence. That's a flat-out accusation."

"Yeah, that's what the police think too."

"What? Harper? What the hell is going on? You *were* there."

I heard Theo grunt a sound of disappointment.

"Yes," I admitted flatly. "And it did have to do with Aiden and Pierre. And the police were there as well. Talked to my friend Manning and Hershey again. I think I got them convinced I had nothing to do with it, that it was just a coincidence, but I think they'd buy more truth in a reality show being 'real' than my story right about now."

"What the hell? So what? Are the police going to show up

here today and haul you off in handcuffs?"

I kinda shrugged, not sure what to tell her. Last night seemed like a lifetime ago and I couldn't really recall the detectives' moods after I had told them everything and walked away. Sure, I gave them everything wrapped up with a nice little bow. They could have bought it all and been done with it. But somehow, I kinda doubted it. And besides, this was drugs at the school we were talking about. Even if they were finished with Pierre's murder, they still had the drug problem which would be an ongoing case for them to worry about.

"Well . . ." Skye slammed my locker door shut on me and started to storm off. "At least you didn't get shot."

"I . . . uh . . ." I turned for comfort from Theo and found myself all alone in the hallway.

Spanish passed without any kind of concern other than a reminder about the oral exam we had due on Friday AKA in two days. I didn't even know what the topic of the conversation was let alone if I could pull it off. Passing between Spanish and AP Chem I should have noticed something was off but was too wrapped in my own little world to notice anything. It wasn't until I switched between AP Chem and Algebra II that I noticed several people standing around and looking at me as I passed through the hallways. You know the look. As if they're talking about you and then try to hide it when you're nearby. Something was up.

I went to my locker, where I saw Theo Lannapo once again standing next to it, to switch my books from my first two classes to the next two before lunch. I once again greeted Theo, who once again remained quiet like he was my own personal bodyguard. I asked Theo if he had seen Jasmine around and I only got a raised eyebrow of intolerance. I shook my head and began to dig through my locker when Amy Song and her best friend, Kyla Lewis, approached me.

Now I had nothing against Amy, or Kyla, but I couldn't tell you how many words the two of us had exchanged throughout our entire lives of knowing each other (since the second grade) probably because we had never exchanged words before. Period. Amy Song was of the upper crust circle of life that ran alongside Jasmine and Madison's group of friends. She wasn't a cheerleader per say, but she was on the student council and was at every school function. Not because she gave a damn but because it looked good on the transcripts and girl was damn well going to do everything it took to get the hell out of here come graduation day. Amy Song felt she was better than everyone else at school. And she had no problem announcing that thought from time to time.

"Is it true you spent the night in jail?"

"What?" I asked, genuinely shocked as I dropped my US History book. "What the hell are you talking about?"

I turned to the girl and could tell there was some sort of genuine interest and almost, well, desire as she spoke to me. Then again, that could have just been my teenage hormones working on their own. Her hair was pulled back out of her face, held back with a stylish clip of some sort. She wore a single wrap that stopped just halfway down her tanned thighs. The wraparound dress was covered with what I assumed to be white daisies pattern all over it. I wondered if this is what they meant by a floral pattern.

"Well, rumor has it you pushed Connor Emerson in front of a moving car last night and that you were arrested."

"Number one, that's total shit. I would never. And number two; if I had been arrested for murder do you really think I'd be out of jail and already back in school? The very next morning?"

Amy made as if she was deeply thinking about this scenario and then that it was too much to comprehend for whatever was truly on her mind. She finally noticed Theo standing behind me, as if he couldn't be seen standing behind me from the moon, then turned back to me as if he wasn't worth the time or effort.

"Have you seen Jasmine around school today?"

"Jasmine?" The look on Amy's face almost made me shrivel up and die right there. "No. She's not here today. She's sick or something."

I made a look of doubt then went back to my locker. Amy exchanged looks with Kyla then turned back to me.

"So . . . do you have a date to homecoming yet?"

If I been shocked when she asked me about spending the night in jail, then this one must have thrown me for a loop. I knew the words that had been strung together to ask the question and yet part of me still had no idea what she had said. Surely, I had misheard her. Or at least I was misinterpreting her intentions. Maybe she was asking on behalf of a . . . friend? Which, truthfully, was no more insane than asking for herself.

"Excuse me?"

Instead of flat out answering me, which is how I would have guessed Amy to answer any direct question, she leaned in against the locker next to mine and batted her big brown and black eyes up at me. Oh, Lord. Please make it stop. Now I wasn't sure, but I could have sworn I heard Theo chuckling behind me.

"I don't even know when—"

"Next Saturday," she piped in immediately, purposefully cutting me off as she knew exactly what the typical boy reply would have been. Though, honestly, I think most typical boys know when most of the major school dances are as it's another opportunity to hopefully get drunk and lucky. "The day after the homecoming game, silly."

"Well . . . I'll have to check my social calendar. I'm not a hundred percent sure what I've got going on that night. Might be busy, you know? Chatting with the police 'n all."

Now I have no idea why I said that, but it seemed to be the right thing as it was the only excuse Amy was going to take for me bailing on going with her to the homecoming dance. If, that was, she really was asking me to the dance with her . . .

"Such a bad boy," she cooed. "Well . . ." She leaned up into me and kissed me partially on my cheek and partially on the side of my mouth, leaving behind what I could only assume was a large smear of red lipstick. "Keep me in mind when you get your affairs straightened out." She and Kyla began to walk on when she stopped and spun around back at me. "Oh, and if you need a good attorney, call me. My dad would be more than grateful to help you out of a jam."

What the hell?

"Well, hello lover boy," came a soft, somewhat gravelly voice that was all show.

I turned around to find Skye Ford standing between Theo and my locker, trying her hardest to hold back laugher.

"Yuck it up," I said as I finished with my books and slammed the door shut, not realizing it had bounced back open.

"Here," she said as she reached up and wiped the lipstick off my face. "Girls."

"Right?"

"So, what was all that about?" she asked as she nodded on after Amy Song.

"That? I have no idea. It involved girls so you know . . . I'm lost."

"Of course."

"She might have been asking me to the homecoming dance. But really I think she was just trying to solicit some work for her father."

"Makes sense," Skye shrugged. "Her father is one of the best defense attorneys in the city. But you sure as hell can't afford him. Maybe if you get in on his daughter's good graces . . ." She winked teasingly at me. "Hey! You're going to homecoming? Since when?"

"Since never. I didn't even know when it was until Amy

just told me. Besides, what do you care? You're not going, are you?"

"Haven't been asked," she fake pouted as she slammed my locker door shut once again and started off for her next class.

"Suuuuure," I called after her. "Like you would ever say yes anyway."

I caught Theo out of the corner of my eye. He was shaking his head at me. Though for over what I couldn't tell.

The rest of the day passed along in the same fashion. Amy's comments had been confirmed by other students and Jasmine's own absence from her classes. She was nowhere to be found on the school grounds.

I ate lunch alone out on the football field bleachers though on my way two different groups of people had inquired if I would join them. Neither were groups I would have joined under any other circumstances, so I played it off that I already had a lunch date.

What the hell was this? For the last two years at this school I was a pariah, a plague to be avoided. I was that kid who found his father in bed with his girlfriend's mother and decided to end it all by driving head on into a tree. And managed to even fail at that. I had been teased and bullied, though to be fair, the Murphys had been bullying me since kindergarten when they were twice as tall as everyone else at that same age. My locker was frequently vandalized, and my P.E. locker was often found open and with either my gym or regular clothes soaking in a toilet or completely gone. No one associated with me, either publically or privately. Group projects in classes were a joke. It had almost gotten to the point where I was invisible at school when suddenly this happens. I get drawn back into everything by Jasmine Fairchild. The police question me and now I'm on everyone's radar again.

What was next?

One thing I did know, Jasmine Fairchild's name was still as pristine as ever as she had had no association with the events at Malia's apartment. Maybe she was on that same getaway vacation her boyfriend Aiden had been on since Monday evening.

Now, it wasn't like the entire school was my friend and wanted to hang out with me. There were still the looks and whisperings, only now it seemed like more people knew who I was and had something to associate with me besides a failed suicide attempt. Though the word around school was people *did* want to know just what my connection to Connor and Aiden and Pierre was.

Come to think of it, I kinda wanted to know the same thing as well.

26

LIGHT UP THE WORLD

The rest of my Wednesday and Thursday went by the same as any other day of the week. Pre-Jasmine's interference with my life, that is. I went to school each day, then went home and did my homework while I worked around the motel.

At school I continued to get the same curious glances and occasional questions but was left alone. Even a few teachers gave me more than a casual glance, signaling that they too had heard the rumors running rampant throughout school.

Friday, I had been yanked out of Algebra II (thank you, Lord) to speak with my guidance counselor, Mr. Lockridge, and some school-appointed grievance counselor (*no* thank you, Lord). That went as expected, which is the way they go. They question, you answer, and they doubt your answers, scribble things down and tell you to continue seeing them for some undisclosed amount of time. What else was I going to do? Argue? Look like I didn't want to receive any help?

My Friday night was just as disjointed as my school days for when I got to the motel, I found Detectives Manning and Hershey waiting for me. They had spoken to my aunt and uncle about the situation (though to what extent I did not know), and I arrived to find them looking just as irritated and inconvenienced as always. At least when the detectives decided to speak to me it was at the motel instead of downtown in some cruddy interrogation room. They had me go over the whole story again; they took more notes and seemed to realize that they didn't have much to go on to argue against my theories with. They may not have liked or totally believed them, but there wasn't much they could do. And quite frankly, at this point, I didn't care. So what? Let them figure it all out. Just because they were adults didn't mean they had the right to bully me into giving them what they wanted. They felt the need to let me know that if I felt I was in danger because of what I knew that they could protect me. Were they kidding me with this shit? Like I hadn't seen almost every mob and crime movie and TV show out there. I knew how it worked. They were full of it and I had no problem relaying my feelings across the many faces I gave them. Apparently, they had already been keeping an eye on Paul-Henri before this whole ordeal began, due to his previous arrests, and had made contact in reference to his brother's murder and the subsequent deaths of Liam and Connor. They in no way let it be known that they were harassing him on my behalf, nor did they inform him of what all they really thought. When it came down to it, they were limited in the amount of actual physical evidence against the man and were left to continue building a case against him. If one even existed. At this point even I wasn't sure what was real and what was part of my made-up bullshit. They let me know they would keep an eye on me still and then left.

That night I slept comfortably for the first time in a week. I hadn't heard from Jasmine since the night she visited me here at the hotel, despite my having left several messages for her. Her sister's phone, which was still fully charged, hadn't gone off since the night Connor died, making me believe my theory about the whole scheme being just that: a scheme. Though, as much as I still wanted to figure out the whys of it all, I was to the point where I figured I should just forget all about it and move on.

I spent Saturday at "work", catching up and finishing all homework assignments as well as starting in on a few upcoming projects. Studying for the PSATs took up my entire afternoon as I had forgotten that we had them coming up the following week. I fixed a few customers' complaints: room five had a problem with their TV, room six a broken light bulb and room nine wanted a new room as they swore, they had seen a cockroach in the bathroom. I assured them that they weren't all that special, that all of our rooms came with an unbiased and equal number of cockroaches.

I was finally settled in for what I thought was the night, lying in my bed watching junk TV on my iPhone when my phone rang with a blocked number. I don't know why or what prompted me to answer the phone. I think I was too much in my zone and did it without much thought or I might have just ignored it. I should have done just that.

"Chance?"

"Humph?"

"It's Paul-Henri." The man paused, probably waiting for an acknowledgement from me. "You know? Pierre's—"

"Yes, I remember. What's up?"

"I wondered if we could talk?"

"About?"

"The status of the case I believe I acquired your assistance with?"

"Don't you read the papers? Or watch the news? Or get Google alerts on your phone?"

"Oh, I'm aware of what's being said. But I'd like your final word on the subject. And to pay you for your services. I always keep my word when it comes to business."

For reals? Somehow, I always thought that paying me for work was B.S. Maybe this was a trap? Maybe he knew I had been the po-po's inside line on him.

"Right now?"

"No time like the present. Come up to my place. I mean Pierre's. I've got a group of your schoolmates over. They're celebrating. Or mourning. Or remembering Pierre and those other two."

"They're having a party to celebrate the deaths of our classmates?"

"More like a celebration of who they were. It's a party. You should come."

"Sure, I'd be invited?"

"I'm inviting you. That's all that matters. Come and find me. We can talk."

I was silent on the phone and Paul-Henri could tell I was hesitant. Why should I? Couldn't Paul-Henri and I just talk at some other time? And why bother? It wasn't like I really did anything. And I couldn't help but feel that this could possibly be a trap. I mean, he did say there were other people around at least. Or was that a lie too? It was rather quiet on his end of the line for a party to be going on all around him. I was about to tell him so when he broke the silence.

"That girlfriend of yours is up here."

"What? Who?" I couldn't for the life of me figure out who he meant when I remembered that the only girl, he had ever seen me with. "You mean Madison?"

"I'm sorry," he chuckled as if he knew I was going to say the wrong name. "I meant the other Fairchild girl. Jasmine."

Ooh. How did he know? And what did he know? More importantly, I *had* been wondering where that girl had been off too. Maybe I could talk to her as well and finish a few loose ends.

"I'll be there I thirty," I said and hung up.

As I had promised, thirty minutes later I arrived at Pierre's place overlooking the city below and indeed there was a party going on. His place was packed with my classmates, each drinking or smoking or doing whatnot. Couples were in corners, trying to sneak in a few minutes alone before being forced to be social. I thought the inside of Pierre's place was packed but discovered it was nothing compared to the crowd on the balcony, which looked to be over its capacity. Students were gossiping and laughing, throwing used butts over the edge of the balcony as they continued to drink and party.

As I entered the place and began to walk around looking for someone, anyone I may have known well enough to strike up a conversation with, I realized something was off about the group of people partying. The light might not have been the greatest, but I was suddenly able to tell that most everyone at the party had on a wig of some sort. There were girls with every length and color of hair imaginable. Short. Long. And everything in between. Red. Blue. Green. You name it. Boys too. As I stood there taking in my surroundings a girl bumped into me and spilled her drink down my arm and she began to laugh. I looked down to see Amy Song wearing an orange and yellow punk rocker-style wig.

"What's going on here?" I asked as I eyed her wig, hoping her guilt of spilling her drink on me would get an answer out of her.

"Pierre's brother moved out a bunch of Pierre's stuff and in one of the closets we found all these wigs," Amy Song laughed as she threw her hands up and twirled around for me. "I mean, how could we let them all go to waste? It's a Wig Party. We can find you one too!"

"No thanks. Have you seen Jasmine here tonight?"

Amy Song thought about this and I could see the alcohol soaking into her eyes with each passing second. At least this time there wasn't the sneering bite that I had received when I asked the question earlier that week at school. Bless you, alcohol.

"Somewhere. Sure you don't want a wig? Everyone's doing it. You need one!"

"Why don't you go find me one," I winked at her.

Amy Song immediately grew the largest smile I'd ever

seen on the girl and she quickly disappeared into the crowd.

I did a once around the party when a girl whom I didn't recognize, wearing a short pink bob, walked up to me and said something. I couldn't hear her over the music blaring and the people talking when she decided to simply point down the hallway. I was about to start for the hallway when I realized I was standing in the exact spot where I had found Pierre's body just several nights earlier. That's when I looked around and noticed the entire place had been done over, each of the tables of knickknack and masks and other desks and assorted furniture had been moved, though had that been done for the party or just in general I did not know. I turned to continue down the hallway when I saw Jasmine, standing in the kitchen with a group of boys standing in a circle around her as she drunkenly laughed at someone's joke. Maybe even her own? I locked eyes with her ever so briefly when she turned back to a boy in a green wig standing next to her, caressing his bulging biceps as he flexed in his football jersey.

Why the hell was I here? I walked away, maneuvering myself throughout the hordes of students in the house as I headed for the hallway leading toward Paul-Henri's office. I passed our school's male equivalent of a Queen-Bee, Brandon Rixton, in the hallway, who all but shoved me out of his way as I practically mounted the wall to get out of his way. Great. Couldn't escape the bullies of my life even when I wasn't in school.

I continued down the hallway, checking each open door until I found myself at the end of the hallway, peering in the back office where I found Paul-Henri sitting behind a desk.

His hair was disheveled, and he had a several day growth that matched the dark circles under his eyes, as if he hadn't been able to sleep since coming back and dealing with Pierre's death. He wore a white button-up Armani shirt that was tucked into a pair of silver slacks and a pair of black leather dress boots.

"Chance," Paul-Henri beamed as he came out from around the desk and took my hand in a fierce shake. "Bon soir. So good to see you. Something to drink?"

"Whatever you're having." I looked around the office. In the center of the room were four chairs, each positioned evenly around a wooden coffee table on top of which was an unfinished puzzle, the majority of the pieces of which were inside the top of the box so I couldn't see what the finished picture was to be.

Paul-Henri poured himself a stiff glass of some sort of imported (and what looked to be expensive) whisky and did the same for me. He handed my glass over and we clinked them before he took a rather large swallow.

"Please. Sit. Sit." Paul-Henri sat on his side of the desk as I took the chair on mine.

I could smell something burning within the room and looked around to find several candles lit, though I had the distinct feeling that each candle had a different smell, thus confusing the scent in the room.

By the time I made my attention back around to Paul-Henri, I found him sitting back in his giant leather chair, his glass resting against his cheek as he stared out into nowhere.

I began to fidget, even as I tried to fight my nerves, and took a swallow of my drink to calm myself.

"Rumor throughout the party has it Aiden Murphy's been missing since Monday night?" Paul-Henri said breaking the silence as he directed his gaze at me.

This I hadn't been expecting. Mostly because I wasn't aware of just what exactly Paul-Henri's connection to our school was other than his half-brother Pierre. I wasn't sure if Paul-Henri had had any other or further interactions with my classmates and if or how he should have any knowledge of who Aiden Murphy was in the first place. Maybe he did have more interactions than I knew. Maybe even including the Connor connection theory I thought was still just a theory.

"Wasn't aware you two were BFFs." I wasn't sure if that was too snarky or not, but I figured I had the drink in my hand as my defense if needed.

"More like . . . business associates."

Ahhh. That clicked. And I'm sure my nodding showed Paul-Henri I understood.

"Should I be worried about him coming after me?" Paul-Henri asked as he took another swallow of his drink and then set the glass back down on his desk.

"I wasn't aware the two of you even knew each other. Let alone any reasons why he might be after you."

"Apparently the police believe that Liam Murphy was the one who killed Pierre. For reasons that they are keeping mum about. And now Liam's dead. So . . ."

"So, Liam kills Pierre and then Connor kills Liam. Why's that leave you open as a target? Connor's to blame and he's dead. Unless you paid him to do the job, which between you and me, I think you could have found more sufficient help in carrying out that job."

"On the contrary. I did *not* hire Connor to do any such thing, but had I done so, I think that would have been brilliant. Liam is dead. Connor is dead. No one around to spill their guts too. La vie est bonne."

"And Aiden would know this. He's a resourceful guy. Even if he doesn't always use every cell in his brain. So, what's this really about? Why do you want to know where he is?"

"He was supposed to come here Monday night and pick up some merchandise from Pierre. Now . . . I've no official way to know if he was here but he hasn't been seen since then and neither has a large quantity of my product. And the only people who could tell me if he was in fact here or not are all dead." He let those final words hang in the air between us along with the smoke from a candle that had just died.

Son of a bitch. Maybe none of what had happened over the last few days had anything to do with anything I originally thought. Maybe this was all about missing merchandise and my entire blackmail scheme was just coincidental timing. Like a magician's trick. Simple misdirection.

Paul-Henri broke my train of thought. "Of course, there is also you?"

"Me?" I almost choked. I reached for my glass, the ice clanking around, and swallowed the rest of it.

Paul-Henri got up and grabbed my glass from my hand

and went for a refill.

"Though not everyone is aware of this, you were here Monday night, correct? The police are aware. But perhaps anyone else who was up here is not. You see my predicament?"

"Not entirely," I answered playing dumb. "Maybe I was. If so, I knew that Pierre would be here. Other than him, all other parties are simple guesses. It's not like I have any proof. I would simply assume Liam and Connor were up here as well."

Just then the images of the license plates I had taken pictures of flashed through my mind. Son of a bitch. Stupid subconscious always trying to give me away.

"And you?"

"I mean, if I was up here that night, not saying I was, but I if I had been, I was never *in* this house."

"You were never in my house? The night Pierre died?"

"No. I was outside all night. I mean I saw people come and go, but it was dark. I couldn't really make everyone out. I wish I could. That would probably help."

"You weren't in here?"

"No," I repeated almost getting tired of the question. What was he driving at? Why did he care if I had been in here or not?

"And Miss Doyle? Was she here that night?" Paul-Henri continued.

"Same as everyone else who was here. By proxy I would assume her to be as well. But I've no concrete proof one way or the other. I never saw her face for sure."

"By proxy could put a lot of people up here that night."

"But all without any physical evidence."

"What about the Fairchild girl?" he asked as he came back with my glass.

This froze me. I had never mentioned to anyone, not even the police that I had found Madison Fairchild up here that night. But if he hadn't known who else had been up here how had he known that Madison had been?

"Don't even take the time to come up with a lie. I know she was here that night. Pierre had spoken about her quite a bit and she was here that day when you and I first met. Don't worry. She's not the one I'm concerned about," Paul-Henri said as he sat on the edge of his desk and stared me down. "I. Want. Aiden. Murphy."

He smiled a slimy, snake-like smile as he slowly spun around his desk and found his way back into his chair.

"Is this another job you're 'hiring' me for?" was more than I could think to ask as I stalled while my brain worked in overdrive.

"If you need to look at it that way," Paul-Henri said leaning back in his chair as he reached into one of the desk drawers and brought out a knife. It was ten inches long, including the handle. He began to play with it as he flipped it from one hand to the other. "I prefer to look at it as applying pressure. You . . . find me Aiden Murphy. And then I won't have to turn the Fairchild girl over to the police for having been at my house during the time of my brother's murder."

"She had nothing to do with your brother's murder."

"That's for the police to determine. Of course"—he paused

as he smiled wider—"we both know I don't care much for the police. I'd be just as happy leaving them completely out of this entire scenario."

"I don't—"

"*Look*, high school boy. You have proved yourself to be quite effective at digging through the muck and outing the truth. I just need you to do this one simple thing, and then we're done. Fini. Okay?"

"So, you say. But what's to stop you from holding this over my head again for some other simple little task?"

Paul-Henri spread his arms wide and smiled. "Absolutely nothing. I guess you'll just have to take my word for it. Homme pour homme."

I sat there, pondering my options and figuring things out. I should have simply said "yes, sir" and walked out. But if I had been that type of guy, I might not have been sitting there face to face with a drug dealer in the first place. This got me thinking about the bigger picture. And then it all clicked together for me.

"You're not the top dog at the pound," I said breaking the silence. It was as if the world had stopped time for a moment. The entire party out on the other side of the double doors had ceased to make any noise. My classmates could no longer be heard. No laughter. No rowdy drunkenness. No mourning for their dead classmates. Nothing.

"Excuse me?"

"I'm trying to figure out why you care so much. It appears you have money. Like Pierre did. But unlike your brother, you've been excommunicated from your family. Sure, you're part of the family, but you did something at some point in time in history that got you deselected as a member of the Chevaliers. You've been arrested. That was in the papers. It was easy enough to dig up. All having to do with drugs. You live on your own. But you're not exactly the building from the ground up drug dealer type. You don't come from a family of dealers and exploiters. Hence the exile and the need to become a dealer. No. You're a middleman. Not someone who's face-to-face with the product or the purchasers, hence the reason why you lost track of your product in the first place. No . . . there's someone higher up than you. They don't know that anything's missing or gone wrong yet. And you're hoping to clean up this mess before they do. Now . . . do we understand each other?"

Paul-Henri reached across the table and grabbed my shirt before I could even blink and had the blade of his knife less than an inch from my left eye.

"So, what exactly is there to stop me from gouging out your eyes right here and now?"

"Absolutely nothing," I smiled even though my body shook like a detached leaf in a windstorm. "But you and I both know you won't. Guess you'll just have to take my word for it. Man to man."

"And why's that? Why wouldn't I pluck out your beautiful baby blues?" He pressed the tip of the knife against my skin mere millimeters below my eye and I could feel the edge of the knife wanting to break the skin and draw blood.

"Because, like you said, who else do you have to help you figure out your problem? And I probably am the only one who can in the time you need it done by."

"Well then . . ." Paul-Henri smiled at me again as he quickly slid the knife across my cheek and let go of my shirt. He had cut me, drawing blood but I wasn't going to die. "Guess you better get to hunting. I'm giving you until the end of Monday to find him. Then the police get an anonymous call about little Miss Fairchild."

"You do realize he's *her* boyfriend, right?" He tilted his head to the side with a perplexed look across his face. "Aiden Murphy. You do realize he is—or was, or whatever tense they currently are—dating Jasmine Fairchild. She is here tonight. I do believe the two of you are acquainted. Why not simply ask her? I don't think there'd be any great love lost if she was to suddenly find herself on the market for a new boy toy again."

"I'd prefer if we keep *her* out of this. If we keep this just between us men. Understand?" I stared at him, wondering how far I should push this when he continued. "Rumors and words have a way of getting back to the wrong people when Jasmine is informed of certain events. She's too connected to the wrong people."

"You mean her father?" Her father did know a lot of people in the D.A.'s office. He had been instrumental in gathering publicity for various cases over the years. And now he was considering running for office.

"What she doesn't know won't hurt her. Look, all you have to do is find Aiden Murphy for me. And she'll never have to know that we were looking for him, or why, or that you were involved or anything else. Her sister doesn't have to be involved in anything else either. I think this is the way we'd all like to keep this. Sewn up as quickly as possible and behind us. Can I count on you to help me with that, Chance Harper?"

Without answering him I turned and walked out the door.

27

COUNT ON ME

Truth of the matter was I had no idea where Aiden Murphy was or where he could even start to be hiding. I would need Jasmine's help in this department whether I liked it or not. I walked back through the thinning crowd until I found her off near the balcony, sitting on one of the many speakers that blared Beyoncé or Maroon 5. I couldn't tell the difference now thanks to the two rather generous drinks that Paul-Henri had bestowed upon me.

Either way, Jasmine sang along to the song as she downed her drink with one hand while holding off some football player with her other. I should have recognized the player but chances were he didn't go to our school. With over a million followers on each his various social media profiles, Pierre's network of kids our age went well beyond our school grounds. And even if they weren't still a couple, Jasmine had been dating Aiden Murphy which would have been enough to keep most suitors from our school at bay, even another football player.

I saw Jasmine wearing a bleached-white wig in the style of a bob haircut that came just below her ears. She had on shocking-red lipstick all of which was complimented nicely by a showy little blue number that showed off all her curves in just the right places and just enough skin in all the others. I walked up to her and leaned in around her glass and whispered into the ear that wasn't being nibbled.

"Where the hell have you been? We need to talk."

She turned her head around, almost moving her entire body to do so, as she stared up at me, her eyes glazed over and she smiled her wide, heart-stopping smile. She reached a thumb up to my check and rubbed it, coming away with a slight smear of blood on the tip and she scolded me.

"Not now. Maybe later. I'm having a good time right now. You should too. So much going on. We deserve a little happiness. Don't we?"

"But I really think we—"

"She said not now!" I found myself being cut off as the football player next to her grabbed me by my shirt and forcibly moved me back away from her. "Ya deaf? Lady said get lost, so piss off!"

Before I could reply he let go of me and turned back to Jasmine who hopped off the speaker and lead him out of the room.

I found my way over to the bar area and mixed myself a concoction containing several mixed liquors in a red plastic cup and then made my way around the room, making note of who was there and with whom. Not for any reason other than to keep my mind going.

Twenty minutes later I had finished my drink and decided to call it a night. There was no real reason I was there. I would just have to find Jasmine sometime over the weekend.

I maneuvered myself throughout the various parked cars that lined the street, making it nearly impossible for any moving cars to get through as I headed up the hill to where I was parked. As I walked, I could hear a couple making out in one of the cars when it began to sound as if the girl was opposed to where the make out session was headed. As I passed by, the objections began to get louder and that's when I could tell it was Jasmine. For some reason I just never think straight when it comes to that girl and before I could even comprehend what I was doing my instincts kicked in and I rushed to the car.

Normally, I would never have had any kind of a chance against a football player, particularly when they're a full grade above me, light years ahead of me in puberty and about double my size. But I had two things going for me. One, he wasn't expecting me. And two, Jasmine had managed to get him into a rather compromised position with his pants down around his knees, thus making his legs intertwined and restricted in their movement.

Now, I had no idea why I went this route, or what would possess me to ever do this to another man, but with the door already open and I needing to get the surprise on him, I grabbed his underwear and pulled them down. It was enough to do the trick as the jock was momentarily startled and whipped his head around, smacking himself against the roof of his car, causing him to fall to the pavement. Before I could give him time to comprehend what was going on, I brought my knee up quick and hard and connected with his jaw, which sent his face slamming into the side of his car and dazing him enough to stop him.

I looked up at Jasmine, with her dress torn and a look of amused surprise on her face. She was about to speak to me when I cut her off.

"Shut up. Let's go."

"But, I—"

"I thought I told you to shut up. I think you've used up all the free passes you have given to you tonight. You don't get a say. Shut up. Let's go."

I continued up the hill toward my car when a few steps later I heard her heels clacking on the pavement behind me. I got into my car and started it, waiting until she got in.

"My knight in shining armor," she said as she got into her seat and did her seatbelt. Her eyes were red and runny, her mascara curving down the sides of her apple cheeks.

"Shut up," I snapped back without much force but still meaning it.

I drove up the hill for a few minutes until I arrived up at Mulholland Drive then turned toward Laurel Canyon. I stared over the cliffs at the city lights of Los Angeles below, the city almost seeming like a scene out of a movie and part of a world I didn't belong to.

We drove in silence until we approached Sunset Boulevard. Jasmine got out her makeup and looked in the mirror in the visor above her and began to reapply. I turned from her and stared out the window. There was a honk from the car behind us and Jasmine turned to me.

"Green light," she said as she reapplied her lipstick with

her still somewhat shaky hands.

"What the hell was all that about?" I asked as I drove through the intersection.

She finished her makeup and put the visor back up and leaned back in her chair, staring out at the passing houses. I couldn't tell you why, but I liked the sounds she was making in the silence of the night. The sound of her rummaging through her purse, fiddling with her makeup. Perhaps it reminded me of when my mother used to do it whenever my father drove.

"Where'd you disappear to the other morning?" I'd finally asked, breaking the silence.

"Do you ever just wish you could be someone else?" she asked, deflecting my question. "Like, have someone else's life? Or one other than the one you were given?" There was tone to her voice that sounded melancholy and distant. As if she was already living another life instead of just daydreaming about it. "I do," she continued. "More than you might think. The girl who has everything. A loving father. Money. Social status at school. And I'd run away from it all in a heartbeat if I could."

"Typical."

"What is?"

"Your reaction. Your thoughts. Sure, I think those things and you know it. The life I've lived. But find me a teenager who hasn't had those thoughts and I'll show you a liar. Even then . . ."

I braked at a red light near Beverly Boulevard. The entire street was dark, save for the occasional streetlamp and a house on our right. A bright neon sign advertised a Psychic living there who could "tell the future" and read all about you "in the cards." The lights inside that house were still on. Even at this late time of the night. Wonder if whoever lived there could tell me where Aiden Murphy was.

The light changed and I continued.

"I know you think I could and just should if I really wanted to," she continued. "That you probably think I'm just being a spoiled bitch who should shut her mouth and accept the golden spoons she's been handed. But life isn't perfect."

"Of course not. But it isn't for anyone. Everyone's got problems. They just got different ones from you and me."

"I'm not brave enough to go out and start over on my own." I could feel her staring at me in the dark. "Let's just keep on driving, Chance. Out of this city. Screw it all. You and me. We can get the hell out of here and go start somewhere new. Just you and me. No one else. Not my sister or father. Just us. We can start over. I've got money. More than enough to get us started. We'll go somewhere where no one knows either one of us. You'll work. Hell, I'll get a job. Earn my keep. I can do it, you know? I'm not that spoiled. I know the meaning of hard work. Just because no one will let me prove it doesn't mean I don't know how."

I stayed silent as I kept on driving toward her house. She knew I wouldn't say yes. Really though, there was no reason why I couldn't. But even if I wanted to I wouldn't. I think deep down inside she knew that. That's why she proposed it right then and there. So, she'd have another reason to blame someone else for her life being shit.

"We were happy, right Chance? Back then. You and me? We had good times. Really good times. We worked well together. Not like anyone else I've known since. We could have that again. You and me. We could. The other night proved it. I know you love me and I . . . I don't think I ever stopped loving you. Not really."

"What about Aiden? And the others?"

"Oh, piss on them. They weren't real and you know that. There was no real future with any of those boys. It's you. You're who I want. Who I've always wanted. You know that."

"The road of life certainly has thrown a lot of curves at us," I said evenly as I mulled over her proposal. "And you and I know that better than most. But the way I see it is if you're still breathing you can always change the course of your life. If you don't like where it's headed, change it. You've no one to blame but yourself. You don't need a companion to choose a different path. And not doing so because you don't have one, well, that's cowardice, far as I can see. No one else can live your life but you. So, you have to make the choices. You make the changes."

I pulled up into the Fairchild's driveway and parked in front of the front door.

"Where's Aiden, Jasmine?" I asked.

"He doesn't matter. Forget about him. Forget about Paul-Henri or Pierre or Maddison or anyone else. It's just you and me. Now. Let's get out of here. We can do it. Okay? Don't leave me trapped here." She stared up at her house, all the outside lights on, while all within were off. I could see the tears streaming down her cheeks.

"Where's—"

"*Why?* Why do you care? He doesn't have anything to do with Maddie's blackmail scheme and that's all you should be worried about. That's why I went to you. So, you could help. Lot of help you were. Couldn't even get that straightened out. Goodbye, Chance Harper." She got out of the car and started for the house.

"Jasmine," I called after her through the open window.

"There's nothing more for you or I to talk about. We're done, Chance. Goodbye. I mean it. This isn't some long goodbye. This one is short and to the point. Goodbye."

And with those words she disappeared into the darkness of her house.

28

HOLD ON TO ME

I was about to drive away when I saw Jasmine's purse down on the floor of the passenger side. I sighed to myself, turned the car off and started for the house with it. I wasn't sure what to do. Ring the doorbell and wake everyone? Knock and do the same? When I got there, I found the front door to be unlocked. I'd just sneak in quickly, put the purse on the closest table or whatever and get out of there.

I'd started to do just that when a few steps into the house I noticed a faint light in the back kitchen, and I heard someone humming to herself. I looked around, mentally scolded myself for my inability to leave enough alone and walked down the hallway.

In the kitchen, sitting at the table was Maddison, humming some nonsensical song as she played with something on the table. There was only the nightlight from the microwave that gave the room a morbid glow. As I inched myself closer to her, making sure not to startle her, I leaned in and realized that across the table she had hundreds of Reese's Pieces spread out, literally covering almost every inch of the table. She moved the orange, yellow and brown pieces around to make various designs, as if making one large singular maze across the table.

"Maddie?" I whispered from behind her. When she didn't respond I went to reach for her. "Maddison?"

"She can't hear you," came a voice from the other end of the kitchen and I jumped and spun around almost letting out a shriek of my own.

Standing in the other entrance to the kitchen, opposite the one I took down the main hallway, was Selena Fairchild. She held a glass of red wine, not her first, as she stood there and stared at her stepdaughter.

"I'm sorry. I didn't see you there. I didn't mean—"

"She zones out. She can't hear you. When she gets like this. In her own little world. I've told James to have her taken in and looked at, but he won't hear of it." She let out a little laugh and took a swallow of her wine. A big swallow. "She has good days and bad. Mostly good though, I'd say. Probably bipolar or something along those lines. Hell, maybe even schizophrenic. I've seen it before. But James won't hear of it. Not his little princess. Says she's just a creative girl who likes to go to the beat of her own drum. Who am I to argue? She's not mine. There's only so much I can do. As the stepmother. Only so much I'm *allowed* to do. The rest . . . well, it's not up to me. I have my rules. And I have to know well enough to color within those lines."

She smiled half-heartedly at me.

"I'm sure I don't know the whole story concerning my husband and his ex and your father. But I got bits and pieces. You can find it if you look hard enough. Believe it or not, I know what you're going through. My father was taken from me too early as well. Only he was murdered when he was in the wrong place at the wrong time, through no fault of his own." She paused for a moment as she turned back and stared at Maddison. She took another swallow then continued. "I thought I was doomed to spend the rest of my life unhappy. But then I met James. He was so broken from his wife's actions. So, shut off from the world. From love. Even from his own daughters. I think it was that condition I found him in that gave me the strength to move on with my life and made me determined to help him as well. We're two injured pawns in the game of life. I think that's where we get our strength. From each other. I'm glad we found each other. I love my life here. Even if it isn't perfect. I don't think life is supposed to be perfect though, you know? What's the fun in that? But I am sorry. For you. I hope you find the strength to continue as well. To be happy again. I think we all deserve that."

She reached up and caressed my cheek before turning and leaving the room. I could hear her making her way up the stairs to the second floor when I turned back and stared down at Maddie playing with her candies. What was going on through her mind right then? No wonder she didn't care what she did or who thought what of her. She was carefree, always had been. No one thought any differently about her. I wasn't sure what to do so I turned to leave when I heard her call out my name.

"What are you doing here, Chancy?" She hugged the back of the chair, her chin over the back of it as she stared up at me with her big cat-like eyes, made more transparent by the thick mascara and eyeliner she had on.

"What are you still doing up? Shouldn't you be getting some rest?"

"What are you talking about? It's barely sundown." She turned from and waived her arm at the open windows in the kitchen. The nearly full moon shone down and I could feel Maddie's face glow with delight as she stared up at it. "Let's go for a swim."

"Maddie, I don't—" Before I could finish, Maddie was out of her chair and opened the sliding glass door, leaping across the wooden deck. She turned on only the lights in the pool and stopped at the edge of the pool and dropped the silk robe she had been wearing to reveal nothing on underneath. I had taken a few steps out into the yard when she dove in and began to swim around.

"Maddie," I whisper-hissed at her. "Maddie. Get out of the pool. Now. Come on."

"Oh, quit being such a spoilsport. Come on in. The water feels great. Come on. I won't tell Jasmine. It's okay."

Dammit. What was it with these Fairchild girls?

"Maddie. Now. Out of the pool. It's the middle of the night. Come on."

I stood there and let her continue to swim a few laps when she seemed to tire herself out. A few minutes later she made her way over to the steps and I met her with her robe as I had not been able to find a towel of any sort anywhere nearby, being as it was the middle of the night and not exactly the time one would be set up for a swim party.

I took her through the kitchen and on up the stairs to her bedroom. She got herself untangled from her wet robe and dropped it to the floor as she slipped into her bed.

"You feeling all right, Maddie?" I sat down on the edge of her bed next to her and moved a few strands of her drying hair out her face. She breathed deeply and pouted like a child as she considered my question. I looked to the dresser next to the head of her bed and noticed in the moonlight several orange prescription bottles of various sizes.

"What are you doing here?" she asked, breaking my focus.

"Nothing. Just passing through."

"Still running errands for my sister?"

"Something like that," I smiled at her as I made sure she was tucked in tight. She hadn't bothered to turn on a light when she entered the room so there was only the moonlight through her window to help me read her face.

"It isn't real, you know? It was all just a scam. She doesn't really care. Not about you. Or me. Or anyone for that matter."

"What are you talking about? Maddie?"

She reached up and kissed me firmly on my lips.

"Out of all the things I could be jealous of my sister for the one and only thing it's been all these years was you. You were good. Better than she ever knew. She was wrong to do what she did to you. All those years ago. To treat you like that."

She leaned back against her pillow and closed her eyes with a smile on her face.

"Maddie? What are you talking about? What isn't real?"

"The pictures. The blackmail. That wasn't even my phone."

I stared at her and she opened her eyes, registered my denial and looked over to her nearby dresser. "See?" She nodded toward her cell phone. "That's mine. Always has been. Never been out of my sight. I'm sure that was just a burner she picked up for her little charade. Not entirely sure *why* she's doing it. I know where she found the photos. Up at Pierre's. But they were none of her business. So why bother? No one else cares. I certainly don't. And despite what she may have told you, neither would Daddy dearest. This is all just some sick game in her head. You can stay with me, if you want? Here. Tonight. If you want? I'd like you to stay. Could you?"

"You know I can't."

She closed her eyes again and I sat there putting the pieces of what she had said together in my head. A minute later I realized she had finally fallen asleep.

"Good night, Maddie."

I left her room, closed the door behind me and made my way down the stairs and out the front door. I got to my car and began to look through my phone, not sure what I was looking for or going to do. Would I really text Jasmine now? Call her? She was probably asleep. And if not, this wasn't really a conversation I wanted to have in the middle of the night in her home with her father nearby. If she was playing me then I'd figure the whole mess out later. I turned my phone off and threw it into the seat next to me where it bounced off and fell to the floor below, face down. Maybe if I hadn't done that, I would have seen the alert on the screen. I had friends nearby.

Funny thing was, when I finally found my phone the next

morning, I would find it out was neither Jasmine nor Madison whose presence I had been alerted to, despite having been at their house.

Apparently, Aiden Murphy had been somewhere nearby.

29

I WILL NEVER LET YOU DOWN

Since Sundays were not school days, they were considered work days and therefore I was usually expected to be at the motel. My aunt and uncle were having a day to themselves, to who only knew where, so I was expected to be at the motel all day. At least I put the time to good use and continued to study for the PSATs.

I also spent the day searching through students' various online social profiles to see if I could get any further on locating Aiden Murphy. Though at this point I was close to not caring who did what with the Fairchild girls, though I had begun to feel protective of Maddie considering her current mental condition. Jasmine, on the other hand, was hiding things from me.

Monday morning, I arrived at school early and waited in the school's parking lot as I surveyed the masses for particular people to arrive. Jasmine. Maddie. Possibly Aiden? When would they arrive? Who would they arrive with? Of the three only one showed up: Madison.

"Hey," I called out as I jogged up to her, walking to class

along with a few of her friends. "Where's your sister?"

"No idea. Probably still at home. Like I give a shit. She's your girlfriend, not mine. But you better watch out for Aiden. He'll kick your ass if he finds out you're asking about her again."

I had a feeling I was back to the good ol' Maddie now. Not the Maddie from the other night.

"Have you seen him? Aiden, I mean? Was he at your house this weekend?"

"No," she said with a scrunched-up face. "I haven't seen that looser in a week. Probably skipped town. Now do you mind? I have to get to class."

I let her go and made my way to my own classes. Rumors were spilling around campus about the police still being interested in my connection with the deaths of my fellow classmates. And Gossip Girl herself, Rebecca Collins, was haranguing me for an exclusive one-on-one interview for the student paper. What for, I've no idea. Apparently, she wanted "my side" of the story.

I tackled lunch out in the bleachers near the football field, though today I had Theo as company. If you could call him that. He hadn't said a word to me when he marched out there a few minutes after me and sat a few steps above me like he was some sort of guardian angel. I finished lunch and was folding an origami penguin to keep my mind off the events going on around me that I had no control over. I had no idea where Aiden Murphy was or how I would find him either. I was basically counting down the minutes until I got that threatening phone call from Paul-Henri and then the police showed up to arrest Maddison for being up at the Chevalier home the night of Pierre's murder. And possibly me for aiding and abetting.

"You look aplexed," Skye said as she sat down on one of the aluminum benches not far from me. She startled me as I hadn't seen her coming and apparently Theo had seen the need to warn me.

"That's not a word."

"Yes, it is. I just said it and used it in a sentence. Therefore, it's a word." I hoped the look I gave was in the general family of: you're feeding me bullshit, right? "What'cha doing?"

"Thinking. Clearing my head. Or trying to. Too much going on. Can't make sense of it all."

"You still in trouble?" I had briefly updated her on the whole situation the day before when she called me at the motel.

"Do I know any other way?" I squished the penguin in my hands. It wasn't working out anyway. "I don't know what to do."

"Maybe . . . and I know this is a big maybe, but maybe, this isn't your problem to worry about anymore. Just drop the whole thing. Call the police. Pass this whole mess off. Who cares? It isn't your shit to deal with. And you're only digging yourself a bigger hole the longer you stay connected with the whole deal."

I raised my eyebrows to show that I had heard her and was considering her words.

"I mean your social status among the masses has risen in

the last week. People know who you are again. Maybe this is a good point to just jump ship. Take one of those floozies who've asked you to the lame homecoming dance and just go. Try to be normal. And fit in. And have a semi decent junior year of high school."

"You don't really think I'm going to go with one of those girls who've asked me, do you?"

"Why not? It's what you want, isn't it? To fit in? To not be looked at and talked about as that boy who tried to take the fast out when he discovered his father and his lover in that creepy motel you now work at. Maybe you never were supposed to help the Fairchilds through this ordeal. Maybe not. What do I know?"

I looked to Theo who was silently studying the two off us but was offering no sage advice himself.

"You going to homecoming?" I asked her, not sure where the interest came from.

She laughed lightly. "I'll be working. No interested parties. I'm still that bat-shit crazy girl who everyone keeps their distance from, remember?"

"I don't think that."

"And look where that's gotten you?" She stood up and stared down at me, and despite the sun trying its hardest to block my view, I could have sworn I saw pity on her face.

"This is kinda what you wanted, Chance. So, take it. Life doesn't give you too many do overs. Especially high school life."

She playfully slugged me in the shoulder before she turned away and walked back to class.

I was in Mrs. Cherry's AP English class with a few minutes to spare before the starting bell rang when Rebecca Collins slammed herself into her seat behind me, all hot and bothered and breathing heavily as if she had run to class.

"Guess you're no longer going to be the token suspect around here," Rebecca smiled as she got out her books and binders for class.

Skye was a row over from us but even her interest had been piqued by Rebecca's comment.

"What do you mean?" I asked without turning around.

"Oh? Are you talking to me now? Because I seem to recall every time I try to get you to talk you avoid me?"

I glared grudgingly at her over my shoulder. I didn't have to give in to her demands. She would have told me eventually anyway. Girl loved to talk. "Fine. I give in. I'll give you your stupid interview. Just give."

"Haven't you heard?" She beamed.

"Sorry. I was actually eating during lunch. I forgot to check Just Jared or Popsugar or whoever I was supposed to in order to get the latest and greatest. Spill."

"Aiden Murphy."

"What about him?" I asked spinning around.

"They found him."

"What? Where?"

"In Mexico. Apparently, he's been hiding out down there since last Monday night. Took a last-minute impromptu trip with some buddies and they've been down there ever since."

Once her desk was set up, she looked to the clock in the classroom and saw she still had three minutes and so got out her phone and began Tweeting or texting or posting something. "Of course the police are looking into him for Pierre's murder. They think he fled after the fact. And since it looks like he didn't cross the border until nearly three in the morning on Tuesday it's a possibility. They say they found drugs on him too." She smiled as she looked from me to Skye and everyone else around us who paid attention. "Guess you're off the suspect list now. Good breaks for you."

Suddenly, for the first time in days I could feel myself breathing normally. Looked like everything would be all right after all.

30

BEGIN THE END

Thirty minutes later my cell began to vibrate. The number wasn't familiar, but the ID had come up as the local hospital. I wasn't sure, but currently Malia Doyle was the only person I knew in a hospital. Maybe she had finally woken up from the doctor-induced coma she had been in. I asked Mrs. Cherry to be excused for the restroom. She sighed at me and then waved me on.

"Chance?" came the voice from the other end of my cell phone.

"Who is this?" I asked as I walked quickly through the hallway for the closest men's restroom. I entered and after searching each stall, found myself to be alone. "Malia?"

"Yes. I need to speak to you. Now."

"In case you weren't aware of this yet I'm in school. Like high school. Classes. Right now."

"I know things. Things you want to know. Things you asked about. I'll tell you. All of it."

"Near death had you deciding to be forthcoming out of the goodness of your heart?"

"Of course not. I need money. Now."

"What? Why?"

"I need to get out of town. I'm not safe. But I don't have any more to withdraw from. The police have everything being watched until I'm cleared and since I'm being charged with drug possession that will never happen. I need the cash and I need it now."

"So, I can be arrested for assisting a felon?"

"You want to know about Flush, right? Paul-Henri and his connection to everything. Jasmine's connection? I can tell you it all. But I need money."

"And what's stopping me from calling the police and just having them get it out of you?"

"I'll never live to make it to the police. I need to get out of town and now. Will you help me?" I considered my options. "Come on, Chance. I know Jasmine paid you for some job. You have the money. She'll repay you. I need it. Now."

"I don't care about any of this anymore. Aiden Murphy's been arrested for Pierre's murder. You and I both know the police will buy all the other drug connections and figure everything else out. Your part included. This doesn't concern me anymore."

"You and I both know Aiden Murphy will never spill his guts to the cops. And they've got it all wrong. Paul-Henri thinks Aiden has something of his, but Aiden was never up at Pierre's Monday night, and I think you know that." I had been wondering about that. Sure, I had seen him pop up on my Facebook app as being a friend that was nearby. But I had never actually seen him. And according to the brief news blip and what little twitter was feeding the masses Aiden was sticking to his story that he had already been down in San Diego with some friends by ten o'clock that evening.

"But if Aiden never took any of Paul-Henri's product then what does he really want?"

"I'll tell you all that. But first, the money. Now. How much do you got?"

"I don't know—"

"I need at least a thousand."

"A thousand? I don't have that kind of money. I'm not a bank you know."

"Fine. What can you get your hands on? Quickly. I need it, Chance."

I don't know why I was even considering this option. "I don't know . . . probably five hundred?"

"Five hundred? Fine. That will have to work. I need you to bring it to me. Now."

"All right. Let me get the money and I'll meet you at the hospital."

"Thanks, Chance." And with that she hung up on me. Without me getting to tell her she'd have to wait until the end of class. It was okay. It was only another forty minutes and then I'd be on my way to her.

My phone made a noise and I saw that I had a missed call and a new voicemail from Paul-Henri. He wasn't sure how I did it but he was thankful for the anonymous tip that turned Aiden into the police. As far as he was concerned, we were square. And if I ever needed anything from him, I was not to hesitate to ask.

Anonymous tip? Who was I to question the Gods above?

If someone had turned him in, that was all the better for me. Why did I care where the help came from? Why did I care who did it or why? I was just happy that it was all done and over with.

And as for Paul-Henri? I figured the less interaction I had with him the longer my lifespan would be.

The bell rang, signaling the end of class, and I bolted out of the room so quickly I could have sworn I heard someone (I believe Skye) call out my name after me but I never turned around to confirm it. I headed for the parking lot and went to the motel to get the five hundred dollars I had hidden away for just such an occasion. I then made my way over to Cedars Sinai hospital near West Hollywood and Beverly Hills.

I noticed two missed calls on my cell, as well as several text messages where fifty percent of the words typed would have been censored even on an HBO show, all from Skye, each one asking what was going on and if I was okay. I texted a quick reply that I was fine and that I'd fill her in later.

It was a little before five and I figured not all that late. By the time I made it to the seventh floor where Malia was recuperating, I noticed an abundance of police walking around.

I tried my best at hiding my face from the numerous officers when I made my way past Malia's room and saw her lying in her bed, her face blue and her eyes bulging. Along with her bed being trashed, there were dark markings around her neck, signs of having put up a fight and been strangled.

But why? And how? Hadn't Malia been under police surveillance since she arrived? Why would Paul-Henri do this? What did he want? He said he was looking for Aiden and he had him. So why this? Unless Aiden didn't have what he was looking for? What if Malia had been right? What if Aiden hadn't been up at Pierre's last Monday night? Then someone else would have what he was looking for.

I made my way back down the hallway for the elevator, pressed the button and waited.

Unless Malia had whatever it was Paul-Henri was looking for and turned it over, which was doubtful as she had been shot and taken directly to the hospital without being able to grab anything before the ambulance ride, then she would have had to tell him where said object was. There was Liam Murphy, who was dead. Connor Emerson, also dead. That left . . . Maddie? But she had been in too bad a state when I found her up at Pierre's last Monday night to have taken anything with her. I would have known. I would have . . . That other mysterious person who had been up there that night. The same person that would have been able to make me or anyone else believe that Aiden Murphy had been up at Pierre's that night.

Jasmine Fairchild.

She was Aiden's girlfriend after all. The chances of him having left or forgotten his cell phone with her, or her even taking it, would have been easy. Hell, she probably didn't even have to do that. She was his girlfriend after all. She probably knew all his passwords. And had she been up at Pierre's last Monday night she easily could have signed him on to his social medial accounts with her own phone and made his presence in the area known. Which was exactly what had happened. I had seen him there. Like she had intended. I had been set up. I was her alibi and the one person who could finger Aiden for being up there even without having seen him. She knew I was logged into everyone's whereabouts from earlier that day when I discussed Pierre's Facebook and other social media accounts.

I punched the wall next to me as I got onto the elevator and pressed the button for the garage. I looked up and noticed two nurses at the station staring at me for the commotion I had just made. I smiled and waved innocently as I pressed the button once more.

As the elevator doors began to open it all came together for me. All of it. Flush. What Paul-Henri was after and why? It had nothing to do with missing merchandise. And it had everything to do with something I had been carrying on myself since that Monday night when I took it out of Pierre's secret drawer within his desk. The ledger. The secret code that everything inside had been written in. Suddenly it all made sense to me. Whose it was. Why they had it. Or, theoretically, I knew the answers to these questions. Now to just go and make sure. But something told me I would need help.

I turned from the elevator and ran down the hall for the first police officer I could find.

"Where are Detectives Manning and Hershey? Are they here?" I all but shouted in the officer's face. Before he could get out a reply I continued. "Detectives Manning and

Hershey? Do you know where they are? I need to speak with them immediately."

"What's this concerning?" the officer asked me.

I waived him off. "Just, where are they?"

"Chance," came a voice from behind me. I turned to find myself face to face with Detectives Manning and Hershey. "What a surprise seeing you here."

"Just who I was looking for. Look, I have something to tell you. And I'm not sure how you're going to take it. In fact, I think I'm about to bring a little dark rain cloud to your day."

"I got a dead witness in the other room, Chance. How much darker can it get?"

"I know. I know. But if you stick with me, I promise, this will all make sense, and will all make you very happy by the end of the day. Double rainbows all around. I promise. So, what do you say?"

31

LOUD LIKE LOVE

It was just after six by the time I'd made it to the Fairchild's home and the sun had already set on this short autumn day. The wind had been picking up all day, threatening to bring in with it more rain, or at the very least heavy clouds. I parked haphazardly on the driveway and ran in through the front door, not caring who was around but hoped the right people were. So far, I had seen no evidence that Paul-Henri or anyone else was around.

"Jasmine?" I shouted as I spun around in the main foyer, looking for signs of anyone being at home from any direction. "*Jasmine?*"

I was about to run down the hallway when I heard my name called out from up above.

"Chance? Chance, what the hell are you doing here?"

Jasmine made her way from her bedroom to the edge of the balcony up above me. She wore a one-piece hunter-green dress that fit her like a glove. Her hair had been done up and she looked as if she had just come back from or was headed out to a party of some sort.

"Where are you going?" I asked, not that I really cared or

knew why I had even bothered to ask in the first place.

"Father's making his announcement later tonight. We've got the party at the Mayor's home. What's going on? Why are you here?"

I started making my way up the stairs, meeting her halfway.

"I think you're in danger."

"What?" She laughed.

"Seriously. Paul-Henri. I think he's after you. I think he may have just killed Malia, or at least had her killed, looking for something. Only it's not what he's been telling everyone he's been looking for all week. And if she did any sort of talking before he offed her, then I think she may have given him the impression that you had it."

"What? Why? What are you talking about?"

"All week Paul-Henri has been looking for Aiden. He thought your boyfriend had been up at Pierre's last Monday night and after Pierre was murdered, he fled with some of Paul-Henri's product. Flush. Don't deny it, I already know. The problem was no one knows what this Flush is exactly. It's a new drug that even the police don't have a handle on. But I've seen it. Both up at Pierre's and at Malia's and even in Maddie's locker at school. And it's perfect, I must admit. No one would ever suspect it. I didn't. That's why I didn't question Paul-Henri's motives, even though it was staring me right in the face. But he wasn't looking for it because he's had it all along. I saw it in his study the other night when I was at the Wig Party." Jasmine stared tepidly at me. She knew what I was talking about. She had been up there at Pierre's that night. She knew all about Flush. "The puzzle pieces. That's it. No one would suspect. They're just puzzle pieces. But that's because no one knew how it was taken. But they're like a pill. You put the puzzle piece on your tongue and let it dissolve. Then you get the rush. The one that makes you get all flushed. Flush. Or PDV as Vice calls it. Pieza de venatus. Or something. I'm sure I'm butchering it. Either way, I don't know why I didn't put it together sooner."

"So what?" Jasmine asked as she continued down the stairs past me. "So what? What's this have to do with Aiden? Or me? Why does Paul-Henri care about us when he has his product?"

"He doesn't want the merchandise because he already has it. What he wants is what he thinks you took from Pierre's Monday night."

"But I wasn't—"

"We both know you were there. That's how you were able to make it look as if Aiden had been up there. Through Facebook, which you knew from earlier that day I had programed to follow. I put that one together already."

Though she hesitated for a moment she knew I had caught her in that lie. "So, what's he think I took from him?"

"The thing I was talking to you and Malia about the other night. The ledger."

Jasmine laughed. "There is no ledger, Chance. I've never seen this so-called ledger and neither has anyone else. That's just a myth that Paul-Henri uses to keep his minions in line."

"Oh, yeah?" I asked as I held up the little black book that I had taken the previous Monday night. Her eyes immediately enlarged, and I could tell that she both knew what it was and why I had it.

"I've seen that before."

"I'm sure you have. It's Pierre's little black book. Holds names and numbers though to what and for what reason I'm still not sure. But it's valuable either way. People have been killed for what's in this ledger."

"No," Jasmine said, confusion clouding her face. "No, that's not Pierre's or Paul-Henri's ledger."

"Yes. Yes, it is. I got it up at Pierre's Monday night when he was killed."

"No. I've seen it before. That book belongs to—"

"Me," came a voice from behind us, cutting Jasmine off and startling the two of us.

Standing there aiming a gun square at us was Jasmine's stepmother, Selena. She too was dressed up, ready for her husband's announcement later that evening, though I had to admit I hadn't seen the great Mr. Fairchild anywhere in the home. Perhaps he was already at the Mayor's house, preparing his speech.

"You," Jasmine said at the same time as me as we both stood there staring at her stunned, though I think I was a little more stunned and Jasmine was a little more miffed. I took the moment to look from Selena to Jasmine and back again, putting together more of the (figurative) puzzle pieces.

"This isn't Paul-Henri's?" I said as I waved the book in my hand.

"No," Selena admitted with a shake of her head and a roll of her eyes that showed all the distain for most everyone she knew and had bouncing in and out of her life. Yes, I read all that in one simple look of her face. She was a thirty-year-old drug dealer who had planned a cover life as the wife of an up-and-comer in politics who had to learn to bite her tongue around two teenage stepdaughters whom I'm sure she loathed. "No, it isn't his. It's mine."

"You're . . . you're who Paul-Henri works for. *You're* the reason why he wanted Jasmine kept out of the loop. Not her father but you."

"Bastard's been trying to get his hands on it for months. That's why I had him set up and found with those hookers and drugs a year ago that got his family to keep him away. Paul-Henri's been a greedy little man who's been trying to— forget about getting his hand in it—but rather, has been trying to take the whole cookie jar. He was supposed to clean up this mess and instead he's digging us in deeper. Sure, the cops knew about Flush, it was only a matter of time, but their knowledge was minimal. Then somehow this whole fiasco unfolds and his connection to the youth market—I'm talking his about his brother, Pierre's friend Connor—goes and gets killed and Paul-Henri begins to unravel. The cops are onto us more than ever before and I can't figure out how this is all happened or why. He's my only common denominator. He had one simple task. Keep everyone in line. And instead it's all turning to shit."

"If the book's yours, how'd he get it?"

"Liam, I'm assuming. Aiden was smart enough to know never to double-cross me. But Liam was young and stupid. Paul-Henri told him about the book, I'm sure. Liam probably figured he'd have more leverage if he had the book himself. But once he got it, I'm sure he had no idea how to read it. So, then he had to take it to Paul-Henri to decipher it and then . . . voila, no more Liam. The rest were just dominos. The butterfly effect from one man's stupid attempt at being at the top. Men are stupid. They don't realize how much work it takes to both get to the top and then stay there."

I wasn't looking at Selena anymore but was staring at Jasmine, the look on her face, the revelations in her eyes. Just like before. Just like with our parents and their secrets. She had always known more than she let on. But she never knew how to act on her suspicions. That's what I had always been around for. I was the instigator. I had unfolded the actions that resulted in the death of our parents but in the end the truth did out. Now, she had a similar problem and she didn't know how to fix it. So, she had sought me out. I saw it on her face. She *knew* about Selena all this time. Somehow, probably one night on the way to or from Pierre's, she had seen Selena from a distance and then began to causally ask questions, putting two and two together. She was clever like that. And in the end, she figured it out all out, that her father and sister, her true family, were no longer safe. That another woman had once again infiltrated their lives put her own needs before those of her families' and sought out to harm them. Only Jasmine wasn't about to let that happen. Again.

"Maddie isn't bipolar, is she?" I asked, stalling for time. "That was just a cover you used on me. She was high as a kite the night of Pierre's murder and I'm sure she was the other night when I saw you."

"No, she probably is bipolar or depressed or whatever the hell teenagers have nowadays," Selena confessed. "But I'm sure the drugs don't help her condition. What's that have to do with anything?"

"You were supposed to be her mother. You were supposed to protect her. And when you didn't Jasmine stepped in," I explained. "She sought out the devil and unfolded a plan to chase the devil away. You. You, Selena. You're that devil. And she realized it. Only you were too stupid to realize you were being played." I turned to Jasmine who had slowly begun to inch her way back up the staircase. "There never was any blackmail scheme. You simply found those pictures on Maddie's phone and probably forwarded them to a burner in hopes of getting me sniffing around. You knew I'd go to Pierre's first because you nudged me toward him and from there you hoped I'd stumble upon everything I did. Oh, I mean, you had no idea that what would happen would happen, Pierre's death, and Liam's and Connor's and Malia's. But you still knew that by the time I finished the truth would be free. And if not, so what? The worse that would happen would be that I was dead. And who really cares if little ol' me is dead, right? You sure didn't? That's why you picked me. It wasn't that you cared, like you claimed. It was that I was expendable. Right?"

I could see her eyes beginning to water up, but she was too good at this game. I saw right through that. Those tears could have been because I simply caught her at her worse. Careless about anyone in her life other than her own immediate family. I had lost mine, so I understood that need to protect it. She had almost lost hers as well. But in the aftermath of that original tragedy she had survived.

"I never meant to hurt you or for you to get hurt," Jasmine blurted out as the tears finally let go like a leaky faucet the landlord keeps promising to fix. "I never meant for anyone to get hurt. I love you, Chance, I do. I promise."

"Aww, you believe that?" I asked turning to Selena. I was only a few steps away from her, still holding up her little black book while she held a gun to my face. Personally, I felt the odds were stacked against me, but I was running out of options and my brain was spinning too fast to get it under control. Out of control cars on an ice slick had a better chance at regaining control of the situation than I did right now. So, I had to play with what I had. Mainly, pitting girl against girl. Stepmother against stepdaughter. The good, old fashioned cat fight.

"Not for a second," Selena almost purred as she kept the gun aimed on me.

"I don't want nothing to do with any of this," I continued as I physically cowered before the woman, holding up my hands in surrender. "I just want to get the hell out of here and finish high school. You can have this stupid ledger. Have no idea what it says any-ways."

"Truth is," Selena hissed as she yanked the ledger from my hands as I continued to cower before her. "It's not even mine really. It was my father's. This whole racket was his. But then he had to go and get himself arrested and killed in prison. What did that leave me, huh? Other than alone and without a family of my own."

Something clicked in my head as I heard Selena pouring out her life story. Something about the tone she was using. There was a reason to this all and it had nothing to do with it being the right season. She had sought the Fairchilds out.

"You blame them," I said shakily as I faced Selena. "For your father's death?"

"James Fairchild is a highly influential man. Strongly motivated and wealthy beyond all means," she said confidently. "Apparently James had some property he needed to unload but it wasn't worth squat. What with all the kids hanging around passing out drugs on the corners of the neighborhood. But once the drug trade got cleaned up the land suddenly was worth millions. He was the one who got the book thrown at my father. Got him life inside. If he hadn't been in that prison, he never would have been caught in that knife fight and I might still have him around. So yes, I do blame them. All of them. But what easier way to get back at a man than through his children? His daughters. At first, I had no idea how I would do this. Infiltrate the family. I mean, I wasn't even around. My father had kept me out of the picture his whole life. Wanted me to be better than the life he had lived to provide for his family. What a hypocrite. But that's a man for you. Then I saw about the Misses dying and I saw all those grieving widow pictures in the paper and it all just came to me. I knew how I would get in. I mean, I didn't always look this good. I had to work at it. But determination in a woman can go a long ways. I mean . . . look at me."

She held up her arms as she showed herself off to us as if neither one of us had ever caught sight of the woman before.

But it was all I needed. The gun was finally off me, out of my face, and aimed into the middle of nowhere.

I bolted as quickly as I could for Selena, and I could see in her eyes the acknowledgement that she had slipped up as she began to aim the gun back in my direction. I thought I yelled at Jasmine to run, but I had no idea what I was thinking and what I was doing or saying. It all played out in slow motion like the final real in a movie as I tackled the wicked stepmother—side note, she may have been evil but out of everyone in the world to tackle I couldn't complain it was that woman—and pined her to the ground. I kept most of my weight and focus on the hand with the gun in it and she surprised me with a sharp slug to my jaw with her left hand. It momentarily dazed me when I felt her grabbing at my face and clawing me with her fingernails. She got her hand in my mouth and I bit down on her, drawing blood which I could taste flowing down the back of my throat as I released the hand holding the gun and before I could think about my actions I swung a fist square in her face, slamming her head against the cold, marble floor. I managed to wrestle the gun from her hand, and it slid across the floor when Selena kneed me in the groin, immediately stopping my attack. She managed to wrestle her way out from under me and began to crawl across the floor toward her gun. I could tell where she was going and while I figured I couldn't quite make it after her before she got to the gun, I knew I couldn't stay put.

"Jasmine, run!" I shouted to her as I quickly got to my feet and managed to hobble out of the foyer into the neighboring room just as a bullet ricocheted off the wall behind where I had been standing just a moment before.

I kept my pace up and continued to hobble my way through the living room and into the neighboring dining room as yet another bullet was fired in my direction, both just narrowly missing me. I wasn't sure if Jasmine was safe, but since I had only heard the three gunshots, and deduced all three had been aimed at me, I figured she was long gone, upstairs. Hopefully calling for the police. Or some sort of help. Speaking of which . . . where were Detectives Manning and Hershey? What kind of help were they if they couldn't even be around for a gunfight?

I made my way through the dining room and just kept on moving around through the kitchen, my sneakers squeaking across the black and white checker-board patterned floor, when I was about to go through the neighboring hallway only to come face to face with Selena and her gun aimed at me. Before I had time to react, she swung the gun at me, connecting square with the side of my face and sending me crashing to the floor. I was dazed and tried to focus up at Selena as she aimed the gun down at me.

"Don't worry," Selena purred at me as she leaned down over me. "You won't be alone in hell for long. Your little girlfriend is coming right behind you just as soon as I finish with you."

Selena raised herself back up and began to aim the gun at me when suddenly Jasmine brought a rather expensive looking vase down on her stepmother's head. Though the vase shattered into thousands of pieces, it only momentarily phased the woman. But it was enough. And I struck out with my foot at her shin and connected with more force than I had been planning. Again, it was enough, and the woman went crashing to the floor, her head connecting with the cold tile, knocking her out but good.

I barely had time to look up at Jasmine when we both heard the cavalry crashing through the front door. Maybe now was as good a time as any to take a nap. My head hurt like hell.

"Wakie, wakie," I could hear the voice that I assumed was aimed at me. Truthfully, I had a hell of a time placing it as it sounded like I was being talked to through several hundred gallons of water. "Oh, here he comes."

I felt an excruciating pain in the back of my head, though at this point from what I could not remember. I could swear my front was where my back was and vice versa.

I pealed my eyes open to find myself face to face with Detective Hershey who had the look of relief come across his face. He looked between me and someone off in the distance that I couldn't quite place yet as everything further than two feet away was still blurry to my eyes. It wasn't until she got closer that I should have realized he'd be communicating with Detective Manning.

"What took you so long?" I asked groggily as I rubbed my face and immediately felt a bolt of pain shoot through my skull. "I almost bit it."

"Oh, quit complaining," Detective Manning said from over Hershey's shoulder. "You're fine. Quit being a baby. We had trouble with your mic. You're wearing it under too many layers. Couldn't get the whole conversation."

That's what I get for taking my time and trying to involve the police. I get threatened with impeding an investigation, strapped with a wire, and thrown in the face of danger. How do I keep getting roped into these situations?

"So, you just felt like dangling me on the edge of a hook a little longer?"

"Well, that, and we were busy arresting Paul-Henri. We caught him outside. Guess your instincts were right. He was coming here with malicious intent," Detective Manning said as she motioned for a paramedic over to come give me the once over.

"Wha?" I asked as I tried to maneuver around the EMT who flashed a light in my eyes.

I looked past Hershey out the front door where I saw both Selena Fairchild and Paul-Henri being guided to separate police vehicles, each one with their hands cuffed behind their backs. I could hear sobbing and looked over to see Jasmine still standing off to the side in the kitchen. Somehow, I couldn't but help feel those weren't real tears of sorrow.

"Wha? How . . ." My head still swirled as I tried to take it all in when I just collapsed on the ground, just giving up. Who cared? It was all over. Time to move on.

"There are a few more questions we'd like to ask you though, Chance," Detective Manning continued as the EMT continued checking me out.

"Right now?" I asked pitifully.

"He's got a concussion," the EMT answered for me. "We

need to take him in. Your questions will have to wait."

I was then walked to the back of an ambulance and as I lay there, I realized I'd never been so happy to have a concussion before in my life.

312

32

DIZZ KNEE LAND

I went to the hospital, got fixed up, was told to rest when the detectives came by and asked their questions. I played dumb, they had my previous explanations and all the rest was on the wire. Let Jasmine do all the lying. Let her squirm her way out if she makes a mistake. Later that evening I was released and sent went back to the motel. Back home.

I spent all the next day in bed. The detectives stopped by once again, wanting to know more; wanting a few more questions to be wrapped up. I knew they'd just keep hounding me until they got what they wanted so I let them stay and we hashed it all out. I kept the charade up as best I could when three hours later, they finally left. Since I had held back as much as I could I can't say they were happy about all my answers, but they were content enough to finally leave me alone.

Thursday, I had to finally show up at school as we had the PSATs that day, though once I finished them, I bailed. I couldn't take all the whispering and staring. I knew they were talking about me. Never I had I wished so hard to be back to the old days, when I ate lunch alone and no one at school had any idea who I was.

Somehow, I had a feeling that things might just work their way back to that sooner than later.

I didn't see Jasmine or Maddison at school that day and rumor had it their father—who had not made his announcement that Tuesday night—had whisked them up and away on a "family vacation." No one had any idea when they'd be back. I figured I could live the rest of my high school days just fine if I never came across another Fairchild girl again.

It was a quarter after nine on that following Saturday evening, the homecoming dance now well into its second hour of boys and girls standing on opposite sides of the gym while spiked punch was snuck around, when I found Skye taking a break from her shift at Curious Coffee by sitting at one of the tables on the back patio and doodling.

"And what are we up to on this fine Saturday night?" I asked as I swung a chair around backwards and sat down at the table. This was the first time since the whole confrontation at the Fairchilds that either one of us had spoken to the other.

"What the hell are you doing here?" Skye demanded of me as she all but slammed her pencil down. I could tell she was drawing some manga-inspired comic-book-type characters, though from my point of view I wasn't sure what was going on in the picture.

I stared at her. I was in a good place. And nothing would ruin this for me.

"Oh, God," Skye said worriedly as she saw the bruises and scratches on my face, and she reached a hand up to my face to get a closer inspection. "Nice battle scars. Especially the one from me."

"You didn't give me any of these," I said confused when she slapped side of my forehead.

"Ass," she sneered as she went back to her doodle. "What the hell *are* you doing here?"

"Did I have a previous engagement I was unaware of?"

She continued to draw when a minute later she took a break and stared up at me. "Homecoming?"

"Oh, that," I waved her off. "Like I really want this mug to be photographed forever so that my future progeny can see what I went through day after day through high school."

"Oh, please. You've looked worse."

I gasped, faking injury by her stinging words as I threw a hand to my chest. "Pa-leze. I've never looked better. It's no wonder the girls of our school have been throwing themselves at me. It's a wonder I wasn't manhandled on my way out here to the patio."

"Uh-huh. My thoughts exactly." Skye went back to her doodle and I looked around at the empty patio and took in the sounds of the nearby waterfall. It was a peaceful night. The first time in a long time that I could recall just feeling relaxed. "So, what's the story, morning glory?"

"The wicked stepmother has been slayed. Heading off to jail. Though I'm sure she'll try to cut some sort of a deal. Of course, Paul-Henri is trying for the same thing. A he said/she said sort of a situation. Unfortunately for Paul-Henri I think

Selena's the sharper of the bunch and she'll get the better deal. Who cares? Just so long as they're gone and out of my life, what do I care what the justice system does with them. Oh, and the police think there's the slightest possibility they may be able to stop the spread of Flush in all the local schools—as if. And the Fairchilds are off on a faraway vacation to Never-Never Land."

"And you?"

"Oh, didn't you hear? I'm going to Disneyland."

She looked up with skepticism.

"Please. Like I could ever afford that," I winked as I looked down at her drawing again. "What's that?"

"Nothing," she said quickly as she went to put it away in her folder of other assorted drawings.

"Wait," I said catching her wrist and turning it enough to see the picture. "Is that . . . is that me?"

She gave up and let me look at the picture. It was. Various versions of me across the page but each one was of me. Except for one that showed a smoldering, vixen I took to be Jasmine.

"These are good . . ." I said getting caught up in the pictures. "But . . ."

"Oh, I just figured since you were going to go get yourself killed, I might as well profit off it," she said with bite as she stood up. "I mean, since you did just bail on me, never letting me know what was going on. How was I supposed to know? You could have been dead. And you could have died. But apparently, I didn't need to know what was going on. Right?"

I could tell she was hurt by my actions and I found myself

at a loss for words. She took the page from my hands and started away.

"I have to get back to work."

"Can I stick around?"

"It's a free country."

I wasn't sure how to reply. I figured she was entitled to her anger. I couldn't really blame her. She had earned it. And I didn't want to make it any worse. So, I figured go ahead and let her vent. It was a good night for me so far so why not make another person feel just as good.

She left me there on the patio. I worked my way back around to her chair and leaned back in it and stared up at the stars again. I wasn't sure how much time had passed when Skye placed a cup of coffee and a shoebox-sized box down on the table in front of me.

"You know, Chance Harper, I realize you don't have a lot of friends. Hell, I'm not sure you have *any*. And guess what? Neither do I. But we do have each other. That's right, Chance Harper, you finally have one friend in your life. Me. Okay . . . and Theo Lannapo, I suppose. I'll give you him too. But as someone who isn't sure how to treat a friend let me fill you in on a little something-something since every now and again a good detective needs a good clue. You don't do what you did to me to friends. If you need help you ask for it."

"If memory serves me correct, that's how we got talking again since last year. I asked you for a favor."

"And I obliged. And what thanks did I get?" She spread her arms out as if waiting for the world to be given to her. "If you're going to go do something stupid and dangerous, and yes, I know you did because I can see it by the wounds on your face and because you're a man and because men are the very definition of stupid. So, if you're going to do something stupid and dangerous let someone know. Particularly the police. But if not them, then at the very least *me!* We both know I could kick a hell of a lot more ass than you ever could." Now she was done lecturing. We were venturing back into *friend* territory. Perhaps that's how it was done between friends. Lecture. Yell. Let it all out. And then back to the reason why you were friends it the first place. "I mean, could you imagine you actually having to rescue someone? Lord have mercy."

"Hey, you know when that end of the world zombie apocalypse happens, you're gonna want me on your side."

"More like you're going to want me to come dig your ass out of the mess you're going to be buried underneath. But don't worry, Chance Harper, if you become a zombie, I will totally end your life."

"Aww, I think that's the sweetest thing you've ever said to me."

We both smiled and let the moment just be for a little while.

"What this?" I asked eyeing the box.

"That's"—she said nodding toward the mug of coffee— "because it's getting cold out here. *That*"—she said nodding toward the box—"I found downtown in an antique shop. It's a puzzle box. I figure if you need to solve a mystery so bad...well, at least this one won't kill you. As your friend, and yes, I am your friend, I forbid you to help anyone else out the rest of this year until you solve *this* puzzle first."

I could see the smirk on her face and the twinkle in her eye. She had me. How could I resist. These crazy girls. If it wasn't one of them, it was the other. I swear, one of these days, one of them was gonna be the death of me.

Oh, but what a way to go.

ABOUT THE AUTHOR

Tyler Compton is the author of three previous novels featuring LAPD Detective Dave Parks. His first book, *The Poisonous Ten*, was released in June 2013 and was named an Award-Winning Finalist in the Fiction: Mystery/Suspense category of the 2013 USA Best Book Awards, sponsored by USA Book News.

The Fast Out is his first young-adult novel.

The son of a prison guard, Tyler Compton graduated from CSU, Sacramento in 2002 with a BA in Theatre Arts and a minor in Film Studies. He currently resides in Los Angeles where he has witnessed various forms of crime, including someone breaking into his apartment while he was in it.

Follow Tyler on Twitter or Instagram @tscompton or visit TylerComptonBooks.com for the latest news and details about future releases.

Made in the USA
Columbia, SC
30 September 2019